CHASING THE DRAGON

BY MARK TOWSE

EERIE RIVER PUBLISHING
Kitchener, Ontario

Eerie River Publishing
www.EerieRiverPublishing.com
Kitchener, Ontario Canada

This book is a work of fiction. Names, characters, places, events, organi-
zations and incidents are either part of the author's imagination or
are used fictitiously. Any resemblance to actual persons, living or dead, or
actual events is purely coincidental. Except all the details about Hell, that
is real.

Paperback ISBN: 978-1-998112-26-5
Hardcover ISBN: 978-1-998112-27-2
Digital ISBN: 978-1-998112-25-8
Edited by David-Jack Fletcher

Cover design by Tom Brown
Book Formatting by Michelle River of Eerie River Publishing

ALSO BY MARK TOWSE

Reviews for Chasing The Dragon

"This book is bonkers...and I loved it! A grungy superhero origin story soaked in blood (and other bodily fluids); Chasing the Dragon has all the gusto of a Marvel comic mixed with the absolute filth of a grindhouse flick. Reformo, a hero as demented as the villains he battles, is all that stands between us and chaos (and tinned peaches)."
- C.M. Forest, author of award winning novel *Infested*.

"SIN CITY meets CARRIE meets WEST SIDE STORY."
- Mort Stone, *The Mort Report*.

"The humor I have grown to love in the author's books is sprinkled heavily throughout this one. I enjoy what it brings to the story and the main character. It's not easy being a superhero, but Reformo gives it his all."
- Diana, *Indie Book Addict*.

"Mark Towse's debut novel is a book you can unwind with knowing you'll have a good time. It combines a good dose of comedy mixed with stomach-churning scenes of violence that made my heart race and kept things exciting. It gave me major Norman Bates vibes but with Towse's signature humor weaved in."
- Rose, *RoseDevoursBooks*.

"If Ken Loach wrote a superhero story sprinkled with tongue in cheek sharpness - or perhaps if Psycho met Unbreakable - it might result in Chasing The Dragon."
- Emma, *Bookstagrammer and Author*.

"Never before has a book managed to make me cry with laughter; cry with pity; and hold my breath simultaneously. It seamlessly combines multiple genres, horror, fantasy, thriller, crime - and of course - Towsey's fantastic humour!"
- Trish Wilson, *Bookstagrammer*.

This one is going out to my father, Michael Thomas Towse.

A common denominator of my work is the thread of humour cutting through the darkness, a gift handed down to me by the aforementioned. My father is losing his way a little these days, but I will continue using this gifted beacon of light to chart my path. Thank you, Dad.

x

And I can't go without saying a big thanks to my mother, Jennifer Syder, the first reader and editor of my work. Without her, this journey would not be possible.

Chapter One: I Hate Jesus

Late October, Thursday, 7:00 PM

Another shift finally comes to an end.

Iciness wraps around me as I step outside into the now lighter rain, the brightness of the moon offering only a temporary distraction from surrounding squalor and dilapidation. It's not so much the smell of fried chicken on my clothes, nor the ever-present scent of piss and liquor that makes me sick to the stomach, but the thickness of the fear in the air. It's stifling, claustrophobic, and relentless. You can almost taste it.

"Gets my fucking goat."

Safe to say, dread's bony fingers have been wrapped around this town's throat for some time, but now the place is on its knees, its death rattles soon to follow.

The dimly-lit faces of my co-workers gawp back as I slide the door closed behind me, their mouths no doubt further polluting the air with their bile and tittle-tattle. Toxic exchanges about the new guy who hardly speaks a word and does what he's paid to do instead of slacking. Only been there a week, but I'm sure they hate me already. How is that possible? I keep my head down, trying to appear as normal as possible, smiling and nodding in the right places. Yes, sir. No, sir. Yes, shove the balls in as well if you like, sir.

People tend to jump to hate at things they don't understand

or that threaten the self-imposed regulations of their tiny little universe. They'll see, though. I'll open their eyes to a bigger world.

They have no idea who I am about to become.

An involuntary snicker leaves my lips, prompting an approaching elderly couple—no doubt on their way home before the unwritten curfew kicks in—to cross the road and increase their pace.

"Good evening," I say, following with a smile.

Nothing.

Residents, who once held their heads with pride, keep their stare fixed on the cracked pavement, afraid to make eye contact, scared of their own shadow. It's rare to catch them outside after seven. The poor things usually huddle together behind thick curtains and triple-bolted doors, watching the *Price is Right* and praying for just one night without harassment and a flaming bag of dog shit through their letterbox. Not too much to ask, surely?

But there's no trust around here anymore, no shared human bond.

During my time behind bars, I pledged to Mother I would do better. Bring some hope back into the world. I'm not even sure what I feel towards her anymore. Too young to understand at the time, I'm beginning to comprehend why she was always so highly strung. Pent up to the point of insanity, she just wanted the chaos to end.

"It gets my fucking goat!" she used to say, eyes wild, fingers white around her feather duster as she eyed the stranger's car parked outside our house. "Without rules, without respect, Simon, we are nothing but animals."

Yes, it's time for me to step up.

As I make my way past the boarded-up windows of once-treasured stores, my eyes draw to the house across the road, the word 'cockmuncher' sprayed across the rotten panels of the fence. A dirty, yellow streetlight shows the paint still glistening as I march across, eyeing the discarded aerosol in the overgrown lawn.

Edith, is it? Yes, Edith, the name of the woman who lives here. Mother knew her. She said the lady had a Shih Tzu that held true to its name, pebble-dashing our driveway with its little brown nuggets one morning. Eighty, if a day—the woman, not the Shih Tzu—and I suspect the old lady munches on cough drops over cocks these days.

Feeling helpless, I bend down and pick up the discarded aerosol.

"I saw who did it." The feeble voice emerges from the partially open door. "Little shit had a skateboard tucked under his arm. One of them inbred faces too."

Over the muffled sound of her TV, I hear smashing glass and howls from night walkers, accompanied by the ever-present soundtrack of thumping bass and distant sirens.

"Did you call the police?"

She offers a croaky laugh. "You're a funny bastard, aren't you? Had an incident last month, and it took two hours before the pigs showed up."

She knows as well as I do most are paid off or have given up the fight. So-called "drug lords" taking over the town, everyone in their back pocket while the place goes to shit. The sirens are just for show, an attempt to placate, but those days are long gone.

"Things are going to change around here," I say. "Mark my words."

"Some twat came to the door a few months ago promising the exact same thing," Edith says. "Shoved a leaflet in my face and told me his party would put this town back on the map. He was in the papers a week later, caught with his pants down in the disabled bogs, some hooker choking on his meat stick. You know—his love truncheon, pecker, womb ferret, purple-headed—"

"Yeah, yeah, I get it, dearie."

"Anyway, certainly not the sort of thing you want to be on the map for." She opens the door a little further, exposing a tuft of hair resembling iron wool, albeit with a blue tinge. "Do I know you?"

"Just know that things will get better."

"Why, are they dropping an effin' bomb on the place?"

"No." I clear my throat. "A saviour is coming."

She sighs, opening the door further to reveal the flickering frown across her forehead. "A bloody bible basher, I should have known. Christ, you've got some nerve, kid, touting the Lord's name around here."

"No, no, no, you've got me all wrong." Time for a change of tactic. "I despise all that stuff. In fact, I hate Jesus."

A strange, garbled croak leaves through the tiniest hole in her lips, and her eyes grow just as narrow. "You hate Jesus?" She takes an urgent step across the threshold, looks to the heavens, and makes the sign of the cross on her chest.

"Yeah, but...but"—some days you just can't win—"I mean the way you can love someone with all your heart but sometimes hate them. You know, like your parents or your partner, for example."

"My parents are worm food, and my Bernard had a coronary four years ago."

Fuck. Fuck. Fuckity-fuck.

As the woman continues her heavy wheeze, I make a mental note that saying things like, "I hate Jesus," will not necessarily win people over. Back-pedalling as fast as I can, I raise my palms in a gesture once again. "Help is coming, Edith. The caped disciple will bring order back to town."

"The caped disciple?"

Knowing I need to work on my PR skills, I offer a feeble nod and keep my mouth shut.

Shaking her head, the old lady puckers her lips again and looks up and down the street before taking a step back into darkness. "Look, son, you might mean well, but you're wasting your time around here. Even God moved out from these parts a long time ago. Found himself a nice little piece of real estate in the nice little town of '*I Don't Give a Fuck.*'

"I'm sorry. All I'm trying to do is—"

"Just drop your leaflet and bugger off, will you? *Antiques Roadshow* is next, and I've got a casserole for one in."

Before I can respond, the door slams in my face. *Stop the chaos.* I guess she's every right to be sceptical, one empty promise after another shoved down her scraggy little throat. And questionable faith, jumping from devout to insincere at the drop of a hat, but again, I guess it's been tested many times living in this shit hole of a town. Feet together, I stiffen my posture, lift my chin, and offer a salute of sorts. "I promise to restore hope, Edith. This town will be good again. I will bring order back, you'll see."

After tossing the empty aerosol into Edith's wheelie bin, I continue on my way, contemplating just how much work is required. Suburbia's soundtrack continues around me as neon light spills onto damp streets, basking them with seediness and giving discarded fast-food wrappers a radioactive tinge. Blurry puddles offer the illusory effect of rippled portals to an underworld, the rain stinging as if tiny acidic tears of the once happy residents, each droplet loaded with a misery beyond memory.

It's chaos, Simon. Anarchy.

Even alleys are alive with moving shadows and whispers, only the desperate or foolish venturing into the darkness. The druggies are starting to come out, too, blood-stained or borrowed cash in their pockets, always on the lookout for more.

Yes, it's time. I will make a change. This town will get its hero.

I can't remember the last time I heard a bird sing around these parts. Or even the last time I heard a laugh not tainted by evil. Perhaps people can still find joy somehow, behind closed doors, their televisions providing a portal into worlds of colour and unfiltered happiness. For me, it was always the latest superhero comic—exciting tales of heroic acts in the battle of good vs. evil. A belief that things could change for the better because Christ knows we needed it. It was escapism without limits, and I guess one thing I'm thankful to my father for.

I'm close. Yeah, here we go. Not this right, but the one after. Red door, if I remember correctly, about halfway down. The house number has slipped my mind, but the address carries too much significance—*Hope Street*. What are the chances?

A shudder runs down my spine as Mother's voice catches me by surprise. *Imagine if everyone did that, Simon. A blind eye here, a blind eye there, and before you know it, we're hiding in the broom closet eating tinned peaches. It starts with the little things, Simon. You must rinse your bowl out. It's just laziness, Simon, a lack of self-respect. Rinse! Rinse! Rinse! Bastards next door parked in front of our house again. It gets my fucking goat! Crumbs on the countertop, Simon. It's chaos! How many times have I told you? And I know you're not fucking stupid. Not like your sorry excuse of a father over there, sitting in that chair while the world turns to shit. Jeff! Jeff! I'm talking to you. Someone's cat has taken a shit on our front lawn. What are you going to do about it? I'll poison the fucking thing, see if I don't.*

"Let me be, Mother. I'll uphold my pledge to you and clean up this town, but please, just let me be."

If you sit back and watch, you'll become just another casualty of the chaos, Simon. You have to set an example. You have to fight. Grow some balls. If you do nothing, you're as much to blame as the others. Don't give up like him over there, the useless sack of shit. A quitter. Always has been, always will be.

"Mama, stop!"

Look at him, just sitting on his fat arse as if nothing is happening. You have to set an example if you want people to follow. Jeff, why aren't you doing something? Jeff! Jeff! Idiots down the street playing their loud music again. It gets my fucking goat! Go and tell them, Jeff. Jeff, can you hear me? Kids playing cricket in the street again. If that ball comes anywhere near my begonias, so help me God. Go and tell them, Jeff. Are you ignoring me, Jeff? Jeff! JEEEEEEEEEEEEEFF! Simon, for the love of God, promise you won't turn out like your weak-as-piss father or his pissant of a brother. PROMISE ME, SIMON!

And that was my childhood—witness to a relentless barrage of instructions and discipline, nervously observing from the staircase as my father absorbed most of the impact. Scared of his own shadow, he became nothing more than a shell. I hated her for it but hated my father more, especially when Mother turned her attention to me when nothing was left of him to peck at.

That's not going to be me, though. No fucking way. I'm the man who will make a difference and put this town back on the map. Just see if I don't. When the sun goes down, no more Simon Dooley. It's time to meet The Rectifier.

The Rectifier.

Rectifier.

Shit! It sounded good the first few times, but now it just sounds lame, like something to treat a breathing condition or crooked teeth. We'll call it a work in progress. After all, Rome wasn't built in a day.

Chapter Two: The Leotard

Behind the door, the TV blares so loudly I'm not even sure they'll hear my knock.

"Hello?"

I rap again, my attention drawn towards the flickering light behind the twitching curtains of the house next door. You see me now, but soon I'll just be a shadow, a trick of the eye, a blur on—*come on, for Christ's sake, it's pissing it down.*

RAP. RAP.

On the verge of the boggy front strip in front of the house, I notice a squished black bag, brown mush spilling onto the pavement.

Chaos, Simon. Chaos. It gets my fucking goat!

To think, all the trouble of wrapping one's fingers around your dog's steaming warm turd, then leaving the bag there, as if it's a job done.

RAP. RAP. RAP. RAP.

At last, the door opens, revealing a woman looking older than time itself, cigarette dangling loosely from the corner of her mouth. She screws up her eyes and begins to examine me.

"Is it ready?" I say.

The lines across her forehead deepen, and she takes a long, slow drag, lending thoughts of a retired detective brought in to solve a crime that's keeping the hotshots from sleep. "You what, love?"

"The costume? Is it ready?"

She's back on the case again, giving it another crack, red veins in her cheeks almost glowing in the dark. "Ah, yes. Leotard man," she says.

"It's not a leotard." It was once but shouldn't look like one now if the old codger's done her job. "It's my costume," I say, puffing my chest out. "Did you put the pockets in as I asked, and add the cape?"

"Wait there, love."

As she leaves in a puff of smoke, I snap my head to the left and inhale air less tainted with second-hand smoke or dog shit. Come on, come on, you silly old goose.

"Can you remember where I put that leotard, Alf?" I hear her say. "That weirdo's back."

"Don't let him in, for Christ's sake," a voice replies, one I assume belongs to Alf.

Arching my neck through the doorway, I can almost taste the stale warmth. Beyond the yellowing hallway, I see an ashtray overflowing with butts and a stack of empty dishes, leftover carnage from goodness knows how many TV dinners. One can hardly blame them for bunkering down, though, losing themselves in any other world than this one.

Chaos, Simon.

But it's just one cup, Mum.

CRACK. How dare you!

Sorry. I'm sorry.

It's one cup now, two tomorrow, and before you know it, you're living in a bloody shit heap, Simon. Nothing but a fucking hippy collecting your piss in empty milk bottles. Is that what you want, Simon? Is it? Because that's what's going to happen.

Sorry, Mum. Sorry.

It gets my fucking goat!

"Here we go, love."

It's less grand than I would have hoped. Lacklustre by superhero standards but better than a bin bag and tape. "Four pockets?"

"Just like you asked, pet. Two on the outside, two on the inside. It's got a zip-up back and a flowing cape."

"Eyes?"

"Red netting, just like you—"

"Wait. Where's the mouth hole?"

"Beg your pardon, love?"

"Has the weirdo gone yet, Janice?" Alf hollers from behind the discoloured wall. "You're letting all the cold air in."

"Mouth hole. A hole for the mouth," I say, trying to remain calm.

"Janice!"

"Hang on, Alf! I'm with a client."

I'm losing it, my jaw beginning to ache from clenching. "Mouth hoooooooooole."

"Just give him the leotard and tell him to eff off, will yer. Our show's starting."

She snaps her head around again. "Will you shut up, Alf? Will you? Will you just shut the fuck up?"

"And it's not a fucking leotard," I shout at the wall.

"Look, you didn't ask for a mouth hole," she says, watery eyes back on me. "If you'd have asked for one, you'd have got one."

"I just assumed you'd know to put a hole there. You know, so one can breeeeeeeathe."

"Gimp suits are not my specialty," she says, folding her arms tight.

"Janice, hurry up."

"Shut up, Alf! Shut up! Shut up!"

Dropping my shoulders, I offer a resigned sigh, running my finger over the material where the mouth should be. "I just thought it would be obvious enough."

"Well, the material looks breathable for a few hours. And if you'd wanted holes, you should have—"

"Can you do it now?"

"Do what now?"

"The hole."

"The hole?

"Now."

"Now?"

"Yes, now."

"I'm sorry, love, but I'm watching—what are we watching, Alf?"

"Fuck all at the bloody moment."

"I have a slot on Thursday morning if that suits you?"

"But it's just a hole. Can't be difficult."

"Not if you want a good job. Now, as I said, if you bring it—"

"But I need it now." I've been thinking about this moment all day; it made my skin sing. "Never mind," I say, close to tears. "It's fine. I'll take it as is."

"That'll be a hundred then." She hands over the costume and offers her crinkled palm, splayed fingers more yellow than the hallway. "Where's the party anyway?"

I lay the cash in her hand. No tip. "Party?"

"Fancy dress."

"No, you don't understand." I correct my posture, thrusting my chest out again and lifting my chin. "I'm The Rectifier."

"Come again? And what just happened to your voice?"

"The Rectifier." It still sounds strained, but I'm sure my vocal cords will get used to it. "I'm bringing hope back to town."

"Janice!"

"Okay, okay." She rolls her eyes. "That man, I tell yer. Well, I'll wish you good luck. Although I think you might be a little late, pet. This town went to the dogs long ago, and they won't give it back without a fight." She looks up and down the street before flicking the cigarette butt onto the pavement.

If everyone did that. Lack of self-respect.

I've seen so many misdemeanours today that made my blood boil, but I'm just a civilian until I'm in that costume. No power. Not long to wait now, though, and my skin prickles again at the thought.

"Well, goodnight, love," she says, now frantically rubbing at her arms. "As I said, if you need a hole for the mouth, or anywhere else for that matter, bring it back on Thursday."

Unable to tear my stare away from the smouldering butt, all I can manage is a weak, "Goodbye."

The TV kicks into action as soon as the door closes.

Chaos, Simon. Drinking your own piss.

Unable to turn a blind eye any longer, I snatch the cigarette butt from the concrete, and lift the letter box. Giggling comes from inside, somewhat reserved at first, but it soon competes with the shrill canned laughter from the TV.

"The Rectum Eater," I hear Alf say.

That's enough to send them both into hysterics, and for me to shove the butt through the door. A small step, but I guess even Spider-Man struggled to cast webs at first, and I expect Superman had his fair share of crash landings and sore retinas. I stand, ready to run, but my eyes fall across the broken bag of dog shit, causing a shudder to run down my spine.

Chaos, Simon. Chaos! It's everywhere you look, spreading like mould. The pull is too powerful—my superhero senses tingling and Mother's voice screaming at me to end the chaos.

The Rectum Eater.

Am I going to do this? Am I? I'm damn sure this wouldn't fall within the superhero code of conduct. Still, until I get that suit on, I'm just a civilian.

Fuck it.

As I pick up the bag and begin forcing it through the letterbox, some of it spills onto my fingers and runs down my arm. *That's it, Simon. Get it all in. Teach them some respect.* It's all I can do not to spew, but I continue digging my fingers into the warmth, knowing becoming a superhero was never going to be an easy ride. *Get in. Get in.*

"Who the hell is that now?" Alf shouts from inside.

Ah, shit.

"It's your turn," Janice says, the blare of the TV ceasing once more.

A simultaneous groan and squeak signify the big guy is on his way. *Come on, almost there. Get in there, you fucker. Get in. Goddamn it, will you just—*

"What in the name of horseshit!" The handle turns, and the door snaps open.

"Captain Justice, at your service," I scream, wiping my shitty fingers across my thigh and making my run.

"Oy," Alf calls into the night. "Come back here, you pervy little twat."

"Small steps make climbable ladders."

"I'll stick that leotard right up your arse."

"It's not a fucking leotard!"

I see hopelessness, a town on its knees in desperate need of a hero. It's overloading my circuitry, wrongdoing wherever one looks. Someone must rise to the challenge and set an example. *Starts with you, Simon. If you don't rinse your bowl, why would you expect others to?*

Glancing over my shoulder, I see Alf still standing in the doorway. I'm not sure why I'm still running; the guy looks three hundred pounds, and that's being generous. One sudden move and Janice would be picking out an extra-large casket for him at the parlour. That said, I slow to a walk only as I turn the corner, the smell of dog shit still strong in my nostrils.

Tough beginnings.

If only they could see what I intend to do, they'd surely get behind me, perhaps even sleep more peacefully in their beds. A rookie move, letting my emotions guide my actions, and certainly not the best start to my public esteem campaign. If there is to be a change and a semblance of restored order, I need the public on my side.

Promise you won't turn out like your weak-as-piss father or his pissant of a brother, Simon.

A scene fills my head, creeping down the hallway for a midnight snack, one of my braver moments, never to be repeated. Heart in mouth, I swung myself into the kitchen, celebrating prematurely by letting out a deep exhale and offering a mini fist pump. The last thing I expected to find was a bleary-eyed and ominously skinny

Uncle Rodney, his head in the fridge, a bundle of blankets hanging around his lower half but well past his arse crack. He seemed much less perturbed, lifting his head from the fridge and offering a toothless smile, blankets dropping to the floor, exposing a limp dick swinging between pasty white stilts. "Simey! Got any peanut butter in here, maaaaaaaaate?"

Mother often called Dad's brother a waste of a skeleton, and I was always inclined to agree—another victim to add to the growing tally of what was becoming a drug-fuelled town. Even Father despised him, but being *as weak as piss,* I guess he didn't have the heart to estrange himself from kin. He made me swear on my life not to tell, knowing Mother would tear him a new one if she ever found out. "Rodney occasionally sleeps things off in the shed," Father said. "It's only now and again. Better than him sleeping on the streets, don't you agree?"

No, I'll not turn out like either of those two. "I won't let you down, Mama."

Fantasising about a long, hot shower, I resume my journey home, observing the chaos. Plastic bags caught in bushes, empty bottles and cans nestled in weeds, graffiti wherever I look, and worst of all, discarded needles and condoms left in plain sight. Making a mental note of it all, I do my best to ignore the car pulling up on the opposite side of the road, taking up two spaces. *Easy, Simon, easy.* I give them the benefit of the doubt, thinking they may check their position and correct themselves, but as they exit the vehicle and slam the door shut, I'm overwhelmed and already making my way across.

You must set an example, Simon.

"Excuse me, sir."

A woman with a crew cut turns around, a white plastic bag swinging in her grip.

"My apologies," I say. "It gets dark early these days, doesn't it?"

"Is that what you wanted to tell me?"

"Actually, no. It's just... Well, you're parked over two spaces, see."

The woman looks over my shoulder and back at me again. "You don't look like a parking inspector, chicken boy."

"That's funny. Chicken boy." Mocking myself still prompts no sign of her breaking her defences. "Could you move it then, please?"

She offers a gentle shake of her head. "I'll be five minutes, tops. I'm just dropping off a food package to some of the elderlies in the high rise."

The skin tightens around my skull. "I'm guessing moving the car will only take a minute. *Tops.*"

She sighs hard, giving me another up-and-down look, eyes stopping briefly on the leotard. "Look, it's been a long day. All I want to do is take this up and then go home."

"Just move the car, then you can continue with your business."

"Five minutes, tops."

"A minute, *tops,* to move the car."

Her forehead creases. "But I'm bringing food to the elderly."

"And I'm bringing hope back to town."

"The only thing you're bringing is a migraine, chicken boy. And what's with the leotard?"

"Move the car."

"No."

"Move the car."

"No."

I feel my blood begin to boil. This woman thinks she has a free pass because she's carrying food for one of the crusties in the tower block. Words start crashing into each other in my head as I try and find a way through all this chaos. It all starts to become too much until lightning finally strikes. "I'll take the food up for you."

"No. We're not allowed to do that. They're used to seeing me, and quite frankly, you'd likely upset the poor dearies."

I hate Jesus. "It'll be fine, I like old people. Give me the food."

"No."

"Why are you being so obtuse?"

"Obtuse? It's taking all my reserve not to thump you."

"I'm not sure you should be working with elderly people."

"I'm not sure you should be breathing."

"Give me the food."

"No."

"Give me the food."

"No."

Once again, overwhelmed, I snatch at the plastic bag.

"You smell like shit," she cries.

We push, shove, twist, and dance amid a series of groans and cuss words, the cape flapping between us. Light rain begins to shower down but washes away neither our dogged pursuit for supremacy nor the shit stains down my fingers. Only as the plastic bag splits, launching the contents towards the sky, do we cease our struggle, observing as gravity comes into play, bringing the Tupperware boxes plummeting towards the ground. We watch in silence as what looks like gravy spills across the road.

The woman offers a snort as she turns to face me, the fingers of her right hand curling into a fist. "Oh, it's on now."

I take a step back. She takes a step forward. I take another step back. She takes two steps forward. I may have mishandled this situation. Perhaps I could have been more diplomatic with my approach. Still, the words in my head are unrelenting, and I know resistance is futile. "You should have moved the car."

And as predicted, the short sentence ignites a fire behind my dance partner's eyes. She offers another snort and begins her charge. Nursing my wounded ego, I turn fast and start my run, meatballs squelching underfoot.

"If I get my hands on you!"

But I'm running like the wind, beating world records. "If everyone did that, the world would—"

"I'll rip yer fucking head off!"

"I'm just trying to bring order. Why can't you just—"

"Oh, just fuck off with your self-righteous goody-goody bullshit."

"Be respectful."

"Kiss my arse."

Her voice is already growing distant, and her breathing is nothing but a wheeze. Taking the opportunity, I look over my shoulder to find her slowing, shaking a fist at the air in front. She finally stops, doubling over, sucking in the town's toxicity.

If only they knew, could see what I was trying to do. Chicken boy, she'd called me. Just like Rectum Eater, it's a name I hope doesn't stick. *Why won't anyone get on side? In this godforsaken town, why wouldn't anyone want to embrace change?* Chalking the encounter as another work in progress, I slip back into the shadows and continue home. Light has albeit faded now, bringing an even more sinister feel to town along with the familiar heaviness in the pit of my stomach.

Chapter Three: Night Creatures

I don't get far before a voice stops me in my tracks. "Spare any change, mate?" Spinning around, I see a scruffy-looking kid in a hoodie emerging from the darkness, desperation behind his eyes. Everything about him is drab, aside from the pristine white sneakers.

"Jesus Christ! Where the fuck did you come from?"

He shuffles from foot to foot before bringing a knife out from behind his back. "Your change."

"Easy kid, easy." Christ, he must be fifteen, sixteen at most. Fucker was stealthy, though, I'll give him that. When the costume is on, I must ensure I'm on my guard. "No need for violence here."

"Give me your fucking change!" He brings the knife over his shoulder, offering a frown as he sniffs the air. "Have you shit yourself?"

"It's dog shit. Listen, I'll give you my change, but on one condition."

"One last time, give us your fucking money, mister," he says through gritted teeth, taking a step forward.

"I will. I will. But no need for violence. I have another—"

We both turn our attention to an approaching police car, the kid lowering the knife but making no attempt to hide it. For a moment, he looks like he might run, but he surprises me by standing his ground.

The cops are slowing down. Christ on a bike, I think they might even be pulling over. Perhaps the tide has turned. Maybe the officer inside is a person of principles, a lone wolf fighting against corruption, honouring his badge and allegiance to serve and keep our streets safe. Together we can bring hope and restore this town to its former glory.

"It's all over, kid," I say.

He curls his lip and frowns. "Fuck off, you creep. And what happened to your voice?"

The vehicle stops kerbside, the kid and I watching as the darkened window slides down. Not before shoving a handful of fries into the hole above his greasy chin, the red-faced driver turns and studies us with what Mother would have coined a 'shit on his shoe' look. Still, hope burns in my belly as we wait for the officer to make his next move.

"Is this man bothering you?" the moustached man asks.

"Well, actually, yes," I reply, full of renewed hope. "I was just walking—"

The officer taps his baton against the side of the door. "I was speaking to the other fella."

The kid shrugs. "He was offering me money for a blowjob."

"No, I wasn't."

"Shut up, you," the officer yells, offering me a snarl and another tap of his baton. "The kid's a minor, you know."

Hardly believing what's happening, I hold my hands up in a gesture of peace. "I don't want a blowjob."

"So you want to give him a blowjob?"

"No! No blowjobs." *Jesus fucking Christ.* "The kid stopped me. He waved a knife in my face and demanded my money."

"Did you give it to him?"

"What?"

The officer stuffs more fries down his gullet. "The money?"

"No. We saw you coming and thought—"

"You best then."

"Best what?"

"Give him the money. The kid's got a knife."

Again, unable to believe my ears, I watch the officer slurping his drink through a straw. He offers a subsequent and elongated belch that sounds like a frog being slowly squashed.

"Is this a joke, officer?" is all I can think to say.

The burly man leans out the window, squinting into the rain. "What's that in your hands?"

"What? Why? He's the one with the bloody knife."

"It's a leotard," the kid answers on my behalf.

"Look, are you going to do something about this, officer?" I look around to see if anyone else is hearing such ridiculousness. "These streets aren't safe anymore."

The cop takes a bite of his triple-stacked burger and begins chomping with loud, wet sounds. "Why are you walking the streets carrying a leotard around with you?" he says, shrapnel spraying onto the street.

"That's not important. What is important is—"

"Cos he's a fucking pervert," the kid says. "Said he wanted to fiddle with me diddle."

The officer gives me another accusatory look, shaking his fat chops, mind made up. "Fucking creatures of the night," he says, hurling his carton out of the window and proceeding to wheel-skid away into the night.

Imagine if everyone did that, Simon.

It boils my blood. Gets my effin' goat. My fists clench, and I offer a garbled growl. As I turn back to the kid, he takes a step back, perhaps sensing my volatility and that he might have picked on the wrong person. And as if my superhero senses kick in, even cape-less, I can see right through him, his narrow and shifty eyes giving him away—he's never used the knife before for anything other than a threat. I imagine him to prey on the fragile, knowing them an easy target with no chance of standing their ground. He must have seen my wiry frame and thought I'd be a soft touch.

"Even Clark Kent got bullied, Simon," I mutter in self-defence, before stepping forward.

The kid narrows his eyes at me as he takes another step back, the knife now shaking in front of him. The tide has turned, my adrenaline surging as I step onto the road.

"I'll give you the money, kid," I say, waving the note in the air. "Just tell me who your supplier is."

He glances over his shoulder. "Don't know what you're talking about."

"A name is all I need." He's about to run. I can sense it. The no-doubt stolen sneakers he's wearing could be about to see their first proper action. "The money's yours, kid, a nice crisp note. Just tell me where you get your drugs."

I almost feel sorry for him now, his breath clouds peppering the air, eyes darting back and forth as he clutches the knife level with his hips. Tripping over his feet, he stumbles backwards, just managing to avoid landing arse-first on the puddled tarmac. As if he recalls the gangster he was trying to be a few moments ago, he points the blade towards me. "Just let me be, mister, or I'll shaft yer."

The kid reminds me of my Uncle Rodney, albeit a much younger version, the drugs not taking full hold yet. It could be the vacant look behind his eyes, the slightly slurred speech, or the burn marks around his fingers. With every fibre of her being, Mother hated drugs. Hated Rodney even more, telling me Father could have turned out just like him if it wasn't for her changing his ways, bringing him up to scratch. If she'd ever found out Rodney sometimes slept in the shed, she might have spontaneously combusted on the spot.

The kid waves the knife in the air again. "I'll shaft yer. Don't push me."

There's an undeniable sense of power and control as I take another confident step towards the boy. When adorned with the cape, I imagine such feelings becoming further heightened, the adoring crowd watching slack-jawed as another criminal falls victim to whatever the fuck I end up calling myself. "Just give me a name, kid."

I see it in his eyes before he turns and makes a move. Acting fast, I snatch at his hood, forcing a garbled rasp, his legs moving in a cartoon-like fashion but getting him nowhere. "Get off me, you paedo."

"I'm not a fucking paedo." But even having to make such a qualification brings me down from my superhero pedestal. "Now, tell me who your supplier is."

The material of the hoodie begins to give, and sensing an opportunity, he leans back and tries to worm himself out. Almost free and probably thinking himself home and dry, he lunges, but I take an urgent step forward and wrap my arm around his neck. Hoodie still draped over his head, he offers a strangled cry and begins clawing at my skin.

"Get off, you fucking paedo!"

Minimising the chance of an accidental stabbing, I grab the knife-wielding arm, bring it down by his side, and force him to the ground. "Help. Help!" he cries. After a last and fruitless effort to wrestle free, his body goes limp, and he begins to sob. "Please. They'll hurt me."

"I'll hurt you." *For the greater good, Simon. For the greater good.* "Now, give me a name, or I'll fuck you up."

He cries out again as I twist his arm. "You're not going to rape me, are you?"

"Christ, no. But I'll break your fucking arm."

"Okay, okay." The kid offers a resigned moan. "I can't breathe." I release my arm from his neck and remove the hoodie. "Talk."

"If they find out I snitched, they'll—"

"They won't. Now, the next words leaving your lips need to be the information I'm looking for or—"

"Bum Fluff."

"Come again."

"That's his name, my supplier. His street name anyway."

"Bum Fluff? Jesus Christ. Is that one word or two?"

"Two, I assume, but I've never had the balls to ask. He killed a kid. Served some time in a young offender institution. Now let me go, will yer?"

"Fucking Bum Fluff. Christ on a bike. Are there others?"

"Yeah, but I have nuffin' to do with them. Look, mister, a deal's a deal. That's my supplier, and that's what you asked for." He tries to wrestle free again, his head snapping left and right, manic. "A deal's a deal. A deal's a deal."

The anger has gone, and I only feel pity for the kid as I release him. Never really stood a chance growing up in a place like this, likely deadbeats for parents or not even on the scene. Judgemental, I guess, but I also know better than anyone just how much of a product of our parents we are.

"Yeah, it is, kid. A deal's a deal. Just do me a favour and spend this on something that won't fuck you up."

He plucks the money from my fingers and steps back, offering a nod, but his eyes give him away again. "You're lucky I didn't stab your arse."

"And you're lucky I didn't rape your arse."

"What?"

"A joke." On consideration, I make a note to also keep such quips to myself moving forward. "Just a paedo joke." Not the type of catchphrase one wishes to be quoted on.

"You're fucking weird," the kid says before turning and making a run, only the whites of his sneakers soon visible. "And you smell like shit."

Small steps make climbable ladders, Simon.

Yes, Mama.

The last of my adrenaline dwindles as I begin the walk home, the cold wind making its way through my depleted shield and seeping through to my bones. As I bend to pick up Officer Pigface's discarded carton, I hear sirens, screams, and burning rubber—all sounds I associate with the opposite of hope. But most of all, beneath all that, I hear the desperate cries of those hiding behind doors, those too afraid even to part the curtains once the sun goes down.

I will bring hope back to town; see if I don't. "I'm coming for you, Bum Fluff."

Only the dogs respond to my voice, a domino effect of well-practiced barks that soon surround me. Usually staying quiet, likely immune to the various creatures of the night, they're really going for it, approaching a never-ending crescendo. Maybe in the same way superheroes have a sixth sense, dogs also do. Perhaps they can sense the imminent change, the storm before the calm. I join in with their barking, howling at the moon, unable to contain my excitement about getting home and trying on my costume.

"Shut the fuck up," someone shouts from high up somewhere. But I'll fly even higher; I'll show them. Pausing for a moment, I lay the costume over my shoulder and place both hands palm down in a dark puddle, doing my best to wash off the remaining dog shit. Yeah, flying high, kiddo. "I'm bringing order back to town," I say before ducking into the shadows. As if sensing the anti-climax, the dogs dampen their applause.

In addition to the hard waste left in this no man's land of a town: Old cookers, dirty mattresses, and turned-over fridges, the pavements and streets are lined with filth. Everywhere one looks, nastiness awaits. I lose count of how many used needles and condoms I pass, unable to bring myself to scoop them up. My recent glove purchase will help, although I need to think long-term and beyond being a glorified street sweeper.

Small steps, Simon.

"But Mama, people won't take me seriously if they see me walking the pavements with a poop-a-scoop."

I try to imagine what other superheroes might do, faced with the sheer amount of shite smudged all over the tarmac. Would Superman laser it with his eyes? Surely that would kick off a stench and a half. And what about Spider-Man? Net it, then toss it in the litter bin? That might work out okay for the solids, but what if said doggy ate something it wasn't supposed to that day? Then it would be—*chaos.*

"Get off, you cunt!"

Snapping my head towards the female's voice, I only see a blur of shadows down the alley.

"I don't want to hurt you. Just give me the bag, bitch."

"Your dead, you are," the woman says. "Fucking dead."

"Oi," I yell, setting off on my hero run, long strides but not too flighty. I send a bottle rolling across the ground, dampening the moans and groans of the continuing struggle. This is it; this is my time to shine, to win favour with the public with or without my cape. Word of a vigilante will spread quickly and along with it, hope. "Leave her be," I yell, noting the outline of a petite woman and, behind her, the rounded shoulders of some giant oaf.

Shit. Fuck.

He must be six foot—what—three, four? I lost a fight to a five-foot Hispanic once. Regardless, I puff my chest out, striding to the damsel's rescue. "I said, get off her."

Beefcake turns to face me, his face all twisted and mean, the word "THUG" tattooed across his neck.

Shit. Now what?

He looks me up and down as though I've turned up to a gun-fight with a stick of celery. "Who the fuck are you?" he asks.

"I'm your worst nightmare."

Before he can mock, something whips across his head, prompting a groan. Hands to his round face, he creases over. "My nose. You broke my bloody nose." The woman offers another war cry, swinging the bag again and catching him in the same spot. "Ow, you bitch! You fucking bitch!" Darkness dripping between his fingers, the tough guy begins shrinking back. Still, the woman attacks, relentlessly swinging the makeshift weapon and landing direct hit after direct hit.

POW! WHAM! SLAM!

Before I even arrive on the scene to save the day, he's lumbering away, offering a series of dampened moans.

"You're dead," the woman screams after him. "Fucking dead, you hear!" At last, her face comes into view, neck straining as she mutters more abuse at her fleeing attacker, an unlit cigarette wedged in the corner of her mouth. "You messed with the wrong woman, you cocksucker. Say your prayers, cos you won't see them coming.

You're a dead man walking, a fucking ghost."

As I arrive at her shoulders, I feel like a spare part, heart thumping, blood whooshing in my ears. "Are you okay?"

She turns, her face taut, eyes still wide, fingers white around the straps of the handbag. "The fucker asked a fair question," she says. "Aside from being his worst nightmare, who the fuck are you?"

"Bit cheesy that line, wasn't it?"

"A tad. Now answer the fucking question."

Who am I? I guess it is a fair question. "I'm nobody. I just heard a struggle and thought I'd come to help."

Her features soften as she studies my face, no doubt realising I don't present a threat. *Oh shit. Shit. Shit. Shit on a stick. What is this? Why do I suddenly feel like this? What's happening to me?*

"What's that?" she says, nodding towards my arm. "Is that a leotard?"

"No, it's—it's—so, you're okay?"

The corners of her lips flicker into almost a smile. "Seen off worse than him before. I'm used to looking after myself around these parts. Dog eat dog and all that." She lowers the handbag and falls back against the wall, her long coat opening to reveal a dress far too tiny for an autumn evening. "Ain't seen you around here before. You new to this shithole?"

"Nope. Been away for a while, visiting relatives and stuff."

"Got a light?"

"I don't smoke."

"What do you do, kid?" She leans forward, a hand rifling through her oversized handbag. She comes out with a lighter and flicks it on, the glow of the flame further softening her face but highlighting some old bruising under her right eye. "I mean, apart from walking the streets looking for defenceless women to save?"

Cheeks burning, I shrug and turn my attention to the stars. "Not much really." Words that carry impossible weight, this moment right here being one of the most interesting interactions I've had in a while. The sheer vastness above, though, makes that okay, the greatest equaliser of all. "I mean, I—"

A blazing trail across the night sky steals the rest of my words.

The woman hustles in close, blowing a smoke ring towards the void. It's a magical moment, one I wish could last forever. "You saw that, too, yeah?" she says.

"Yeah. Amazing."

"Must mean something, that."

It means we're in love. I read it somewhere. It means we're destined to be together until the end of time. "Some people believe it's the souls of the dead, reminding us they are still there, watching over us."

"I fucking hope not," she says, offering another smoke ring.

"Well, it's just a theory." *Smooth, Simon. Smooth.* I hold back a cough as tobacco layers at the back of my throat. "My mother's up there somewhere."

"Well, maybe she's trying to tell you how proud she is." Her smile widens. "Rescuing me from the big nasty man."

"No matter how hard I tried in the past, I could never make her proud. But I'm going to do my darnedest to change that."

She wraps a hand around my arm, making me think how little kindness she must have seen to warrant something so forward. "You're different, aren't you?" she says, resting her head against my shoulder, eyes still on the stars. "I can't really get a read."

"I want to make a change. Bring hope back to town."

She snickers, turning her gaze towards me, eyes so pretty but full of pain. I'm a sucker for the eyes, that old chestnut of them being the windows to the soul. And I've always been a good judge of character, preferring to stay quiet, listening, watching, looking for the dark ring around effervescent souls. Only a quiet sadness exudes from the woman's tough exterior, a gentle soul who somehow stumbled through the gates of Hell.

"You think I'm nuts, don't you?"

She shrugs, taking a huge drag on an already half-gone cigarette. "Par for the course. What did you say your name was?"

The Redeemer? For fuck's sake, that sounds like I fly around cashing in coupons all day. Better than Rectum Eater, but still not

press worthy. The Reinforcer? No, that sounds like an odd job person.
"Simon. My name is Simon."

"Pleased to meet you, Simon."

I'm a romanticist and always have been. I think I like the idea of falling in love more than I would the process, but I'd be happy to be proved wrong. My expectations have been set low for some time, knowing reality has different plans for those brave enough to be optimistic. Walks on the beach and nights spent making love in front of an open fire are all great for movies, but I've seen what real life has in store for people around here, and it doesn't come as advertised on Facebook. "And you?"

"And me what?"

"What do they call you?"

"People around here know me as Crystal." She turns her stare to the ground, loosening her grip on my arm. "But my real name is Vera."

I open my mouth to fire a question, but suddenly things become *crystal* clear.

"Something to say?" she asks, her face semi-hardening again.

"I like both names."

"You're judging me, but you don't know me," she says, sliding her arm away. "It's just survival."

"I'm not judging you, honest. It's just that"—I reach for her, but she turns away— "it's just all part of the chaos. But I'm going to make it better. I'm going to—"

"Bring hope back to town." She flicks the cigarette towards the bottle and digs into her handbag. "I think you might be a little late, Simon."

Studying the cigarette butt, I bite my lip. *Let it go, Simon. Let it go.*

But if everyone did that.

"You're not the first person to say that tonight," I say, looking her dead in the eyes. "Look, I know you think I'm crazy, but this town needs something, and everyone else has given up. If I can even create just a ripple of hope."

"And you think parading around these streets wearing that leotard will help?"

For the love of God, it's a cape. "I have to do something, Vera. I can't just—Jesus Christ, is that a rock?"

"Sure is." She wrestles the oversized pebble from the zipper. "Can you hold it while I get the rest of my cigs?" The weight of the stone makes me wince as she drops it into my palm, visions of it heading towards Beefcake's face like an out-of-control comet.

"I always wondered what women carry in their handbags," I say, noting the bundle of notes she swipes to the side. "I've seen pads, rape whistles, make-up, and phones, but I've never seen a boulder before."

"You have to be on your game in this type of neighbourhood," she says. "Excuse the choice of phrase."

Words bounce around my head like unexploded grenades. I bite my lip again, turning my stare to the stars, hoping for a repeat of the magic and another opportunity to huddle up close.

"It was never really a choice," she says, her voice quivering as she continues her hunt. "Sometimes life carves a path so deep it's impossible to climb back out."

"I'll help you." This isn't good, I'm going off-course. It feels like a test, and I'm faltering at the first hurdle.

She turns to face me, the lighter shaking in her hands, her shield well and truly down. I've just met this woman, yet it feels like we're sharing something beyond just the same moon. "What makes you think I need—" Her shoulders go first, and the rest of her body follows, an otherworldly high-pitched wail beginning to emerge from this small bundle as though such distress has been trapped inside for far too long. Draping the leotard—cape—over my shoulder, I wrap my arms around her.

"This isn't me," she says. "I'm as hard as fucking nails."

"I know. I saw you handling that oaf before." Over the smell of tobacco, I get the essence of mango and raspberry. "I think it might be me. Someone said I was easy to talk to once. Initially, I took it as a compliment, but she followed up by saying only in the way she spoke to her dog when nobody else was around."

Vera offers a half laugh, half sniffle. Yes, I feel a strange bond with this woman, as though my success as a superhero directly correlates to her happiness. That isn't how it should be, but it is what it is. I need to rescue her, and properly this time. Not for love. Well, maybe for the thought of it.

"This really isn't like me," she says, smudging her mascara as she wipes the back of her hand across her face. "You've caught me off guard. I hate being weak. Fucking hate it!"

"You're far from weak, Vera." We stay like that for a while, her head nestled into my neck, my arms wrapped around her shoulders as I look towards the sky for another sign of eternal love. This is way off plan, certainly missing from the superhero to-do list. That said, it's the happiest I've felt in some time, and it seems cruel that such a moment will have to end. It's wonderful. Magical. Part of me even thinks—

"Can you smell dog shit?" she says.

"The place is rife with it."

"I better be getting back." She gives a gentle push away, and brushes herself down. "He'll send people out looking for me if I'm late. More about my takings than anything else."

The first grenade explodes in my head. "Why do you do it?" And the second. "There must be another way." And the third. "You're too good for this."

She steps back into the darkness, her face creasing into what I know to be resigned disappointment. I want to suck the words back in, but I know it's too late.

"I'm sorry."

I've failed her, my questions translating as: Where's your self-respect, and why have you given up? *If everyone did that.*

She takes another step back, hardness creeping across her face once more. "I thought you were different, Simon."

"I am. I just—" Desperation forces my hand, a bluff I know I can't win. "Why don't you stay at my place tonight? Not for anything, not for that, just to—"

"You don't understand," she says, her face disappearing into the shadows. "I'm with him now. It's safer that way."

With him? Who's him? Please tell me it's not Bum Fluff. Please, please, please. "Is it Bum Fluff?"

The chink of her heels on the cobbles pauses. "What do you know about Bum Fluff?"

"That he's a dealer," I reply, resisting the urge for untimely sarcasm. "That he's scum, lowest of the low. Getting kids so hooked on stuff they're forced to rob just to feed their addiction."

"Bum Fluff is small scale, Simon, trying to make a name for himself. It might even have been one of his goons that tried to steal my takings, but I doubt it; he should know better than that. If it was, he'll get what's coming to him."

"So, who are you...with?"

The harshness of her heels against the stones starts again. "Stay out of it, Simon. All this superhero bullshit... It isn't the movies, for Christ's sake."

"Wait! Just tell me where I might find Bum Fluff." *Christ, you couldn't write this stuff. What next? Woolly Crotch? Fanny Stubble?*

"I think you might be one of the nice ones, Simon, and I couldn't bear the thought of you getting hurt."

"I'm going to try anyway," I yell into the darkness. "You'd only be saving me time."

"Fine. If you want to get yourself killed, then try by the water." Her voice grows distant and tortured. "There's a broken streetlight where they—" Her words fade into incoherence.

And just like that, she's out of my life. Most think me too odd, casting me aside before putting in the effort of digging past the trauma. But how she looked at me and relaxed in my arms after almost being mugged—nestling in close, and sharing her vulnerability—made me feel like the most important person in her life, even if for a split second. Shooting star aside, I've never felt such a strong connection. *Oh shit. Shit. Shit. Shit. I'm falling into that trap, imagining endless days of laughter and sweet nothings. Will I ever see her again?*

You have a job to do, Simon, a pledge to uphold, remember?
Yes, Mama.

Time to focus. No distractions.

Try by the water. My first solid lead. If it weren't for the funny feeling in my stomach and my elevated heart rate, the superhero part of me could almost convince the rest that the interaction was only to extract information.

"I will make a change," I shout towards the stars. "Just see if I don't."

No further sign comes from the night sky, but this journey is already well under way. I have a name and now a location.

Small steps, Simon.

"Yes, Mama. But please remember I lost a fight to a vertical-ly-challenged Spaniard." That was before I started working out, though, I tell myself. And once I slip into this cape, I will become someone else. And may God help anyone who stands in my way.

To the sound of sirens and the soft patter of rain, I resume my journey home, ignoring the refuse, even the cat-sized rat on Second Avenue. The straw that breaks the camel's back, though, is the bottle of yellow liquid I find inside the bus shelter down Main Street.

Before you know it, you're living in a shit heap—a fucking hippy, collecting your piss in empty milk bottles!

"It gets my fucking goat."

Chapter Four: Tough Beginnings

Finally home, I shake myself off, wipe a smear of shit off my costume, and run upstairs, eager for the transformation. As usual, the racket from next door causes the walls to shake—*All that bloody music*—but excitement and adrenaline rise as I eye the costume spread across the duvet.

It's happening. It's finally happening.

I strip off in front of the full-length mirror, part self-admiration for my new frame and part sorrow for the shy and squeamish young boy who first walked the corridors of the youth detention centre.

Okay, not The Rectifier. What then? Captain Justice has been done, you muppet! The Shadow? Nope. Been done, too. The Silhouette? Too jazzy. Unable to wait any longer, the hairs bristling on the back of my neck, I carefully lift the costume from the bed and slip my arms through.

Oh, yes!

It's as though electricity runs through my veins. I feel alive, reborn. I feel—

"I'm a fucking superhero."

Left leg in, right leg, now time for the head. Jesus, it's tight. *Breathable, my arse, Janice. See how you'd like it with your tar-stained lungs.* "Come on, you fucker."

Sucking my stomach in, I get the zip to the halfway point, but it's in no man's land now. Offering a groan, I push my right elbow back with my left hand, just managing to pinch the end of the metal with the tips of my fingers. "Come on, you zippy little bastard."

Finally, I'm in.

Sweat running down my back, I collect the contents from the bed and force them into my pockets.

It's done. The transformation is complete.

I allow myself a few moments to take in my reflection—a shiny Lycra-ridden hybrid of Batman, Spider-Man, and Death. Not quite how I pictured it in prison, but the dirty-yellow light from above adds a glossiness to the understated muscle definition. Don't get me wrong, I'm no meathead, but prison teaches you how to defend yourself, and I'm a far cry from the nervous, puffy-faced, doughy-bellied kid that first entered those double doors and took a beating from the tiny European.

And it comes to me in a flash.

"The Reformer!"

While running on the spot, I give the cape a quick swish. Looks: seven out of ten. Flexibility: seven out of ten. Breathability: two maximum. Maybe okay for the short term, but I can only imagine if I have to chase someone down.

Full of anticipation, I cross the invisible threshold into my small but immaculate kitchen.

The world is chaotic enough without the need for disarray in the house, Simon.

Hand steady, I stretch my mouth as wide as the fabric will allow. The saying 'Don't try this at home, kids' runs through my head as I hold a steak knife to my face. I'm grateful the material easily cuts as I glide the blade across the mask, creating only a tiny slit but enough to get some extra air in. It could be better, but I doubt anyone will even notice in the dark. The gloves follow—just your everyday gardening type—but ones that have been tried and tested.

That's it, then. I'm ready.

Unable to contain my excitement any further, I coil my fingers around the shiny handle of the back door, admiring the mysterious figure reflected in the glass. The Reformer—he lives in the shadows so residents can live in harmony. Inhale. Exhale. Inhale. Exhale. He's just a man with a dream. Without further ado, I open the door to a mouthful of crisp air and an earful of *bloody loud music.*

I'm only two steps out before The Reformer is called into action. "I hope you're going to pick that up," I say jovially to the old man down the street.

"Fuck off," he replies, dragging the wide-legged dog into the night as it continues to defecate en route.

Bigger fish to fry, though, I tell myself, setting off towards the waterfront. My stomach turns over, but at the same time, I feel more than ready. In prison, I spent so much time fantasising about this day, and it's finally here.

The Reformer.

"The Reformer. Keeping the streets clean." *Nah, tag line makes me sound like a road sweeper.* "The Reformer. A shadow in the dark; you'll never see me coming." *Jesus, that sounds like the rapist's mantra.* "The Reformer. Bringing order and hope back to town." *Yes! I like it. I like it a lot.*

As I walk past rattling windows, it takes all my resolve not to rap on the rickety door, my nerve endings shredding and my fists clenching with the beat.

Jeff, can't you hear that bloody music? Are you just going to sit there? Noise pollution was high on the list of Mother's greatest pet peeves, and by Christ, she had many of them. *Why should everyone be forced to listen to it? All day, every day. If you were a man, Jeff, you'd do something about it. Jeff! Are you listening, Jeff?*

Cape fluttering in the light breeze, I make it three feet past before her voice becomes too much to bear, even giving the spine-crushing bass a run for its money. Another side mission, but this one personal. Even superheroes need a restful night's sleep.

Tap-tap-tap.

The rest of the street appears quiet, but shifting shadows tell a different story. Creatures are stirring, and before long, mischief will run rife. *Keep emotions out of it*, I tell myself. Firm but fair; the public must be on side.

Tap-tap-tap.

Come on. I'm freezing my tits off here. Ear to the door, I hear shouting above the music. What sounds like a child's bawl adds even further intensity to the chaos. I knock harder, but the music shows no signs of quieting. Tensing the muscles in my right arm, I run my left hand over the Lycra, enjoying the rippling bicep. Firm but fair. Firm but fair.

You have to stand up for what you believe in, Simon, or they'll walk all over you. You have to set an example. If you don't, you'll end up as weak as piss, just like your father.

Inhale. Exhale.

Just as I'm about to unleash hell on the door, the doorknob twists, revealing the watery eyes of a little boy wearing an oversized diaper, his hands behind his back and a faint orange dusting on his skin. Beyond him, discoloured walls are tarnished further by handprints and tendrils of spilled drinks. The carpet is threadbare and old with faded-pink swirls only just distinguishable and matted with hair. A dog, perhaps? But I hear no barking.

And all that bloody music, Simon.

Light flickers against the wall, the TV no doubt playing to itself in the lounge. The kid's saviour likely, offering a glimpse into that much better world.

"Hey, kid."

"Who you?"

I've seen the boy a couple of times before, being dragged indoors by a small man with a tattoo on his neck. Looks like a mean son of a bitch, and far from father material. Not anticipating my first proper interaction as a superhero would be with a child, I swallow hard and crouch to his level, Lycra pulling way too tight against my crotch. "I'm The Reformer," I reply, my voice much higher than in the many rehearsals.

The kid's watery eyes give me nothing for a while. "The Wee farmer?" he says, bringing the packet of Cheetos from behind his back and shovelling in his catch.

"No, I'm the—oh, never mind." Another fucking name in the trash can. "How old are you, kid?"

"Four," he says, spraying powder into the air. "Just Wee-formo better."

I consider his response carefully. Re-formo. Re-formo. I'm Reformo, and I'm bringing hope back to town. Reformo at your service. Reformo to save the day. Short and punchy, it's a winner. "Kid, you're on. Reformo it is."

He offers a giggle and a squelchy fart. "Silly mon-key."

"Indeed. Is your daddy in?"

He shakes his head, his body appearing to contract as though shrinking in self-defence. The boy suddenly looks ridiculous, far too big to be sporting a diaper. He scratches his belly with orange fingers, and I notice the light-green bruising below his ribs.

"Anyhow, you know my name now. What's yours?"

"Jayden."

"Well, it's nice to meet you. And I mean no offence when I say this, but I'm pretty sure you've shit yourself, Jayden."

He nods. "Wait for Mummy."

"Where is she?"

"Through there." He points to the rear of the house. "With Terry."

Terry? Perhaps not the father, after all. "Is Terry your dad?"

"My dad's dead."

I nod, offering a sigh. "The music is very loud."

He nods and gives his belly another scratch. "Terry like it loud."

"Mind if I turn it down?"

He offers a resigned shrug. "Okay."

As he leads me to the lounge, I almost regret putting a hole in the Lycra, the stench of fast food, cigarettes, and whatever else lurking within the carpet fibres, assaulting my senses. Two dead fish float in the tank towards the centre of the room, the water too murky to see if others are alive.

It's chaos, Simon; the whole word gone to the dogs, I tell you.

I wonder how the kid bears it, but then I figure, if you dipped your fingers in enough dog shit, you'd become immune to it after a while.

"There," he says, pointing his finger at the bookshelf full of DVDs and the illuminated phone. Poor kid looks terrified, slumping further, likely in anticipation of what's about to unfold. "Terry not likey," he says, bottom lip quivering.

Reformo not give fucky. "It's okay," I say, reaching over and raking my fingers through his scraggy black curly hair, wincing as they get stuck halfway. "No need to be scared. I'm a superhero, Jayden."

His eyes light up, but after looking me up and down a couple of times, he turns his attention back to the TV and the smiling muppets around the piano. "Nah."

"I am, I promise."

"Fwy then."

"I can't fly."

Jayden shrugs. "Bring fwishes back to life then."

My turn to shrug. "I can't do that."

"Laser hole in wall."

"Just wait, Jayden." I hold my finger in the air, and the kid follows the tip as though expecting a bolt of fizzing red light to emerge at any second. "Give me a countdown, kid," I say, reaching for the phone from the shelf. "Go on. From five." I'm all in now, about to go head-to-head with my first evil villain.

The kid turns again, his eyes widening as he sees me holding the phone over the fish tank. His head begins to shake, and he begins stepping back, scratching frantically at his belly. "Terry get weeeeal angwy."

"Do you think it's fair that everyone down the street has to listen to Terry's music?"

Sucking the orange from the middle finger of his left hand, the kid appears to be considering his response. He pauses to scratch at his nest of hair. After a few moments, offering another shake of his head, he lowers himself to the carpet and sits cross-legged, his face becoming distressed as the shit no doubt rides further up his flesh. *The Muppets* are putting on a hell of a show but failing to overshadow the shouting from deeper within the house.

"Good boy. Okay, from five, Jayden." I nod for him to begin.

He averts his gaze from me to the phone and back again, a smile replacing the worry as though he thinks I might be playing; the silly man wearing a tight black costume about to feed Terry's phone to the fish.

"When you're ready, Jayden."

He coils his orange fingers around his toes, his grin disappearing. Perhaps for further assurance that things will be okay, he looks at me again, eyes exuding fear as he rocks back and forth. Uncertainty begins twisting in my stomach, but I nod regardless.

"One," he finally says.

"No, Jayden. Start at five and count down."

He looks at me and shrugs.

"Okay, let's do it your way. Start from one, and on five, we do it, yeah? Can you count to five? Can you do that for me, Jayden?"

"One...two—" He pauses, eyes so wide, his head offering a gentle shake.

"It's okay, Jayden. It's okay."

"Thwee."

"Good boy. And what comes after three?"

"F-fwour." He glances towards the back of the house, his rocking intensifying.

"Go on, Jayden, it's okay."

He screws his eyes shut and offers a shudder. "Fwive."

There's a delay before the *music* finally cuts out, and *The Muppets* retake centre stage, putting to death an old classic. Jayden snaps his eyes open, his rocking at an end. Did the kid think I was bluffing? Superheroes don't bluff, kid. He begins dragging himself backwards, the already vile carpet drinking the light brown liquid dripping from his thighs. As the voices get closer, he nestles behind a shabby old armchair, breath held.

"Put that music back on, you little shit," a male voice yells.

Terry, I assume. "Don't make me come out there."

The boy sniffles, pushing himself against the chair as though trying to become part of it. Making a point of leaning over, I offer another rustle of his matted hair. He's shaking, breathing heavy. Snot inflates and deflates in both nostrils. "It's okay, Jayden." The welt towards the bottom of his spine makes my skin crawl. "I told you, I'm a superhero."

"I wish," he mumbles.

As footsteps pound, causing pictures of faraway landscapes to rattle against dirty walls, Jayden tries to stifle his sobs with an elbow. Poor kid doesn't stand a chance. I snap my head towards the approaching shadow to see Terry—Tattoo Man—gracing us with his presence.

"What the fuck?" He looks me up and down from the doorway and blinks hard as if his eyes are playing catch up. He's about the same size as the angry Spaniard, give it or take an inch. The same belly, too, held in by a too-tight and stained white vest. "Do I know you?" he says, face twisting into ugliness.

"You do now, Terry," I reply, cool as a fucking cucumber. "People call me—" My voice cracks halfway, so I make a point of thrusting my chest out and tensing. "People call me Reformo."

"How the fuck do you know my name?"

"I'm here to restore order and hope."

Terry looks down towards the battered armchair. "Jayden, did this man touch you?"

The boy stands, still trembling, heavy diaper looking weightier even with what must be a pound of shit running down both legs. He opens his mouth and closes it again, red track lines running across his chest as his scratching intensifies further.

Fingering a strap over her shoulder, a woman joins *Tattoo Man* at the doorway. "What's going on? And who the fuck is that?"

The villain doesn't take his eyes off me. "Says his name is Returdo. This man touch you, Jayden?"

"It's Reformo, actually."

"Shut the fuck up," he says through gritted teeth. "Jayden, tell me the truth, or so help me God. Did this man touch you?"

The boy looks at me and back to Terry, finally offering a gentle but unmistakable nod.

"I did, but not like that." My voice cracks again. "I just ran my fingers through his hair." *Ah, shit.*

"You filthy fucking pervert," the woman cries. "Is that what you do? Sneak into houses and touch kids like some sort of—some sort of paedo Santa. Terry, shall I call the police?"

"No, Violet. He's in our house, on our turf." The man crunches his knuckles and removes his shirt. "Anything goes."

"Your music—it was too loud." Fight or flight. Fight or flight. I turn to the door but know this journey will be over if I run. And this is not the headline I wanted: Reformo—he'll sneak into your house and touch your kids. "I just wanted some order, some respect."

"What you're going to get is a good whooping."

This is it. My first fight as a superhero. Inhale. Exhale. Inhale. Exhale.

Noticing the teardrop under his eye, I freeze for a moment, the taste of prison at the back of my throat, a bitter blend of blood, tobacco, and detergent.

Remember the pledge you made when you were there, Simon.
I'm scared, Mama.

"Don't kill him, Terry," Violet cries, but her eyes and snarl convey a different message.

After that short fight with the short Spaniard, we became friends of sorts. "Luca" became my little European Mr. Miyagi, telling me something in broken English about having to strike first, always taking the opponent by surprise, even if you think you'll lose.

He's coming!

Fear rides up my spine. *Promise you won't turn out like your weak as piss father.* Terry readies his short but bulky arms, reminding me of a dinosaur cartoon I used to watch.

Teardrop! Teardrop! Teardrop!

But before he can even get off a punch, I swing—THWACK—catching him square on the jaw and sending him crumpling to the carpet. Face down in Jayden's shit, he tries to push himself from the ground, but his arms fail him, and his eyes all but spin in his head.

GROOOOOOAN.

The jaw—a favoured weak spot by most inmates and caught just right—can turn someone's lights out. I've seen it for myself, on the inside, but on those desperate occasions that I had to defend myself was never able to master it. It seems that wearing this costume carries some extra clout, placebic or not.

"I am Reformo." Hardly believing it was that easy and over so quick, I crouch beside Terry, unable to deny a fleeting sense of supremacy. *Teardrop.*

"Get the kid out of here, Violet," the man rasps.

"Probably a good opportunity to get Jayden cleaned up and change his diaper," I say, eyeing the woman sternly. Turning my attention back on the kid, I note his changed demeanour and the sparkle in his eyes. "Told you, Jayden." I offer him a wink, but my stomach turns, imagining how much heartache and pain the kid has already experienced. Against the backdrop of the TV, more bruises present themselves, all the colours of an evil rainbow. "It's okay now, Jayden. I told you it would—"

"Wassout!" the kid cries.

I snap my head around to see Terry on his knees, swinging a dining chair towards me, his mouth contorted with rage. Before I can raise my hands in defence, black spots fill my vision, delayed pain surging across my skull and neck. *Fuuuuuuuck!* Face down on the carpet, it's my turn to taste Jayden's Cheeto-infused shit.

"You come into my house," Terry screams, "turn my music off, and touch my kid."

Skewed priorities, Terry, but that's about the sum of it. "I just want some order." Beyond Jayden's wide eyes, I see muppets, all smiles, mid-way through another number.

"I'll fucking kill you!"

"Geroff him," Jayden cries. "Leave him lone."

In preparation for the pain, I screw my eyes half-shut and roll over to my back, the chair leg missing my head by inches. Terry straddles me, trying to use his bought-and-paid-for belly to keep me pinned, but with superhero strength I roll us to the right, offering him a swift elbow in his roundness as we plummet. POW! He releases a gasp and loosens his grip, allowing me to get on top and drive a knee into his chest. BAM!

"I'll fucking kill you!" he screams.

"You have to respect your neighbours, Terry."

"I'll rip your fucking head off—"

"It's just a matter of decency."

"—and then shit down your neck."

"Drinking your own piss from milk bottles."

"What the fuck are you on about?" Spittle sprays from his lips as his face grows redder still. "Arrrrrrggggggggghhhhh!"

Just as I feel some semblance of control, something shatters across the left side of my face—CRACK—a wave of delayed pain spreading inside my head. As Terry tries to buck me off, I study the broken shards of the lampshade on the carpet.

"Get off him, you pervert," Violet screams.

The angry little man beneath me tries to capitalise, his contrastingly big hands punching at the air as I dodge and weave like a master. WHOOSH. WHOOSH. WHOOSH. Already gasping for breath, his eyes grow wide, but the punches keep coming, albeit weaker, each attempt missing me by a good few inches.

FZZZZ. FZZZZ.

I've seen that before, in prison, when they realise they've bitten off more than they can chew, lack of cardio taking a big bite out of their fat arse.

FZZZZ. FZZZZ.

I tense my arm, creating an audible crackle of the muscle, and, making a meal of it, bring my fist to shoulder level. Violet's now nowhere to be seen, but Jayden moves in closer, his eyes full of awe as Terry's fists continue weakly glancing off my chest. It's a beautiful and high-energy scene that eradicates any doubt.

"From five, Jayden."

The boy smiles and nods. "One, two—"

"You're fucking dead, kid," Terry screams, but his words carry as much impact as his fists.

"Thwee." Jayden continues. "Fwour, fwive."

Terry tries to protect himself, but my fist finds a way through, connecting with his chin. CRACK! And another. BANG! And another. WHALLOP!

"Let's see if we can find your phone, shall we, Terry?" I drag him to his feet and lead him to the fish tank. "Jayden, are we warm or cold?"

The kid snickers. "Warm."

"I think it's in here, but I can't be sure." I grab the guy's ponytail and dunk him into the murkiness, sending dirty water spilling over the edges. He strains against my grip, kicking at air, lashing with his arms, bubbles rising to the surface to the sound of his muted and watery screams. My arm sings, but the strength of a hero ebbs through me. I twist Terry's head until his lips press against the glass. "Look, Jayden. What type of fish is that?"

"A Terryfwish." The kid laughs again, doubling over, his palms pressed against chubby kneecaps.

"Leave him be!"

I snap my head towards Violet, a gun shaking violently in her hands. Needle marks puncture her arm, some going all the way to her shoulder. "But I'm bringing hope back to town," I say, realising at face value that might be a bit of a leap of faith. "You're better off without him, Violet. Trust me, you can do better. If not for you, for the kid."

There's a knowing in her eyes, but still, she waves the gun and takes a nervous step forward. "Let him out of there, or I'll shoot."

Weakening my grip, I allow Terry to come up, noting the teardrop is now nothing but a smear. Would you fucking believe it? Gasping for air and hacking out dirty water, he shakes off like a wild wet dog. "I'll fucking kill you, you fucking—"

I drive him under again—all that shaking for nothing.

"I'll fucking do it," she says, curling a finger around the trigger. There's fear in her eyes, but I don't think it's for me. "I'm not playing."

"Violet, don't be silly. Just put the gun down." There's no way she's going to do it. I've seen this scene countless times in the movies, and they always break down and collapse to the floor, begging for forgiveness. "I just want the message to be received, Violet. It's just a matter of respect for yourself and others."

"Three."

Not in a million years will she do it. "Violet, there's still time to change."

"Two."

What if she does, though? "Together we can restore order, Violet."

"One."

Oh fuck, I think she might do it. "Think of your son."

The gun explodes, somehow putting a hole in the ceiling and sending Violet to the floor in a heap. "I'm sorry," she cries. "I'm sorry." Close but no cigar, Columbo. Throwing the gun against the wall, she contorts her mouth into a cry, but all I hear is a loud ringing and the voice of my mother screaming for the chaos to end.

Jesus fucking Christ.

White dust rains down from the ceiling as Jayden rushes to his mother's side, an instinctive need, come hell or high water, to be close to her.

The silly bitch just tried to shoot me. The silly fucking bitch just aimed at my head and fired. "It's okay, Jayden," I say, somewhat relieved to be able to hear Kermit's rendition of *Take Me Out to the Ball Game.* "Things will be different now."

Almost forgetting about Terry, I lift his head out of the water. He gasps for air, spewing some murk from his mouth and nostrils.

"Had enough, Terry?"

"You have no idea what you're getting yourself into," he croaks. "You're dead. A fucking dead man—"

And down he goes again. Jayden looks at me and offers the biggest smile, his eyes sparkling with renewed awe and wonder, as a child's should be. "Wee-formo," he says.

"That's right, Jayden. Reformo."

"Wee-formo," he repeats, offering a little jump on the spot. "Wee-formo. Wee-formo. Wee-formo." He suddenly remembers his whimpering mother and wraps his chubby little arms around her. "Wee-formo save day, Mummy."

"Can you give me another five, Jayden, please?"

The kid grins. "One...two...thwee...fwour...fwive."

And out Terry comes. "Now, this is a very important moment," I say, close enough that the arse-hat will feel my breath on his slimy skin. I lean in, giving him a few seconds to collect himself but still hovering his head over the water. "I need you to listen really carefully. Can you do that, Terry? Can you listen for once?"

He spits out more of the light brown liquid and offers a snarl. I plunge his head towards the water until the tip of his nose touches the surface.

"Okay, okay," he whines.

Mother was right. After one cup comes two.

This encounter was only supposed to be about the bloody music, but I know it's much more than that now. If this poor kid is to stand a chance, Terry needs to disappear for good. I see promise in the mother's eyes but only bitterness and sorrow in this human muppet before me.

"Let's try that again. Are you ready to listen?"

I feel him wilt, the last of his bravado floating on the tank's surface with the dead fish. He flexes his jaw muscles, perhaps a swan song to his manhood, following with a gentle nod.

"Good boy." Oh, the control, the power. *Mercy be, Mother, can you see me now?* "That child is not property, he is a blessing. And you don't deserve such grace." I move in close again, bringing my lips within an inch of his ear. "This is the last time you'll see either of them," I whisper. "Do you understand me? Do you catch my drift?"

His eyes widen, and his jaw falls slack. "You mean to kill me?"

Eyes burning into him, I let the thought linger in his head. "Not today." My voice finds its groove, low and husky. I'm well and truly in character, living the fantasy. "But if I ever see your face around these parts again, I will not hesitate. Do you understand?"

Terry looks at Violet, who turns her stare to the dirty carpet. Perhaps there's a realisation they'd be better off without this bully, or maybe she's just coming to terms with how strangely the night has panned out. I guess it's not every day you shoot at a man in Lycra.

"Catch my drift?" I repeat. To add weight to my threat, I butt my head against his—WHACK—driving our skulls into each other. "DO YOU CATCH MY FUCKING DRIFT?"

He nods, offering a garbled croak that I assume translates as a "Yes."

"Good boy. You have one minute to get your belongings and scoot. Starting now."

As I release my grip, Violet scrambles from the ground and staggers to Terry's side in a move that I take to be purely habitual and with fear of potential backlash. Raising his hands, he offers a growl, slinking off towards the back of the house. I swear I hear him begin to sob.

"Wee-formo save us." Jayden slaps his shitty hands against his shitty thighs, happy as a pig in—mud. "Wee-formo save day."

Eyeing Jayden sitting on the floor alone, I can only hope Terry's tears are remorseful, but I'm guessing they're more due to dented pride at being slam-dunked into a fishbowl by a man in a leo—costume.

"Your son needs his diaper changed, Violet," I say. "There's a good four or five loads in there. Pick up your game, love."

Eyes streaming, she turns towards Jayden and nods.

"You're better than him, Violet. Jayden deserves better, too." My campaign has only just begun, but it feels good. "I'm not a believer in miracles," I say softly, "but small steps make climbable ladders."

She lifts her gaze towards me, eyes full of hope and awe. That's it! That's the look I've been waiting for!

"Thirty seconds, Terry."

He mumbles something incomprehensible, but the shuffling sounds intensify.

"And do me a favour," I say, returning my attention to Violet.

"Please keep the music to a reasonable level. People around here have to sleep."

She nods again and brings Jayden towards her bosom. The kid doesn't seem to mind, letting himself go floppy and running a shit-stained hand down his mother's side. It's a beautiful moment, not Polaroid-worthy by any stretch, but a snapshot of hope.

With fifteen seconds to spare, Terry emerges from the back, still muttering under his breath, a dirty backpack slung over his right shoulder. As he makes for the door, eyes straight ahead, I notice some algae draped over his left ear.

"Fwish man," Jayden says.

"Fuck off, kid." He wraps his yellow fingers around the grimy handle and without offering a glance behind, snaps the door open and steps out. The cool breeze is welcome, helping to displace eye-watering air.

"So that's it, is it, Terry?" I say. "No goodbyes, no empty promises of coming back a better man? No tears? No kisses or hugs?"

He turns and curls his top lip, eyeing Violet and Jayden locked in a loving but somewhat vile embrace. "You did me a fucking favour, you freak." And with that, the door slams behind him, sending Jayden into rapturous applause. "Fwuck off, Twerryfish," the kid says, extending an orange middle finger towards the door.

Violet looks lost, confused, the reality of the situation kicking in. I want to tell her everything will be okay, but that's down to her now. All I can do is give people a fighting chance.

"Stay strong, Violet. He needs you." It's time for me to move on, the night has just begun. Bum Fluff is out there somewhere, and I need to take him out of action. "My name is Reformo, and I'm here to bring back hope." I offer a nod to both and a clumsy swish of my cape. Work in progress, but for now, it will do. "And for the love of Christ, change the kid's diaper, will you?"

With a final nod, I leave back into the shadows of the night. Adrenaline surging, I feel charged, full of power. I inhale, all the usual scents of fast food and piss filling my nostrils, but something else is in the air now. Could it be the faintest whiff of hope?

Even the rain has stopped.

Back to stealth mode, I slink against walls and duck down behind garden hedges. I feel powerful as I head towards the main road, my senses heightened to any possible distress calls. I'm everywhere and nowhere, invisible to all. But rest assured, Reformo will be watching, and you'll never see him coming.

Reformo—it's a bloody winner!

And just like that, a side mission presents itself.

"Excuse me," I say, stepping from the shadows and puffing out my chest.

The two girls turn, offer each other a glance, and up their pace.

"No, wait." I reach down and pick up a discarded fast-food carton. "I think you dropped this. Easy mistake to put right."

They offer no acknowledgement, upping their pace again and mumbling between themselves.

"Hey. Hey, come back." I march after them, duplicating some of the walks of the many superheroes before me. What a cop-out, though, a damned oversight. I need to work on my own, something unique that kids will copy in playgrounds as they chant my name. "Littering is not acceptable. It's all about respect."

They're slow-jogging now, heels clopping against the concrete, legs angled in a way nature never intended. "Fuck off, you creep," one of them shouts.

I up my pace, grateful for the cushioning of my spray-painted sneakers, and joyous at the sound of my long cape fluttering behind. I'm gaining fast, but we're getting closer to the main road. "Wait. I just want to restore order, stop the chaos."

They've parked there again, Jeff. Can you hear that music? Mowing their lawns at this time of day, Jeff! Their leaves are dropping in our yard, Jeff! Jeff! Jeff! Simon, get your elbows off the table. Simon, you can't eat ice cream in here. SIMON, LOOK WHAT YOU'VE DONE NOW! No, I don't want other people trudging through my house. I don't care if other people have their friends around.

"Wait!"

Bloody dogs barking all bastard day, Jeff. Can't you do any-

thing, Jeff? Jeff? Can't you be a man for once, Jeff? Jeff! Jeff! Jeff!
Jesus-motherfucking-Christ! You and him—just the same—weak as
piss. Peas-in-a-mother-fucking-pod.

My arms are pumping so fast that I can imagine taking off.
"You must come back and do the right thing."

The blonde girl on the left glances over her shoulder while
reaching into the handbag clutched in her left hand. She looks
terrified, eyes wide, her face taut and twisted.

"No need to be afraid. I just need you to—"

And just like that, with a scrape of the heels and a high-pitched
cry, darkness swallows her.

"Cassie!" her friend cries, staggering to a halt and offering
a look over her shoulder. "Get up, Cassie," she yells, her arm outstretched, panic drawn across her face.

"It's okay, I mean no harm." I lift both arms in a gesture of
peace, the food carton still clutched in my right hand. "I just need
you to put this in a trash can."

They both look towards me, eyeing me head to toe and back
again. "I have a rape whistle," the blonde says from the ground,
working a twig from her hair.

"I'm not going to rape you." My intended words of comfort
have no effect as she fumbles through her handbag and brings the
whistle to her lips. "Honest."

Cassie scrambles to her feet and brushes herself down, nose
wrinkled, top lip pulled over. The fear is all but gone. Something
else is in her eyes now. "You made me snap a heel. And look at the
state of my hair, you fucker." Looking me up and down again, her
lip curls further across. "It's ruined. Absolutely ruined." Her jaw
clenches. "What are you going to do about it?" She steps towards
me, eyebrows meeting in the middle as she pulls more foliage from
her blonde streaks. "Huh? Well? These shoes were eighty pounds,
and the hair nearly two hundred."

Wait. What the fuck is going on here? "I just want you to put
your litter in the right place." I thrust the carton towards her again.
"It's just a matter of self-respect."

"Did you not hear me, Mister?"

"But I'm Reformo, bringing hope back to town."

The red-haired friend offers a snicker. "Fuck's sake, have you seen yourself? I mean, where did you get that outfit? Perverts R Us?"

"Unless I get two hundred and eighty quid from you," blondie says, kicking off the broken shoe and taking another step towards me. "I'm going to blow this whistle and tell people you were chasing us down. My friend, Janet, here, will call the police, too."

"But that's, that's—"

"The price you pay for chasing after young girls, you paedo," the redhead says.

What is it with all the paedo comments? The way people are carrying on, you'd think every man and his dog was fiddling these days.

As if to show she isn't bluffing, Blondie—Cassie—inhales, puffing her cheeks, the whistle between her lips.

"Wait," I cry, wondering how the bloody hell it came to this. "I don't have any money on me."

"Well, we have a bit of a problem then, don't we?" Janet says, hands on her hips, scraping her shoe against the kerb. "Bloody dog shit everywhere, they should do something about it."

"Listen, I think we've got off on the wrong—"

"Shut up, perv." The annoyance of the defecation not helping my cause, Janet turns to her friend, face twisted into what I can only describe as quite a bloodthirsty expression. "What do you reckon we should do about it, Cassie?"

Blondie picks up on the intensity, pulling the whistle from her lips and placing a hand on her chin. A true evil villain if ever I saw one. "A kick in the bollocks."

"What?"

"We'll call it quits if you let me kick you in the bollocks."

I search her eyes for a sign she may be jesting, but she looks as serious as a heart attack. You couldn't write this stuff.

"And Janet, too," Blondie adds.

It was all going so well, but this has turned into one hell of a curveball. Two perhaps. The sentence forms in my head, but I can't believe the words will leave my lips. "If I let you kick me in the bollocks, will you bin your trash? One kick, mind."

"Deal," Blondie says. "Hold this, Jan." She offers her friend the unbroken shoe.

"You put that in the trash, though."

"I said I would, didn't I?" She begins taking long, backward strides.

"Hey, you didn't say anything about a run-up." I hand the carton to Janet, who offers a disconcerted smile. "Cassie's a blue belt," she says. "Self-defence is important when there are so many creeps around. Hell of a kick on 'er. Saw her break a piece of wood last week."

I brace, cussing myself for not having padding installed around my vitals, but at the same time, wondering how I could plan for this sort of occasion. She's ten yards away, raking her right foot along the ground like a bull preparing to charge, wisps of breath emerging from both nostrils.

I'm a superhero. I'm a superhero. Feel no pain. Feel no pain. Oh shit, she's coming.

With lips curled over gritted teeth and emitting a guttural growl, she looks like a soul possessed. Janet's egging her on, chanting her name as she claps her hands. I feel my nuts shrivelling into my stomach lining. *I am Reformo. I am Reformo.*

WHAM!

Oh, sweet Jesus of fucking Nazareth!

A long exhale leaves my lips as I drop to the ground in the foetal position, cupping my tenderness. Waves of pain wash over me, building to a nauseating, overwhelming crescendo as though my stomach is about to implode. I let out a groan, willing for the impossible burning to end, but it just gets deeper and deeper, burying into me and opening new corridors of pain.

"That's what you get, paedo," Cassie says. "Your turn, Janet."

"I think he's done, Cass."

As I squirm on the ground, the pain finally settling into a dull throb, the two girls give each other a high-five and giggle as they walk into the distance. I see Janet discard the carton over the bushes two gardens down.

"It's just a matter of self-respect," I cry, the irony far from lost.

They turn, both offering the middle finger.

I roll into the shadows, waiting for the throbbing to subside. Part of me wants to go home, rip off the costume, and never set foot outdoors again. But then I remember Jayden's face—the look of awe and wonder as he let himself believe. "Nobody said it was going to be easy." Wincing at the fire in my groin, I push myself to my feet and walk down the street, but not like a superhero.

It isn't long before I find my next perpetrator.

"Excuse me," I say, hobbling out from the shadows and thinking a different approach might be in order.

The woman turns, and I'm grateful she's old and likely too frail to run. "I thought Halloween was next month?" she says, taking in my costume.

"That's a beautiful dog."

"Polly. Yes, she's our sweetheart. I couldn't imagine life without her."

"A terrier, isn't she?" Mother wouldn't even let me have a goldfish.

"That's right. Do you want to pat her?"

"That's okay. Thank you, though. She really is stunning."

"Thank you."

"Yes, quite adorable." I stand and nod for a while, hands on my hips. "It's just, well, the stuff that comes out of her arse, not so much."

"Beg your pardon, dear?"

She was hearing me perfectly fine until that point. "The shit on the floor," I say, pointing towards each mound for maximum effect. "Imagine if everyone let their dogs shit all over the place without picking it up?"

The old lady turns her head towards the small pile, yanking at the mutt as it reacts to something in the distance. "Hmm." Patting at her coat pockets, she looks at me and back at the dog shit again. "I seem to have forgotten to bring poop bags today." After stroking her chin for what feels like an eternity, eyes still on Poppy's *pebbles* and her face a picture of fake concern, she says, "I'll come back with one in the morning."

"No need," I say, unzipping one of my sewn-in pockets. "We all get caught out from time to time." Reformo at your service. "Here you go."

The dog continues its struggles. "Poppy," she yells, finally lifting her stare to me. "But they're just little pebbles, love."

I smile. "Only they're not pebbles, are they, dear? They're excrement. Crap. Faecal matter. Little balls of shite, is what they are."

"Poppy!" She looks edgy now, uptight, deeper wrinkles forming around her pursed lips.

"Here you go," I say, waving the bag before her. "Just pick it up. Do the right thing and embrace the warmth of your doggy's doo-doo."

Eyebrows meeting in the middle, she offers the dog an extra hard yank before lifting her watery eyes towards me again. "Who are you, anyway?"

"I'm glad you asked. My name is Reformo, and I'm here to bring back hope." Further down the street, I hear glass smashing, but I maintain my stare, determined to chalk this one up as a victory. At least she hasn't asked if I'm going to rape her yet. "Small steps make climbable ladders," I say, thrusting the bag towards her again.

Reluctantly, she takes it, offering an exaggerated sigh and a look that could kill if she had lasers for eyes. FZZZZZZ. She grimaces as she crouches, scolding poor little Poppy once again as the little rat dog almost takes her off balance.

"Respect for others starts with yourself," I say, watching her wrap the bag around the poop, ensuring she collects every pebble. "Now, tell me you don't feel better about yourself."

She rises, offering an unconvincing nod and wrinkling her nose, the swinging bag of poo pinched between her fingers.

"Awesome. Now please spread the word that Reformo is—"

"Help," someone cries from the darkness. "Help!"

To the sound of screeching tyres ripping down the street, I turn to see the silhouette of a man running, a flabby arm in the air. "The fucker stole my car!"

I see no headlights, only the vehicle's dark outline. "Tell them Reformo is in town." And with that, I rush into the road towards the approaching engine noise. "I'm here to bring back hope." But it occurs to me as I stand here, gentle breeze flapping at my cape, that I'm dressed entirely in black.

They'll never see me coming.

"Get out of the road, you bloody lunatic," the old lady cries from behind.

But Reformo doesn't run; besides, it's too late now. I see the thief's face, and he finally sees mine. Eyes wide, lips pulled back over his teeth, he swings the wheel to the right, sending the car into a fishtail.

Oh, shit.

Brakes struggling against the wet ground, the car begins to spin.

Oh fuck. Oh fuck. Oh fuck.

I can only dive—POOINNNG—screaming as the car slams into my lower half—SMASH—"FUUUUUUCK." Just in time to see the hooded thief throwing open the car door and making his run, I lift my head from the murky puddle. "In the name of Reformo, stop," I cry, pushing myself up but crumpling back into dampness as a wave of searing pain takes my breath away. "Tell Bum Fluff I'm coming for him."

The scoundrel turns and offers the finger, such a reaction telling me he knows BF. For what good it does me.

"Stop, thief!" The old lady barks and hurls the bag of poop towards the runner, her feeble attempt falling well short.

"I hope you're going to pick that up," I rasp, prompting the woman to deliver a scowl and my second middle finger of the day.

Sirens emerge from somewhere not too far away, and I can't

help thinking about the commendations I'll no doubt receive for my bravery. *Can you see me, Mama?* Halfway through running over my acceptance speech in my head, my train of thought is interrupted as a bald, fat man wearing underpants arrives on the scene.

"Fuck's sake," he says, slowing to a trot until he doubles over and begins hacking at the ground. "What the bloody hell were you thinking?"

"No need to thank me," I say, pushing to my elbows. "I'm Reformo, and I'm bringing hope back to town."

The old lady offers a roll of her eyes.

"You've put a dent in my car," the bald man says, running his balloon hand across the paintwork. "A bloody big dent."

"Oh, yes," the old lady says, "Won't be a cheap job either."

"But I stopped him. You asked for help, and I saved the day."

"I didn't mean for you to stand in front of the bloody thing."

"You have your car back," I say through gritted teeth, struggling to my feet. "I stopped him, and now the police will catch him."

"I never called the police. The bloody tax has expired, and I'm up to my tits in parking tickets." He folds in half again, coughing a glistening globule of thickness onto the tarmac. "So who's going to pay for the damage now?"

"Asked me to pick up my dog's shit, too," the old lady chirps. "Scared the hell out of me, jumping out on an old lady in the dark."

"I'm Reformo."

"Bet they're only little pebbles, aren't they?" Captain Underpants says, eyeing the rat dog. "Aw, what a cute little pup."

The old lady nods. "I'm still shaking. Won't be able to sleep tonight."

"You're a meddler, mate," the man says. "That's what they should call you—The fucking Meddler."

"I was just trying to help," I say, limping back towards the shadows. "It's just a matter of respect."

The man offers a snicker. "What self-respecting man jumps out on old women dressed like something from an eighties bondage movie?"

"Small steps make climbable ladders."

"The Meddler," the man screams back at me. "Are you going to pay for my car or what?"

And I'm back in the darkness, limping towards the main road and the bridge in the distance. This superhero lark is even harder than I anticipated, but I won't give up.

"Fucking Meddler!"

Christ, his voice carries. Yes, the public is yet to fully warm to me, but I need to give it time. Word will spread like wildfire when they know I've taken Bum Fluff down. Hope, too. It will burn this town to the ground, and we can start all over again.

"I'm coming for all of you."

CHAPTER FIVE: BUM FLUFF

The water in the distance shimmers, a trick of artificial light lending to a time when this place was once picturesque and sought after. This point of view, this time of night, and one could almost forget the rot that works through town. Even the shit smell is fading as I approach the footpath leading to the water.

"My name is Reformo. Re-formo."

The look on Jayden's face is the night's highlight so far. Another to add to his collection—the tooth fairy, the Easter Bunny, Father Christmas, and now a real-life superhero who slam-dunked his stepdad into a fish tank. *A Terryfwish.* What a story to tell; damn shame the cute little shit-monster can hardly talk. And I don't expect Violet will be too forthcoming with the details, people around here keeping tight lips, loose ones sinking ships.

Inhale. Exhale.

A couple of used needles lie on either side of a scraggy tuft of grass, a luminescent orange wildflower emerging from the depravity. But hope is as treacherous as love—you can fill your heart with it, but there's no guarantee it won't snap its head around and swallow you whole.

Get a grip, Reformo. Focus. Focus. Focus.

Voices in the distance. Two, maybe three. Out-of-control vegetation on either side restricts my view, and broken bollard lights offer no support. Likely a good thing; they'll *never see me coming.* Following the path, I keep my head down and ears open, my heart thundering in my chest, self-doubt running its icy fingers up my spine for the first time, prompting a series of shudders.

What if there are three of them? I don't have super speed or strength, no night vision either, no accelerated healing, just a pocket full of poop bags and the element of surprise.

There!

I can see the top of their heads now. Fucking hell, *there are* three of them, all wearing hoodies and huddled together in a way that couldn't make them look more suspicious. It makes me wonder why they even bother meeting off the main drag, especially after my recent experience with Bad Lieutenant. Call it intuition or my super senses kicking in, but my attention falls on the one wearing the baseball cap. Finding the perfect vantage point, giving me a full view of the muppets, I settle in behind the hedge, Lycra once again trying to push my balls through my stomach lining.

Inhale. Exhale. *You are Reformo. Good always wins out.*

Just as a cramp begins setting in, there's movement. In what looks akin to a spot of playground bullying, two of them direct a series of shoves and slaps towards the wannabe gangster with "Watch Your Own Back" on the reverse of his incognito, bright-yellow hoodie. There's no retaliation, no attempt to save dignity, so I can only assume the one doing most of the pushing is the head honcho, at least of this little entourage.

Fuck-a-doodle-doo, is that a knife?

Moonlight catches the blade as the guy with the baseball cap gets in the face of the yellow-hoodie man, issuing what I assume to be a series of aggressive but muted threats and further polluting this town's air with vileness.

What's my plan? What's my fucking plan?

I could maybe handle one of them, but three, and at least one with a—*Shit, yellow hoodie guy is on the move and coming this way.*

Inhale.

There's a flicker of light against the backdrop of black water.

Exhale.

Not taking my eyes from the approaching orange dot, I nestle into the darkness, wincing as sharpness scratches my left side. Already smelling tobacco carrying on a light breeze, I hold my breath, knowing the game's up if he sees me.

Christ, my poor bloody nuts.

Perhaps thirty feet away, I hear the kid mumbling under his breath, smoke clouds dissipating behind him. *Shit. Shit. Shiiiiiit.* The moon suddenly seems brighter, as though trying to expose me. Crouching further, I stifle a cry, my contorted limbs and testes screaming for mercy.

"Don't ever come back short again," a voice yells from behind the hooded man, who is less than twenty feet away. "Or I'll cut off your balls and feed them to my dog."

Cussing, the man continues his approach, taking a kick at a crumpled can and sending it into the hedgerow only a few inches behind me. "Fuck you, Bum Fluff. Fuck you," the guy mumbles.

Looking about the same age as the kid who tried to mug me before, he draws level, hands planted deep in the hoodie's pockets. The thought crosses my mind that I could follow him, take him from behind when he gets further down the path. And just like I did with Tattoo Man, I could threaten him, run him out of town. *Run him out of town?* But he's just a guppy in the pond, and I'm hunting sharks.

"Stupid fucking name anyway," the guy says, kicking out again, sending a burst of orange petals spilling onto the grass.

Motherfucker!

He fades out of sight, pride no doubt dented, his only success of the evening to win a fight with a flower.

Down to two, yet I've no urge to roll the dice. Even though I came out on top of my last few fights in prison, thanks to my Spanish friend, they were mano a mano and weapon-free. Don't get me wrong; I'm not a troublemaker. Hate violence, to tell you the truth, but tough guys looking for fights generally pick the ones they think they can win. Meatheads tend to use the "scrawnies" for stress relief, but sometimes they mistake lean for skinny and get their arses served.

Here we go. Here we go.

Hoodie number two leaves, heading east alongside the wall. As I stand, my body trembles, a release for the adrenaline that's been building within. This is it, the time is nigh. A glance over my shoulder confirms Yellow Hoodie is well out of sight, perhaps off to drown his sorrows or beat up a bunch of daffodils.

It's just him and me, the head honcho—baseball cap man—aka Bum Fluff.

As a rather icy blast wraps around me—perhaps my heightened nerve endings more vulnerable than usual—I make my way forward, still under the thicket's cover. My target makes a phone call, perhaps to one of his thugs, maybe to the one who pulls his strings. There's a chain of command, always is. Saw it in prison. Saw it at home.

He perches on the edge of the wall, legs dangling over the other side, the brim of his cap rising and falling. It's now or never. After taking several deep breaths, I finally come out of cover, cape swaying behind just like in my dreams. *Look, Mama, I'm doing it. Told you I'd do better.*

As he turns, I crouch, heart in mouth, balls back in my stomach lining.

Inhale.

Eyes lingering in my direction, Bum Fluff slides his other hand into his pocket.

Exhale.

At last, his attention moves back to the phone call and water, and I take the opportunity of staggering to the next base, a graffiti-riddled park bench with the word "cockmuncher" written across the top panel. The fucker's prolific, I'll give them that. Before I can decide if cockmuncher should be one word or two, the phone call ends, and Bum Fluff lights up a cigarette. He blows a smoke ring towards the moon and lets out an exaggerated sigh. The contemplative thug.

Taking a minute to slow my breathing, I double-check to ensure we are alone. Clear. Not another soul in sight. Stealth mode activated, I push away from the bench, staying in the shadows of the trees, using the thickest tufts of grass to disguise my footfalls.

Twenty feet.

Another smoke ring circles the moon before being taken away by the light breeze.

Fifteen feet.

He looks quiet and poetic sitting there. But knowing the shit heel's name starts with Bum and ends with Fluff takes the edge off.

Ten feet.

With gravel ahead, leading up to the small wall, I slow my approach. *Now what? Not like I can fucking fly the rest of the way.* Inhale. Exhale. As I arrive at the last of the grass, my eyes burn into the back of the villain's head. FZZZZZZ. I spy the knife resting on the wall beside him, blade pointing towards the water.

That's a big knife, Mama.

I knew you were as weak as piss, just like your father.

It feels like I'm playing a game of Grandmother's Footsteps as I edge forward, avoiding the larger of the stones. Still no plan. *What the hell am I going to do, tap him on the shoulder and tell him it's his turn? He's got a fucking knife, for Christ's sake.* My balls move even higher as I imagine the blade slicing through the Lycra and into my milky skin. *Shit. Shit. Shit.*

I could reach for the knife if I got close enough. Or there's the option of kicking it over the edge, ensuring neither of us takes one in the gut. *Steady. Steady. Ste*—CRUNCH. Bum Fluff snaps his head around and grabs the knife from the wall in one smooth motion.

"Who the fuck are you supposed to be?"

He's bigger than Tattoo Man. Wider, with just as thick arms. Younger, too. Not that I haven't had worse come at me, but it's the knife I'm worried about. It leaves too much to chance. "I'm Reformo," I say, hoping the announcement will make him come peacefully.

"Is that a leotard?"

"I'm bringing order back to town."

"Is this a wind-up?" A smile breaks across his face as his eyes begin searching the shadows. "Fat Tony, is this your doing?"

Fat Tony. Hardly original, but at least it sounds more gangster than Bum Fluff. And it's another name for the list. "Put down the knife."

He's still unconvinced, eyes darting left and right, an inane grin stretching across his face. "Seriously, mate, you know it's not Halloween?"

"Put down the knife."

"Are you some sort of rapist? Do you fancy a piece of Bum Fluff? Is that it?"

What the hell is it with all the raping? When did people stop taking wallets and purses and be on their merry way? "I'll ask one last time... Put down the knife."

"That's not a question."

"PUT IT DOWN!"

"You're making a big mistake. Do you know who I am?"

"I know who you are." *It's chaos, Simon. Chaos.* "And I know what you do. But I'm here to put an end to it. I'm Reformo, and I'm bringing—"

"You're dead fucking meat is what you are." The grin fades as he begins a slow approach, gravel crunching like bone in his path.

Mama?

You must set an example, Simon.

Have you seen the size of that bloody knife?

Piss weak, just like your father.

The blade protruding from Bum Fluff's clenched fist appears even larger now. Five inches? Six? The scars running across his right cheek, one down to his chin, all point to Bum Fluff having seen action.

"This doesn't have to happen." I hold my hands out, declaring myself weapon-free. "You could turn your life around. We could unite, start teaching kids about the harmful effects of drugs and clean up these streets. What do you say?"

"Look, I don't know who the fuck you are, Mister, but I see you ain't right in the head. But mental or not, you can't come on my patch and expect not to get shanked."

Moonlight falls across his face, picking up the few hairs across his lip. *Jesus Christ, how fucking old is he?* "It's not too late," I say. "This town can be good again. We could start a youth centre. Get funding from the council and buy a table tennis table."

"Table-fucking-tennis. You're off your fucking rocker, mate." He tosses the knife between his hands, finishing with an impressive spin. "That might keep you happy down at the local funny farm, but folks can see angels with the stuff I sell."

"I just want some order."

"Well, you're in the wrong place, mate." He stares me down, flexing his jaw muscles. "Now, you have two options here: run like the fucking wind, or have that lovely leotard cut to shreds."

"It's not a fucking leotard."

This time, I move first, feigning to the left but attacking from the right. Bum Fluff tries to alter course, but it's too late, the knife cutting through the air, the blade missing my side by nothing more than an inch. We come together, the flurry of hairs on his lip dancing on the breeze. He grits his teeth and tries to whip his arm back, but my fingers coil around his wrist.

"I'll fucking kill you!"

"There's still time," I say. "It doesn't have to be like this."

"I'm not spending my days playing fucking ping pong."

"We could get a pool table."

We dance under the moonlight, fighting for supremacy. I can feel his muscles against mine, bigger but softer. Behind us, the water shimmers between light and dark, a perfect setting for the battle of good against evil.

"Why the leotard?"

"For the last fucking time today, it's not a fucking leotard!"

We continue our tussle, advantage swapping back and forth until I finally feel some give in his arm. He's tiring; all show and no stamina. Desperate, he pulls his head back and attempts to bring his skull into mine, but it's a half-assed effort that misses the target. Face red and twisted, he offers a war cry, wrestling his left arm free and getting a decent punch off into my midriff—WHACK—but I'm up to a thousand crunches a day. He tries again—POW—his forehead creasing as the blow bounces off my chest.

This fight is already over, and the kid knows it; I can see it in his eyes. Still, he strains, veins popping in his wrist and neck as he tries to wrestle free his knife-wielding arm. He offers a garbled moan and throws a knee, but I twist my body, resulting in nothing more than a glancing blow.

"Just leave me fucking be, Mister." He claws his fingers across my face. "I know people."

"Thought you were a tough guy, Bum Fluff? All those scars and big muscles." Our struggle brings us to the water's edge, spilling some gravel into the blackness.

"Wait until Butter Balls hears about this."

Butter Balls? For the love of—"Drop the knife."

"Fuck you!" Another ineffectual slap glances the side of my head. On recoil, I grab it, locking him up almost entirely. He grunts and attempts another knee, but his eyes widen as I push him off balance towards the water's edge. I'm in total control; the only thing between him and an early bath.

"Drop the knife."

"I can't swim!"

"What?"

"Not even a lap."

"Fuck me." Perhaps it's just me, but such a revelation suggests incredulous stupidity. It's almost akin to Superman setting up camp on planet Krypton. "Drop it!"

"Butter Balls will be all over you like a rash."

"I don't give a fuck. Drop it."

"Please let me go."

"DROP IT!"

The undeniable fear behind his eyes gives way to the kid he once was, just another lost soul in this world of chaos, too many wrong paths taken. "Look, Mister, you don't understand. If I don't get the cash, I'm dead."

"Reformo. My name is Reformo."

"Whatever." Eyes wide, he arches his neck, studying the soft blackness below. "This won't end well for either of us."

"You have to promise. You have to swear you'll stop dealing." I inch forward, sending Bum Fluff back until the heels of his pristine sneakers hang over the wall's edge. To the right of his foot, a large hole punctures the concrete. There are more on either side, cavities once home to iron rods that supported a safety barrier. But nothing about this town feels safe anymore.

"Last warning. Drop the knife."

Bum Fluff holds on tight, his other arm still outstretched, redundant; blade pointing towards the moon. "Drop the fucking knife," I scream, years of frustration, anger, and torment releasing into the night.

The moment I've been waiting for—demanding—is upon us now. His right palm opens, and the knife slides out, clattering against the wall before falling to the gravel.

"Good boy. Small steps make climbable ladders."

"Huh?"

"Swear, Bum Fluff. Swear you'll stop."

He looks down at the water, his Adam's apple suddenly very prominent. "She won't let me."

"Who?"

"Butter Balls."

"Butter Balls is a woman?"

"No, not a woman, a fucking savage."

"Tougher than you?"

"I'm not really tough."

"What about the scars? The muscles?"

"Had the scars done down at the arcade; made them put me under to do it. Five hundred big ones."

"You paid someone five hundred quid to do that to your face?"

"Yeah, but you can see more hair on a porn star's fanny than on my lip. Adapt and survive, Mister."

"Reformo."

"Reformo."

"And the muscles?"

"Steroids. I'm pumped full of 'em."

"Knew it!"

"I can't walk for more than five minutes without cramping. That's why we meet here; my house is a couple hundred yards up that way."

"Jesus Christ."

"I'm scared, Mister Reformo. Real scared."

"Just Reformo. Of me?"

"Well, a little bit, but mostly her."

"Leave her to me."

"You don't understand what you're getting yourself into."

"If everyone turned a blind eye."

"Have you a death wish?"

"I just wish for order."

"Please let me go."

"Swear then." Patience running thin, I lean him further over the water. More gravel spills over. "Swear you'll quit."

"Please, she'll—"

"SWEAR!"

"Okay, okay." He lets out a garbled cry, eyes wide as he surveys the blackness beneath us. "I swear. I swear."

"I swear, Reformo."

"I swear, Reformo."

"To help end the chaos and to bring hope back to town."

"To help end the chaos and to bring hope back to town."

His words are like music to my ears. *Did you hear that, Mama?* My second bad dude of the day, and the night is still young. I'll not end up like my father. Who's next on the cards? Fat Tony? Butter Balls? Not weak as piss. Not like *him.*

As I bring Bum Fluff back from the edge, I feel his body offer a little shudder of relief, his pulse working overtime. PUMP, PUMP,

PUMP. We unlock, and I take a few steps back, allowing him to suck in some air and recompose. He looks on the verge of tears.

"It won't be easy, but you'll be a better man for it." It feels good, this post-fight pep talk. Now that I have his respect, I expect my words are taking on new meaning. Perhaps, he even feels hope trickling through his veins. "And if we make a stand together, show these bullies that we—"

Knife back in his hand, he rushes towards me, letting out a high-pitched croak. It's a desperate noise, sounding more like a disgruntled wild pig than a seasoned drug dealer's war cry. He nears, and I sidestep, my cape fluttering like a bullfighter's muleta. Olé! I feel graceful and composed, whereas Bum Fluff staggers across the gravel, just managing not to go arse over tit. He yells to the moon, and we turn, ready for our second round.

"Don't do it, Bum Fluff."

"I have no choice."

It would feel akin to a medieval joust if it weren't for his sneakers, baggy pants, and baseball cap. Here we are, two enemies in a stand-off, ready to rush each other. But my only weapon is a dream, one to end the chaos and make it safe for people to walk the streets without fear of being robbed. Or raped. I'm unsure what compels me, but I also offer a howl to the moon.

He comes at me, knife above his shoulder. Once again, I sidestep, but his reactions are quicker this time. SWISH. It feels like nothing more than a solid kidney punch, but as Bum Fluff turns to face me, his eyes widen, and his mouth hangs open. "Fuck," he says. "I'm sorry."

My left leg buckles. I feel lightheaded. Blood leaks from my side onto my hands. "You stabbed me."

"I'm sorry."

"After you swore, too." It's all I can do to stay standing. I'm in a different world, drifting through a montage of scenes from my childhood.

"I'm so sorry. It's just that Butter Balls would—"

Bum Fluff's voice grows distant. I'm back in Mother's universe. The time I came home from school with only one gym shoe. "Where's the other?" Mother said. "Where's the other shoe?"

"I don't know, Mama. Is it not in there?"

That look she gave me, as though I'd just outed her as dumber than a box of rocks. And to this day, I swear she offered a little growl. Before I knew what was happening, I was in darkness, the bag wrapped around my head.

"Can you see it, Simon? Can you see the fucking shoe?"

I knew crying would do no good, only serve to work her up even more. "No, Mama."

"What's that, Simon? I can't hear you. Is the fucking shoe in there or not?"

"No, it's not, Mama."

As though things had gotten too much for her, her voice began to crackle. "Are you sure? Are you sure it's not in there?"

"Yes, Mama."

The whimpering started then. "It's chaos, Simon. Losing things. Carelessness."

"Yes, Mama."

Soon it was a full-blown sob. "A total lack of self-respect."

"Yes, Mama."

Only when I promised to return to school and search through lost property did I see the light again, and my mother's reddened face. So, back I went, my stomach twisting at the thought of being unable to find it, the prospect of suffering Mother's rage, disappointment, and outright fury with the world all over again. Thirty minutes passed before Karl North and crew vacated the school gates and fucked off to whatever place they decided to make their next living hell. It always struck me as odd how school bullies and those protesting to hate school spent so much bloody time there, even after the bell had gone. It just didn't add up. But then I remembered Father saying something about prisoners unable to bear the thought of being on the outside.

Complete chaos, Simon.

Anyhow, coast clear, I headed for the gymnasium, shuddering

at the thought of returning home without my shoe. My heart sank when I found nothing in the lost property locker. I remember sitting down, my eyes beginning to fill with tears.

And then I heard footsteps.

It was the caretaker, John. I can't recall his last name, not even sure I knew it, but seeing that shoe dangling from his left hand, I swear, a little bit of wee came out. I was giddy, ecstatic, and I'd have likely gone down on my hands and knees and barked like a dog for that shoe if he asked me to. I'd have—

"You should leave." Bum Fluff's voice makes it through, albeit distorted and distant, the fog of the past dissipating. And just like that, I'm back, the cold wind lapping at my face, halogen-speckled darkness spinning around me. Pain bites at my side as I drop to my knees. "You know I can't do that."

The kid shrinks into himself, knife still clutched firm in front, the tremor unmistakable. "I don't want to kill you... I've never killed anyone."

"That's not what I heard." I lift my hand from my side to see darkness blacker than night leaking to the ground.

"Yeah, well. Can't believe everything you hear."

"So you haven't killed anyone?"

Offering a sigh, he shakes his head and lowers the knife. "It was supposed to be an easy exchange, but things got messy when one of theirs recognised my younger brother, Tommy, for having it away with his girl." He kicks at the gravel and switches his gaze to the stars. "My knife is just for show, meant to scare people off, and it did just that. But Tommy still had hold of one of them. I screamed for him to stop, but he had to go one step further and stick the fucker."

Cold wind steals the silence, pushing us forward to the next scene.

"Fucking idiot," Bum Fluff mutters. "He always took things too far. Anyhow, I doused my knife in the kid's blood and told Tommy to leave town."

"Why did you take the blame?"

"Tommy was my bro, man. Loyalty is everything when it's all you got."

Even in my current state, there's a temptation to correct Bum Fluff's grammar, but I figure he's just quoting lyrics thrown down by some pimple-covered freak living with parents who can't wait to get rid of them. More warmth leaks down my side, making me wonder if I'm dying. Either way, I need to wrap this up.

"He OD'd shortly after, and our little secret died with him," Bum Fluff continues. "As I said, he always took things too far. Just kids, lost, abandoned, not a chance in hell." On what looks to be the verge of tears again, he raises the knife and swishes it through the air, lashing out at his perceived weakness. "I knew I'd only do a bit of a time, still being a minor. Butter Balls was waiting for me when I got out. Said she would look after me, set me up with a proper crew this time."

"It's not too late; you can start again. Use your skills for other means." My words sound contrived, and even I don't believe them.

As if in agreement, Bum Fluff raises the knife even higher, and grits his teeth. "You don't understand. Before all that, I was nothing. Less than nothing. For the first time in my life, I have a purpose. No longer a nobody, a somebody."

Even with the claim, I see the child in his eyes, fear pouring from them. I'm unsure what scares him most, but I know chaos is to blame for everything he's become. *Chaos, Simon.*

"Just walk away," he says. "I don't want to hurt you again, but I will."

Grimacing, I push myself up, observing the beauty of the night as though my last few moments on Earth. The colours on the water, the sharpness of the moon above, and the gentle sway of the longer grasses in the breeze are all somehow mesmerising. Even in the shittiest of locations at the shittiest of times, Mother Nature seems capable of providing something for us to marvel at; perhaps a swan song to me before my curtain comes down.

"I'll do it," Bum Fluff says. "Don't test me, Mister."

The cold wind wraps around us again, whistling a haunting soundtrack for the final scene. "The name is Reformo." I'm reminded again of what the Spaniard would tell me if he was standing by my side, albeit in broken, poetic English: "Strike first, even if you think you lose." Wincing with pain, I make my charge, head down, offering a war cry and perhaps my final attempt to make Mother proud.

Bum Fluff's eyes grow wide. He brings the knife high, but by the time he summons the courage to strike, I'm on him, my fingers coiled around his wrist as we dance again, albeit towards the water and with even greater urgency. He launches a knee into my groin, the resulting pain off the charts, but I bite down hard on my lip and offer a growl. With all my might, I continue pushing, gravel crunching underfoot until we arrive at the water's edge, locked in a stalemate of trauma and disillusionment.

"What is this to you, anyway? Why can't you just let me be?"

"A blind eye here, a blind eye there, and we're hiding in the broom closet eating tinned peaches."

"You are fucking mental!" Letting out a garbled scream, Bum Fluff brings his knee into my side—THWACK—causing a renewed explosion of pain that spreads through every part of me. He senses his opportunity, snapping his arm away from my weakened grip.

I'm sorry, Mama.

Screwing my eyes shut in preparation for the blade, I lash out, my knuckles singing on connection. My life flashes before me, Mother standing at the door, ready to bring the bag onto my head.

SPLASH! Splash. Sp—

I open my eyes to a sea of black and silver but no sign of Bum Fluff. The wind wraps around me again, iciness snapping me from the water's smooth hypnotic motion. Standing at the edge, my hand throbbing, I scan the flatness, expecting to see a head breaking through, mouth forming a scream. But all I find is the semi-submerged baseball cap.

"Bum Fluff!"

I look to my left, right, and over my shoulder, but no sign of the kid.

"Bum Fluff!"

Silence greets my cry. Panic and dread initiate the familiar response of elevated heart rate, dizziness, and nausea. Further flash-backs play in my mind. The time I spilled ice cream on Mother's best carpet. The time I knocked her porcelain frog from the mantelpiece, shattering it into countless pieces. *Have you no control, Simon? Are you fucking stupid? Look at me when I'm talking to you, will you!*

Sorry, Mama.

I know I should be doing something, but my limbs feel leaden. I'm here but not, a prisoner of my own body, shackled to the past and the desire to be anything but a disappointment. Only my sting-ing hand seems to exist in this surreal plane. Why am I not moving? What would young Jayden say if he could see me now, frozen at the water's edge while someone drowns? Helpless, I continue staring at the half-submerged baseball cap, a childish and ridiculous thought swimming through my head: Bum Fluff doesn't float.

The knot twists in my stomach, forcing me to double over and observe my darkened silhouette in the water. As pain shoots up my side again, I press my fingers into the wall, a dry gag working its way to my throat and merging with the breeze. *Come on. Come on!* Will-ing myself to get a grip, I remind myself of my pledge to Mother to do all that I can to restore order. Nobody said it was going to be easy.

Three.

Two.

One.

Iciness steals my breath, the shock enough to awaken me from my melancholic stupor. I begin thrashing my arms against the surface, my legs working—inefficient and out of sync—as panic overwhelms me.

"I am Reformo. I'm a goddamn fucking superhero." The words bring a moment of calm, allowing my heart rate to return to somewhere near normal. But just as I begin treading the water, the theme tune from *Jaws* starts playing in my head, filling me with thoughts of my blood leaking into its darkness. *No sharks in these waters, Reformo. Get a bloody grip!*

Inhale. Exhale.

No sign of Bum Fluff. Could I have knocked him clean out—

caught him on his glass jaw? "Bum Fluff!"

I begin to wonder how long it takes for someone to drown. All that time dithering on the side while the death clock was ticking. *Weak as piss.* Praying to see the kid's docile but panicked face, I scan the surface again, but all I find is his stupid cap and a plastic bottle.

There's no choice, I know it. Like it or lump it, it's all part of the stupid superhero code. I take in a few deep breaths, and several more, before ducking under, trying to resist the temptation to come straight back up. Two seconds later, my head is out of the water, and I'm gasping for breath and clutching at my wound.

"I am Reformo. I am Reformo. I AM REFORMO!"

I count to three and try again. Just blackness, a merciless void offering nothing but pressure on my lungs and confirmation that I'm far too late. Nevertheless, I dive deeper, arms outstretched, hoping to brush against the person that stabbed me only moments ago. It's disorienting, nothing to guide me, and no way of knowing if I'm swimming in the right direction. And each stroke, more difficult than I ever remember, the iciness of the water zapping at my strength.

Come on. Come on.

The cape feels clumsy and clingy as I change direction, the material wrapping around my head. I panic, arms and legs lashing out in all directions as an overwhelming urge to inhale kicks in. *I don't want to die, Mama. I don't want to die!*

After what feels like a lifetime, I drag the cape from my face, but I'm exhausted, endless oblivion offering no respite, my life force still trickling into the icy water. And then, without realising, it's Mother I'm trying to find. I picture her drowning in a sea of chaos, her mouth forming an order-starved scream, as she desperately tries to claw her way to the surface. *I'm coming, Mama.* But chaos is everywhere, there's no escape. My chest tightens, my head feels like it might explode. She grabs my leg, taking me further down. *No, Mama, let go. Let go, Mama.* But she strengthens her grip, and I'm drowning with her.

The pressure becomes unbearable.

LET GO, MAMA!

And finally, after a series of kicks that exhaust me further, I'm thrashing through the water with no sense of up or down. But the pressure. *This can't be how it ends; it can't be.* I picture young Jayden's face, excitement in his eyes, a finger up a nostril. *My name is Reformo, and I'm here to bring back hope.* Aiming for the tiniest speck of light from above, I kick my legs even harder.

I'm not going to make it. This is the end of the line.

My mouth opens, and I feel the water rushing inside.

Sorry, Mama. Sorry, Jayden.

But just as I come to terms with it being over before it's begun, a blast of cool air wraps around my face, and a series of violent hacks explode from my lips. I'm alive. I'm alive! Reformo lives to fight another day. In an urgent search for oxygen, I spit out more water. The air so icy it prompts another series of explosive barks. But I am fucking alive. "Do you hear me, everyone? I'm alive, and I'm bringing hope back to town!"

It's a strange and joyous moment, only dampened by thoughts of Bum Fluff, another scan of the surface revealing nothing. Hoping to see something apart from the stubborn baseball cap—bobbing up and down on the surface—I continue treading water, trying my best to ignore the growing pain along my side. But as if the shock is beginning to wear off, fed up with being on hold, my body begins to shake, a sign my engine might soon die. Desperate and weak, I swim towards the steps on the far wall, the night's events flashing through my mind. Limbs again feel leaden, each stroke draining what little reserve I have.

Crystal?

The sight of her standing on the edge of the wall, arms folded, gives me a second wind. Pain and iciness still grip me tight, but there's an ounce of tangible warmth making a fight of it.

Jesus Christ, I think I'm in love.

THRASH. KICK. THRASH. KICK.

So much for not getting distracted from the mission.

THRASH. KICK. THRASH. THRASH. THRASH.

It is. No doubt. It's l-o-v-e. You idiot Reformo, you've only gone

*and fallen for her. Unmistakable. Unshakeable. The kind that hits you
between the eyes. Shit, what's her real name again?*

"What the hell are you doing in there?" she yells.

"Freestyle." I've read about it. From the moment I laid eyes
on her, I've had a funny feeling in my stomach. Mama said there
ain't no such thing; the goggle box making us believe there is for
the sake of consumerism, but I know how I feel. Only felt it once
before—Nicola Taylor—the only one who didn't laugh or sneer
at my awkwardness in the school playground. She even came to sit
next to me one day, her perfume making the concrete spin around
the bench.

"Ain't no good will come of it," Mama used to say. "Probably
talking about you behind your back, making fun of your big ears."

I didn't even realise I had big ears until that point.

"Can't trust anyone in this world," she used to say. "The fewer
people you have in your life, the less chaos there is. You're better off
alone."

Mama didn't let people into the house, so making friends
was almost impossible. The few I did make got sick of inviting me
to theirs all the time, and even Nicola gave up on me, choosing to
spend her time at that goon Johnny Wilson's house. He went around
school once telling people he slipped her a finger, but rumours are
that he got it in the wrong hole, thus the nickname Johnny Shitfin-
ger. It stuck for quite some time afterwards.

I look towards Crystal to see her crouching. "Hurry up and
get out of there, will you?" she says. As my fingers clasp around cold
metal, I almost laugh with relief, noting the tiny gaps between each
rung.

Small steps make climbable ladders.

"You stupid goon. Don't you know you'll catch your death?"
After a shake of her head, Crystal unfolds her arms and flicks her
cigarette to the ground. It's impossible to ignore the irony of her
words, what with her wearing nothing but a boob tube and an
oversized belt.

I pull myself up using my last ounce of strength, coiling my fingers around her offered wrist. Both our faces crease as she yanks.

"You're hurt?" Her perfect, manicured eyebrows meet.

At last, on solid ground, I double over, taking in as much icy air as possible, grateful not to be hacking it straight back out again.

"Are you hurt?" she asks with more urgency.

"A little." Straightening up, I note the unforgiving hug of the Lycra against my groin. "It's freezing," I say in defence.

"Let me have a look."

"At what?"

"The wound."

"It's nothing." But the pain is back in full swing, and I know my eyes give me away. To another wave of agony, instinct draws my hand to my side, and it's all I can do to stay on my feet.

Crystal moves to my side and gently brings my hand away. "Jesus Christ."

"Just a flesh wound."

"Okay, Rambo."

"It's Reformo."

She sighs. Face still creased, she snaps her head left and right, and as though she can suddenly feel the cold, a shudder works through her body. "Let's get you out of here. We need to get that stitched up."

"We?" We. We are a "we".

"I'm assuming you can't really fly, but can you walk?" She leans towards me, and I let her take some of my weight, grimacing as my feet meet the gravel. Entwined, we make our way down the winding path, the proximity to her and the pleasing odour of her perfume masking Bum Fluff behind a temporary blanket of mind fog. L-o-v-e. Moon basking us in romantic radiance, it's a perfect first date, discounting the stab wound and scattered drug needles.

"This is my fault." She turns to me, the same vulnerability in her eyes that I saw in the alley when she dropped her guard. "Should have known you'd be stupid enough to look for trouble."

"You came back for me." My words sound weak, my voice taking on the form of the nervous and awkward school child from many moons ago.

Can't trust anyone in this world, Simon; their truth hides behind layers of lies and fake compassion.

Shut up, Mama. For one second, just shut the fuck up. "You came back for me because you—"

"I don't want to know what happened by the water," she says, "but you have to promise me that's the end. Promise me you'll stop all this silliness."

Feeling like a broken record, I pursue clarity. "Why did you... come back for me? Why do you care?"

She looks to the ground and shrugs. "I just don't want to be responsible for someone else getting killed."

"I think I'm in love with you."

She eyes me again, offering a gentle shake of her head. "What?"

I swallow hard. *Is that a smile or a grimace working across her lips?* "I think I love you."

"You don't know me."

"My senses are tingling."

"Are you sure it's not your dick?"

"Uh-uh. I'm numb below the waist."

"You're mad."

"What makes you think that? My late night dip in the water or—" I try and swish my cape, but it's mostly stuck to my legs, the feedback of pain causing instant regret.

"Come on, you fool."

As we approach the end of the path, the first few boarded-up windows coming into view, she turns, offering a sigh. "Seriously, though. You have to stop all of this."

Does she mean my advances? Has our fleeting romance already come to an end? "Huh?"

"This place isn't movie land, a playground for superhero wannabes. People get hurt. Killed. I've seen so many horrible things, Simon."

She remembered my name. She remembered my fucking name!

"Promise me, Simon."

This is amazing. While she evaded any return thoughts on my declaration of love, the fact she remembered my name speaks volumes. Now I just have to remember hers.

"Simon!"

I smile, still riding high on my first date for years. And if I'm being honest, only my second ever. As if it was meant to be, her real name slips into my mind as soon as I open my mouth. "But what about all the chaos, Vera?"

"For Christ's sake, Simon, you're not a superhero." She begins half-dragging me along with her. "You're nothing but a delusional dork in a leotard, an overgrown boy with his head in the clouds."

The elation of taking up a place in her mind begins to fade, her words cutting like the wind. A delusional dork. An overgrown boy. That's what I get in return for my declaration of love. Not quite like the Hallmark movies from yesteryear they made us watch in prison.

"Wait here," she says.

The pharmacy has one window boarded up and the other with a crack running from top to bottom. Places used to close for such repairs, but there seems little point now. Shivering, the cold working to my bones, I observe the street and the shifting shadows. One can almost smell the mischief, the badness in the air. Senses tingle.

"Oi, you!"

I snap my head towards the voice but see no one. It sounded like a child. Footsteps ahead, what sounds like a can crushing underfoot. "Me?" More stomping to my left. And now behind.

"Yeah, you."

"What?"

"Throw your wallet on the ground and walk away," the voice says.

You've got to be fucking kidding me. Pissed, I thrust my palms out, declaring my empty-handedness. "Haven't got anything on me. Now just fuck off, will you!"

"I'm serious, Mister. We'll knife yer."

Anger shrouds all judgement. "Can't you come up with something more inventive, or are you just too fucking dumb?"

More footsteps. A series of whispers, a cough. "We'll knife yer."

"You've said that already."

Silence.

Sensing the indecision, I adopt my stance, ignoring the pain as I thrust my chest out. "I'm Reformo, bringing hope back to town."

After more prolonged quiet, I hear feet pounding against the pavement, a distant voice confirming their retreat. "Your dick is like an inch big, *Retardo*."

"YEAH, WELL, I'M FUCKING FREEZING!"

The bell sounds behind me. "Who are you shouting at?"

I turn towards Vera. *Simon and Vera, sitting in a tree.* "Just more creatures of the night. Christ, what do I owe you for all that?"

"A promise."

We make it back to my place without any further threats of violence, and I take a moment to enjoy the lack of booming music from next door. I picture Jayden sitting in front of the TV in his clean diaper, eyes on the screen but mind on the mysterious man in the cape who saved the day. His mum is preparing supper in the kitchen, humming a country song about a woman taking her life back. *Fuck, yeah! Reformo bring hope to town!*

"You okay, Simon? You look a little shaky?"

Concrete begins to spin around my feet. "Fine." The soundtrack of the night is becoming drowned out by an intense ringing.

"Simon?"

My leg buckles to the sound of Vera's drawl, lava-lamp-like blobs starting to swim around the edge of my vision. "Totally fine." Feeling myself beginning to sway, I launch my bloodied hands towards brickwork that sinks into blackness. "Actually, I think I might—" Pain swells behind my eyes, but panic forces them open. Black floaters reappear but in abundance. "Sleepy time." I blink rapidly, but they begin to expand, merging into a single cloud.

Chapter Six: The Bed Leg

I recognise the stain on my ceiling that resembles a runny egg. "What happened?" My left side lights up as I try to move, igniting my head further.

"You passed out; been laid out for some time. Here, take these."

"Vera. Lovely Vera."

She smiles and nods. "Hit your head pretty hard. You kept muttering something about a boy. Jayden? And something about a pledge to your mother." She takes a sip from the Spider-Man cup and passes it to me. "You're much heavier than you look."

"I'm sorry about this."

"No need to apologise. But hopefully, this will stop your silly arse ideas of saving the world. Once and for all."

I'm unsure how I didn't notice something so gaudy before, but I can't take my eyes off the oversized jewel-encrusted watch hanging from her wrist. "Did *he* buy you that?" I ask, nodding towards the monstrosity.

"Yeah."

"It's shit."

"Thanks."

Gritting my teeth, I force myself to my elbows, noting the small tea towel covering all that remains of my dignity. "Seriously, though...thank you, Vera." I pop the four tablets in my mouth and swallow on the second gulp, observing the excessive padding running down my side, all kept in place by a ridiculous amount of insulation tape.

"I did my best, but I'm no nurse. You cried a little, kept saying, 'Sorry, Mama' over and over. How do you feel?"

"Like someone who's been stabbed. How bad is it?"

She smiles. "Just a flesh wound, like you said. You were lucky."

"Is that lucky? Surely to be stabbed in the first place negates any luck."

"Only it wasn't bad luck, was it, Mister? Poking around, sticking your nose where it doesn't belong."

"Do people pay extra for that?"

Vera ignores me and lights up a cigarette, prompting Mother's voice to explode in my head. *Smoking in your abode, Simon? What is the world coming to? Are you going to do something, or are you as weak as—*

"What time is it?"

"A little after midnight," she replies.

I offer a smile. "Why a tea towel?"

"Could only find two normal towels, and I used them to dry you. I couldn't find your underwear either. Or anything suitably small."

"Yeah, well, as I keep saying, it's cold."

"Freezing even."

My smile widens. "I want you to know where my underwear is."

"I think that's possibly the most romantic thing anyone has ever said."

"Seriously. Why don't you move in with me? I'll protect you."

"With a tea towel?"

"If that's what it takes."

"I'll say one thing, you certainly keep the place very neat. And please take that as high praise coming from someone with OCD."

"It's not too much of an ask, the place having the square footage of a postage stamp."

"You got any food? I could eat the scabs off a tramp's head."
She takes another drag of her cigarette. "Tell me about your mother."

"My mother's dead. There's some leftover take-out in the fridge."

"I was looking for a little more than that."

"There's quite a lot left. And there's some nice bread in the—"

"I mean about your mother, you silly bastard."

"Why?"

"It's called a conversation, Simon, and I think we're at that stage in our relationship." She rifles through the fridge, turns her nose up, and closes the door without taking anything. "Scabs it is. It's just that I have a sneaking suspicion your dead mother is somehow involved. And what is this silly pledge you were drivelling on about?"

Mention of my dead mother aside, I'm still floating on her use of the 'R' word. *Our relationship.* We're in a relationship. In a ship, having relations. It makes me feel all warm inside, even the pain beginning to numb. "It's a long story."

"I've got a few minutes."

"What if I say I don't want to?"

"I didn't want to drag your sorry arse all the way back here, but I did."

"Fine." Offering a smile to hide the sadness, I take a long breath. I've never spoken about Mother to anyone, knowing it would be traumatic but also difficult to relay her impact on our lives. I try and arrange some words in my head, a lump swelling at the back of my throat. Vera touches my arm, and it's enough to induce the first tears.

"It's okay, Simon," she says, bringing me into her bosom. "You can trust me."

And I spill to her breasts, words running into each other as I nestle further in, her perfume providing some anaesthetic for the pain that tortures me. She listens and nods, stroking my head, offering comfort that was nowhere to be found during childhood. "It didn't take much to set her off, something so trivial as a teaspoon left on the counter or a wet towel hung incorrectly. Hard to explain to those who never got to witness her wrath, but she had a way about her that made me feel at once guilty and terrified. I know that probably doesn't make much sense."

"No wonder you're so fucked up," she says.

"One wrong move and darkness would blanket the house for an undetermined period; it was horrible. She was far scarier to me than any monster on the television or archvillain from one of my comics. I remember jumping on the bed once, pretending I was leaping from building to building in pursuit of a supervillain. The sound of the delayed crack will stay with me forever, Vera. I pissed myself. Pissed myself for crying out loud!"

"Oh, Simon."

Christ knows what Vera thinks of me, but my words won't relent. We are in a *relationship,* though. "For the next few weeks, each time Mother entered my room, I'd perch on the end of the bed, heart in mouth, praying she wouldn't notice the slant. A bed fucking leg, for Christ's sake. It took about three months to save enough pocket money to buy a plastic replacement."

"I think everyone has a healthy fear of their parents."

"You think I'm exaggerating, don't you? I knew you would, I knew you wouldn't get it. It was endless, Vera. If a dog barked, she'd bark with it until it stopped. If a fly got in the house, she'd buzz around Father manically until he got off his 'sorry arse' and did something about it. If someone parked outside our house, she'd make our lives hell, launching a barrage of abuse at Father, calling him every name under the sun." *Weak as piss. Weak as piss. As useless as a glass fucking hammer.* "And God forbid if someone played their music too loud, she'd be in our ears screaming for the chaos to end. It was horrible, Vera, she was—"

"Okay, okay. Breathe, just breathe. And the pledge?"

I recoil, trying to regain some composure. "That I would do my best to help stop the chaos."

"Why? Why would you want to help her after all she put you and your father through?"

More words threaten their relentless attack, but I swallow those down. "She was my mother, Vera." And I fear it's the only way to quieten her.

"Your father?"

"Dead. And better off for it."

She blows a deep sigh and takes another look at that god-awful watch. "I should go."

"Please stay. What about you? Your parents?"

"Well, they're alive, but to say our relationship is strained is an understatement. They know what I do and disapprove, although happy to take the bundles of cash I drop off."

"I'm sorry to hear it."

"Still love them, though. Life isn't perfect, Simon, and it never will be. Reality doesn't work like that." She kneels beside the couch and offers yet another sigh. "Look, whatever little fantasy is looping inside your head about people being able to walk the streets without looking over their shoulders, or couples holding hands on park benches declaring their love for each other, you need to snap yourself out of it. Do you understand? You can't fix this place. It is not fixable, Simon."

"A blind eye here, a blind eye there, and before you know it, we're hiding in the broom closet eating tinned peaches."

The slap across the face is unexpected. My cheek burns, and water fills my eyes.

"You're fucking impossible," she says. "Christ, I'd strip your mother down if she was here now."

I can't help but smile at that last comment, even with all the ringing in my head. "You make a mean nurse."

"This isn't fucking funny, Simon. This is reality. This is Hell. I belong to someone, a nasty little shit with a short temper, but he's all I've got." She reaches for my hand but thinks better of it. "There's no room for love around these parts, only alliances."

"But I love you."

She slaps her forehead this time and offers a garbled cry. "Christ's sake, will you get a grip? Are you not hearing what I'm telling you? I already belong to someone. And if he knew I was here with you, there'd be bits of you spread all over the floor." She bites a lip as if on the verge of tears. "He'd bag them up and feed you to the butcher's dog."

As another wave of ringing subsides, I reach for her hand, but she pulls it away and gets to her feet.

"Please take this as a warning, Simon. I don't know what happened down by the water, and I don't think I want to. But I assure you of one thing, you carry on running around town in that leotard, and you are going to end up—"

"In the butcher's dog."

She looks at her watch again. "I must go."

"Will you get into trouble?"

"My takings will be down."

"There's some money hidden in the cookie jar. Take what you need."

"I can't do that."

"You're worth every penny."

She smiles and heads into the kitchen area. "How old are you anyway?" she says, placing her cup on the counter. "Keeping cash in a cookie jar. Where do you keep the rest of it? In your thermals? Tobacco tin?"

"Funny." I push myself up a little further, enjoying the womanly smell of the place. "When will I see you again?"

"Not a good idea."

"Depends on who you ask."

"You don't listen, do you?"

"Pardon."

"I said you—" She groans, taking a stash of notes from the jar and putting the lid back in place. Lifting the cash in the air, she eyes me, expectant. "I'm expensive, not your typical two-bit whore."

"Don't say that word."

"I'll come by later this morning, but only to drop something stronger for the pain. I'll text you before I leave so you'll know to expect me. What's your number?"

"I don't have a phone."

"Say what now?"

"I don't have a phone. Never have and never will. They only facilitate the chaos."

"You are the strangest person I've ever met, and by Christ, my job puts me in front of some weirdos."

"I'll take that as a compliment." I let my head fall back into the cushion. "You love me, though. I know it."

"I give up."

"Don't."

The door squeaks open, allowing the cold air to rush in. "Stay out of trouble," she says.

"Pardon."

"I said—oh, fuck off, Simon." The door clicks behind her.

"Goodnight, my love."

The pain has ebbed a little, but I suspect it will only be a short respite. Still, the moderate throbbing allows me to close my eyes and romanticise about my future with Vera. Fate? Kismet? A love story for the ages of two tortured souls finding each other in the chaos. I can't explain it or get my head around it, but I guess that's the magic of love. And I'm not a fool to think such enchantment won't eventually wane, but I'm okay with that.

L-o-v-e.

I imagine us doing ordinary things together, such as coffee and breakfast, choosing new salt and pepper shakers, watching the local news—some reporter going on about how the town has changed, how civil and proud folk are becoming all over again. And Vera and I will sit on that park bench, holding hands for all to see. Just see if we don't.

How could you, Simon?

Stop it, Mama. Be nice.

Getting stabbed and falling in love with a hooker... If that's not a definition of chaos, I don't know what is.

"Give me a chance, Mama. I've just started. I'll fix it all, I promise."

But I have a side mission now. Mama might not like it, but she'll have to lump it.

Thoughts turn to the waterfront. The sound of my fist on Bum Fluff's jaw—CRACK! His impact with the water—SPLASH! Then nothing. Is that murder? Manslaughter? *Shit.* Whichever way you look at it, I killed a man. No, a boy. A man-child?

I KILLED A MAN-CHILD.

As the last of Vera's scent fades, and as if her presence had cast a softening haze, her absence allows the true implications of the night to hit home. Panic ensues, but the pain keeps me pinned down.

He wouldn't give, wouldn't see sense, Mama. I had no choice, did I? Guilt begins to gnaw, and moisture fills my eyes. Familiar territory but no easier to manage. "It was for the greater good." I sniff back my tears, knowing this is far from over. Small scale, perhaps, but Bum Fluff worked for someone, and once they realise he's missing, things will take a turn. Paranoia, revenge, and chaos will run rampant.

Sometimes, things will get worse before they get better, Simon.

It doesn't feel right, Mama.

All part of the healing process, Simon.

But, Mama, I killed a man! Child. Man-child.

Did anyone see me down by the water? Did anyone hear us fighting? Jesus, I'm so tired. Just need to close my eyes for a little—

Chapter Seven: Goodbye Reformo

I jolt awake, my senses tingling, pain exploring my side.

"Hello?" Wincing, I push up to my elbows, using my generously-sized ears to track the shuffling noise behind the door. "Who's there?" The handle turns. I know it's locked, though. I heard it click shut behind Vera. *Oh, in that case, you're safe, Simon. Burglars would never dream of breaking into a locked house.*

I feel helpless, a sitting duck.

Teeth pressed into my lip, I throw a leg from the couch, a thunderclap of pain riding through me. *FUUUUUUUUUCK!* But before I can even think about thrusting myself forward and making a play for the kitchen drawer, there's an explosion of frosted glass—CRACK! The front door swings open—SLAM! Immediate iciness trespasses, along with two men wearing ski masks, one carrying a baseball bat lined with dark stains.

My heart rate skips to the max. Blood whooshes in my ears. Enter witty superhero mode, albeit one with their cash in a cookie jar and holding a tea towel across their crotch. "I'd be having a word with your travel agent if I were you guys. We haven't seen snow for nearly a decade."

"Shut the fuck up," the one wearing the blue ski mask yells. He approaches and presses the bat hard into my chest, forcing my head against the cushion and a tidal wave of agony. "Looks like you're having a bad night already, and I'd hate to make it worser."

"Worse."

"Exactly." He runs his eyes up and down the clumsy dressing on my side. "What's with the tea towel?"

"There's cash here, Tom." Red Mask lifts the wad of notes into the air, likely the easiest money he's ever made.

"Don't use my real name, you idiot."

"Soz." Hurrying to load the cash into his pockets, Red Mask clears his throat. "What's your made-up name again?"

"It's a bit late for that, isn't it, you dumb fuck."

"Sorry, Tom. I mean, sorry—"

"For the love of Christ, just stop talking, will you?" Blue Mask—aka Tom—presses the bat down further. Instinctively, I want to rip it from his hands and drive it into his skull, but this isn't *fantasy land*. It's two against one, and I'm still wearing the results of my last set-to. "Should have given the kid your wallet," he barks at me. "And you shouldn't have called him dumb."

"Over two thousand pounds in total," Red Mask says. "Jackpot."

"That was your kid outside the pharmacy?" I try to keep my breathing calm. "Is that why you're here? Because I wouldn't let him mug me?"

Tom leans over. "Made him look a right ninny in front of his mates. And around here, reputation is everything."

A plan forms in my head like a comic strip, a series of images playing out, from me lying on the couch to the two goons tangled up on the floor, little birdies circling their heads. "Christ, you must be proud," I mutter. "Can't imagine what other wonderful things he will go on to achieve in life."

I can't see Tom's face, but I know he's frowning underneath the mask. His breathing becomes quicker, too. "Nobody calls my kid dumb."

"I didn't actually call him dumb; I was just enquiring."

With his pockets lined with my fried chicken money, Red Mask hurries to the door. "Let's go, Tom. I mean—oh, fuck it. I'm starting to get a bad feeling about this."

"I can't let you leave with that money, I'm afraid." My words emerge without a single quiver. And even though my cape is sodden and slung over a chair in the far corner of the room, this superhero is never off duty. "Put it back, leave, and we'll say no more about it."

"Kid said you were a loon," Tom says, pressing the bat down harder and moving his face closer to mine. "Strutting around town in a leotard, your little pecker on display for all to see. He thought you were a paedo until he caught sight of the whore you walked home with."

"Don't you dare call her that!" I try to get up, but he digs the bat into my chest.

"Crystal? Everyone knows she's had more meat in her than a butcher's bin. Do you remember that time we cashed in at the races, Bernie? We gave her a right good spit roasting."

"You fucking fuck!"

"Tom, let's go." Red Mask coils his fingers around the door-knob and peeks through the window. "All this adrenaline is playing havoc with my guts."

"You're not going anywhere with my money, you dumb bastards."

Tom shakes his head, half-breathing, half-growling. "I said to myself I'd go easy on you, the state of you already. But you are really beginning to piss me—"

SNAP.

It's a perfect hit, the tea towel snapping across his eyes. Taking my chance, I swallow a scream and thrust myself from the couch, wrapping my hands around the baseball bat. We're dancing now, albeit to a hushed set of repetitive lyrics from Tom's accomplice: "Had a bad feeling about this. A bad feeling. Baaaad feeling."

"Don't just stand there, Bernie. Get him!" Tom screams through an incessant wink.

"A bad feeling. Reeeeeeeeal bad feeling."

I can tell by the look in his good eye that Tom realises he's underestimated me. I've seen it a lot over the years, the way their faces—their eyes—change. He removes a hand to take a swing, but I duck down, bringing my elbows into his side. POW! Still holding the bat, he topples across the couch with a garbled croak, veins popping in his neck, legs kicking frantically.

"Do something, Bernie!"

But Bernie is still muttering under his breath, his hand frozen to the knob. Probably not the right line of work for him, but there isn't much to choose from around here. "Baaad feeeeling."

"Get the fuck off me." Spittle sprays from Tom's mouth as he lashes out, his left boot catching me on the arm, albeit nothing more than a glance. He snarls and tries again, his right foot landing square on my left thigh this time, adrenaline giving way to a surge of pain that buckles my leg.

FUUUUUUUUUCK!

He strikes again, catching me in almost the same spot, black floaters returning and the room beginning to spin. Pain rips through me, spreading like wildfire. The bat slips from my grasp, and before I know what's happening, a pair of arms wrap around my chest, rendering my top half useless, Bernie finally joining the fight.

"I'll fucking kill you," Tom says through gritted teeth. "Keep hold of him, Bernie, this fucker's gonna pay."

Another comic strip plays out in my head, just as bizarre as the last. And as Tom scrambles from the couch, I prepare to thrust my legs from the ground towards his chin. *Wait for it. Waaaaait for it.* I launch, my head snapping back, a simultaneous cry ringing out in front and behind. "I am Reformo," I yell with pride, my shrivelled pecker jiggling between my legs, "and I'm bringing hope back to town."

Twisting my body fast, I ease out of Bernie's grip.

"No, wait," he says, a hand to his nose, eyes watery and wide with expectation. "Please don't." He takes a small step back, raising his empty palms. "I'll give you the—"

WHACK! Perfect strike to the jaw, and he goes down like a two-bit—never mind.

From the couch, Tom offers a moan, forgetting about the

baseball bat and more concerned with collecting his teeth from the suede cushions. He wrestles off the ski mask and tries to press one back into his gum, offering a series of muted gargles as watery blood spills over his fingers. Finally giving up, he turns towards me, his face now unsymmetrical. "As good as dead you are," he says with a slur. "Once they find out about this, you're—"

"Who?"

"Should have just given the dickhead your wallet."

"Once who finds out?"

"You have no idea, do you?"

I take a stride towards him. Christ, this place is a mess. Dirty footprints on the floor, blood and teeth everywhere. Not to mention the dirty cup on the counter. *Rinse! Rinse! Rinse! For the love of Christ, rinse, Simon!* Mama would turn in her grave if she had one. *Chaos. Total bloody chaos.*

"Tell me."

"Fuck you!"

"We can do this the easy way or the hard way." My words are too contrived and uninspired. I'll work on that. "Once who finds out?" Could it be old Butter Balls?

"They are nowhere but everywhere. Eyes in a thousand places, ears all around."

I lean in close, the smell of blood in my nostrils. "No riddles. Who are they?"

"They are called The Dragon."

Ah, about time. An adversary with a worthy name. "And where do I find this *The Dragon*?"

He offers a tearful snicker. "You don't find them, they find you. And they will. You can count on that."

"What do they look like?"

"Nobody knows. Even those on the top layer of this racket don't know The Dragon's true identity. They are but a ghost."

"Look, you can shroud this punk with all the *Scooby-Doo* vibes you want, but I've seen all sorts of folk claiming to be more than what or who they are. We all breathe, bleed, fart, and eventually expire, so please spare me the theatrics and spill."

"I've told you all I know. They run this town and will take anyone down who tries to get in their way. It's just the way it is, the way it's been for so long. You don't realise how dead you are, do you? Have you been living under a rock?"

"Never mind me." I draw in closer, scooping the baseball bat from the floor. "You'll have to give me something more, Tom."

"You're dead. Soooo dead."

"Last chance, Tom." I run my right palm up and down the maple, letting him know my patience is running thin. I don't think I'm bluffing. Readying my swing, I deeply inhale.

And just like that, he wilts. "Alright. Alright. You're fucking crazy."

"Just getting started, Tom."

"Look, I don't know much, only that The Dragon has a hand in it all—drugs, weapons, women. They have a hierarchy, layers of people looking after each unit, and security always in tow. And then there are the mugs on the street like me, the expendables."

"Who's your employer?"

He offers a sigh, his shoulders sinking further.

"Is it"—*Was it*—"Bum Fluff?"

At first, he gives me nothing, but after a few seconds concedes with an imperceptible nod. "I report to him. Not much older than my son. Loaded with testosterone, but as dumb as a bag of hammers. All his firepower used for downstairs action, if you know what I mean."

"He worked—works for Butter Balls, yeah?"

He snaps his head towards me. "How d'you know that?"

"Where can I find her?"

"I don't know."

"Where?"

"I don't fucking know, okay!"

"This might hurt a little." I shuffle my hips from left to right, tapping the bat against his crown.

"You wouldn't."

I swing—WHOOSH—the bat missing his scalp by less than an inch. "How many teeth have you got left, Tom?" Retaking position, I nod, letting him know the next one will find its target.

"Okay, okay." He sniffs his snot back up, taking out his frustration by driving a fist into the suede again and again. "Fuck! Fuck! Fuck!" Composing himself, he takes a couple of deep breaths. "You'll most likely find her hanging around at the twenty-four-hour launderette, the one over on Smith Street."

"Glamorous. Why a launderette?"

"She owns it. It started as a good cover operation, back when the police still gave a fuck. She's usually there in the early hours, you know, once all the clubs have closed."

"Alone?"

"Never. At least two cronies in tow. Proper meatheads, too."

"What does she look like?"

"Oh, you'll know her when you see her. She'll make your hairs stand on end, and that little pecker of yours will shrivel up to nothing. Bad to the bone she is, not an ounce of compassion." He shuffles to the edge of the couch, caressing the swelling on his cheek but somehow managing to find a smile. "And she will tear you in half when she finds out about this."

"And above her? Who does Butter Balls report to?"

"I don't know."

As I raise the bat again, he brings his hands together as if in prayer. "Honest. The less I know, the better. That's how I see it and how it is."

The door handle turns, as do I, half expecting Butter Balls and entourage to burst into the room, guns blazing. *Eyes in a thousand places, ears all around.* But it's Vera, a white plastic bag swinging from her spindly wrist. "What in the world is happening here?"

"Fuck off, whore, this does not concern you," Tom says from behind.

Against the code, but impossible to control, I wrap the bat around his face—KERPOW—sending more teeth shooting from his mouth like shrapnel. One lands in the glass fruit bowl, making a gentle tinkling sound until it disappears within the mound of seedless grapes. "Don't you call her that," I cry, the bat shaking in my grip. I lift it again, offering a high-pitched roar.

"Simon!"

Arms still trembling, uncontrollable rage firing through my limbs, I step over a very still Tom. "It gets my fucking goat." *Chaos. Chaos. Chaos.*

"Put that bat down and get some pants on."

Even though her voice is harsh, it still has a soothing effect. I let the bat slide from my grasp, wincing as it clatters against the wooden boards. Mess surrounds me, chaos everywhere I look. Offering a desperate squeal, I crumple to the floor in a heap, spying at least three bloody teeth against the wooden grain. Mother was right: The whole world has gone to the dogs. How on earth did I think I could save it? *It is not fixable, Simon.* Mama, I don't know if I can do this.

"You can't stay here, Simon."

I keep telling myself superheroes don't cry, yet the tears flow as raw as a child's. "It hurts." And I'm not just talking about the burning in my side.

"I know a place," she says, latching onto my arm. "I take clients there sometimes."

"I can't do this anymore. I thought I could."

She tugs again, but I refuse to move. "Simon, get off the floor and put some clothes on."

"I killed a child, Vera."

"Who?" She joins me on the floor, eyes wide and full of concern. "Who, Simon?"

"Bum Fluff."

"Is that how you ended up in the water?"

"It was an accident. He tried to stab me."

"Bum Fluff isn't a child. He's scum."

"He's a man-child."

"A what?"

"I thought I could make a difference, Vera. Thought I could turn things around."

"We really have to leave."

"I'm pathetic. A failure. Weak as piss, just like my father."

She pushes herself to her feet. "Get off that fucking floor. Now!"

Her tone startles me. Not the soft one I've been used to. Perhaps the one she reserves for clients who get over-zealous with their fondness. Regardless, it has the desired effect, making me stand and head towards the bedroom. After slipping on some pants and a shirt—groaning and wincing in pain—I slide out a bag from the bottom of the cupboard and stuff it with as many clothes as possible.

"Come on. We've got to go."

"Coming." Feeling as vulnerable as a child, I drag my wrist across my damp eyes. *Are you crying, Simon? I didn't raise a child to blubber. Toughen up and grow some balls. No wonder the world's turning to shit.* The sight of the needle in Vera's left hand only accentuates the longing for a lost childhood. "I hate needles."

"I hate having sex with strangers, but we do what we must. Come here."

"What is it?"

"Fentanyl."

"How did you get it?"

"Not important. This should work quickly."

As the needle sinks into my side, I keep my stare fixed on her. "Thank you, my love," I say, basking in her scent.

"You're welcome. What happened here anyway? Looked like a scene from Dahmer when I came in, what with you standing over two dormant men with your tackle hanging out."

I can imagine some people considering her face severe and devoid of compassion, but I see well beyond that. Years of fending for herself have taken their toll, but her eyes are the giveaway—at least for me. She knows I'm safe, and it's as if the shield behind them drops, allowing me to see into her soul. They make me want to climb through and nestle inside her, and—Christ, I even sound like

Dahmer now. "They broke in, wanted my cash. Bernie's got most of it stashed in his pocket."

"Bernie?"

"Yeah, I know. Tom and Bernie, about as adept at a life of crime as their names suggest."

"We can't come back here," she says, rifling through the still man's pockets. "Is there anything else you need?"

"My Spidey mug."

"You're a fucking child."

"And leave them with two hundred."

Vera's face crinkles.

"Long story." I nod towards my bedroom. "There's more cash hidden in there—top shelf of my left cupboard in the yellow sock. And in the shelf below that, there's a—"

"Tobacco tin?"

"Close. An old coffee jar behind the sneakers."

"You've got to be fucking kidding me."

"See. You know me so well. It's a match made in heaven."

She sighs and disappears through the doorway. "It's a ten-minute walk, I'll get you a jacket."

A night of attempted heroics and this superhero, Reformo, gets stabbed and ends up relying on a hooker-not-girlfriend to nurse him to health and find a hiding spot. Funny enough, I've not seen that movie trope before. As Vera continues raking around in my wardrobe, I study the dishevelled costume strewn across the chair, contemplating whether this is the end of Reformo. No longer looking glossy and worthy of greatness, the cape appears dirty and seedy, a perfect representation of this shitty little town.

I have failed.

Weak as piss, just like your father.

I tried, Mama, I really did.

Just another casualty of the chaos. A quitter, Simon.

Stop it, Mama.

Quitter! Quitter! Quitter! Always have been and always will be.

Mama, I tried.

Stop whining, you quitter.

Mama!

"Are you okay?"

I lift my gaze to Vera and offer a gentle nod, watching as she shoves the last of the notes into her boob tube. The thought of clients doing the same, perhaps even into her knickers, is too much to bear.

"Ready?" she asks.

"I really don't want to put you in any danger."

"Danger is my middle name," she replies. "I've been trying to change it for years, but it kind of sticks."

I can't help but snicker. "Bit corny."

"And this from a man promising to bring hope back to town."

"Touché. Thanks, Vera."

"I'm doing this on one condition," she says, eyebrows huddled together. "Number one: you drop all of this superhero bullshit. Number two: it's only temporary until we decide on a long-term plan."

Offering a pitiful nod, I try and ignore Mother's continuing tirade.

"I need you to say it, Simon. I need you to say, I promise."

"I promise."

"To never again run around town like a twat wearing a leotard."

"Easy there."

"Say it, Simon."

"I promise to never again don my cape and try to save the world."

"Burn it, then."

"What?"

"The leotard. Burn it."

"I've already promised."

"Do I look like someone who has never had a promise broken before? Burn it, Simon."

Quitter! Quitter! Quitter!

She's serious, I can see it in her eyes. The shield is down, but sparks are emerging. Hardly believing the dream is over before it's really begun, I step over Tom and approach the chair. With every step, I feel heavier, the burden of failure weighing me down. My mind provides a reel of childhood memories, the majority sad and from within the four walls of my room, only the occasional ray of light breaking through. *Fantasy Land,* as mother used to call it.

Jumping from chair to chair when she was out, pretending I was Superman. SWOOSH. Using my dad's old fishing nets—*Spider-Man at your service*—to catch the pretend villains. SWISH. Using bat shapes cut out from textbooks to create silhouettes against the wall with my torch. *Don't worry, folks; Batman is here to save the day.*

"We should make a move, Simon."

Noting the shredded hole down the side, I collect my cape from the chair. "It's still wet...I don't think it will burn." *Hate fire. Hate it. Hate it. Hate it.*

"Cut it, then."

"Alright, alright." I take the scissors from the perfectly arranged cutlery drawer and hold them to the fabric.

"Do it."

It feels disloyal, as though I'm turning my back on the only real friend I had during childhood, the only thing that could pull me from misery. *Always living in fantasy land, Simon. Just like your father, the good for nothing.* Each bit of fabric falling into the sink feels like a candle of hope extinguishing.

"Again."

Tears fill my eyes, and the ever-present knot in my stomach twists. SNIP. SNIP. SNIP. Unable to let it go, I pinch the last piece between my fingers.

"I think I love you, Simon."

Did she really just say that, or am I too plugged up with Fentanyl? Struggling to breathe, I watch the black material fall against the wood.

"I've tried to fight it, I really have," she says. "But ever since we met, I think I've known."

CHASING THE DRAGON   111

I turn towards her, my stomach doing somersaults. My entire life has been one disappointment to the next, futile efforts to try and please Mother, the only woman that's ever really been in my life. But to arrive at this moment, all feels worth it.

"I mean, I know you're weird. Oh, so very weird. And I don't mean just a little bit loco; I mean full-on running through the streets wearing—"

"Can we cut back to the part where you said you loved me, please?"

"I said I *think* I love you."

"Good enough for me. Can we kiss?"

"For Christ's sake, now is not the time. And let's not get overly gushy about all of this. I can't explain it, can't rationalise why my heart has been stolen by a twat in a leotard, but there you have it. Come on, we have to go."

A twat in a leotard. Twat in a leotard. Yet somehow, spoken by Vera, the words carry immense compassion and fill me with joy. Love works in mysterious ways, I guess. As we step outside, I'm overwhelmed with the feeling of floating rather than walking, only some of that I put down to the drugs. The cold, too, doesn't seem to be penetrating as much as it has, not with Vera by my side.

Can't trust anyone in this world. The fewer people you have in your life, the less chaos there is.

But I love her, Mama.

You're just part of the chaos now, a quitter like the rest.

But I love her. I love her.

"I don't like this." Vera snaps her head in all directions, her pace quickening. "I should have gone first and have you follow afterwards."

"But we haven't seen a soul."

"It doesn't mean to say they haven't seen us."

Her comments provide a flashback to the pharmacy, the faceless voice emerging from the darkness. Hairs bristle on my neck as I begin searching the night, my superhero senses susceptible to even the slightest of noises.

"It's not far now," she says, all but jogging.

Reality grounds me further, the thoughts of staying in a place where "Crystal" does her entertaining, sending a series of shivers down my spine. *Don't say it. Don't say it.* As we walk the damp streets, our heads still snapping towards every noise, words continue rattling around in my head. The struggle is always futile. "This place. How often do you—"

"Simon, don't."

"What? I'm just taking an interest in—"

"It's just business, that's all. There's no red light or jar of condoms by the side of the bed, if that's what you're thinking. It's just a room. And it's just business."

Arms still entwined, our bodies a little further apart than when we started, the usual smells of piss and fast food float across, along with the occasional howl of night creatures. A drizzle coats us as we pass by iron gates and boarded-up windows, fake security for residents who likely still sleep with one eye open.

"I'm sorry. I had no right to ask that."

"It's okay."

"It's not." *If you do nothing, you're as much to blame.* "I was out of line, and for that, I apologise."

She shakes her head. "It's just survival. What's the alternative?"

"One thing has me confused, though," I say, intending to make things lighter again. "If you really are as expensive as you make out to be, how come you don't own a bloody car?"

"Cheeky bugger. Where's yours anyway?"

Blushing, I turn my stare to the ground. "I can't drive. Never learned how."

"I guess you wouldn't need to, what with the cape and all."

"Funny."

"I do have a car, actually," she says. "A year-old Mercedes, but *he* fitted it with a tracker to go with the one on my phone. He knows everywhere I go and how long I spend there."

"You're kidding."

"Wish I was. If I need to get my hair done, nails, even coffee with a friend, I have to give him advance notice or—"

"Or what?"

She shrugs. "So now you know what we're dealing with, you'll know why I don't want any connection to you traced back."

"This is insane." *Chaos.* "It's not acceptable, Vera. It's not right."

"It is what it is, Simon." She unlatches and nods towards an unlit building perhaps a hundred yards away. "There it is, just above the 'Shop for Sale' notice. I'll go first and let you in through the back way."

"Couldn't I just be one of your clients?"

She shakes her head, solemn. "Too risky. Come on, we have to be quick. I have a booking in forty minutes."

"It's a bit late, isn't it?"

"For dinner, yes. Not for fucking."

"Riiiiight."

"Get a grip, Simon. Focus. The car is at least a ten-minute walk away, and I already need to make up a reason for why I keep going off the grid. He's not stupid, and besides, he has eyes everywhere."

"I hate the fucker."

"Follow me in five."

With now only a dull throb echoing through my body, I watch my love head towards her occasional place of business. *Vera, Vera, Vera.* My only glimmer of hope in a world full of darkness, but she belongs to somebody else. *Belongs. Belongs. Belongs.*

"It's just not right." *Not for fucking.*

A breeze blows across, carrying a waft of shit from the gent's public toilet near the arcade. It escorts me back to recent events and the sight of Jayden in his overloaded diaper. "Wee-formo save us! Wee-formo save day!"

There's a sudden urge to scream, but I swallow it, setting my bag down in the driest patch of ground I can find. A pile of clothes, a wad of cash, and a Spider-Man mug are all I have to my name, my old place out of bounds. How long can I hide? Tail between my legs, running scared from chaos, where to from here? *It's everywhere, spreading like mould.* There's no escape.

A burger wrapper does its best to carry past me on another icy blast, but I snap it from the ground and crunch it into my pocket. *How long now?* Turning my head towards what sounds like a bottle smashing, my heart takes things up a notch, an accompanying pulse throbbing in my ears. Without my cape, I feel powerless, fear riding through my bones.

Scared of your own shadow, just like him over there.

Come on! Come on!

Alright, that's long enough. Expecting voices to emerge, calling me out and announcing my presence, I skip across the damp tarmac like a ballerina needing the toilet. Further pungency, only magnified, greets me at the alley's opening, leading me to believe many people have been caught short around here or have given up and called it home for the night.

"Hurry up, Simon."

"I'm coming." Stepping over the needles, used condoms, and God knows what else, I note the graffiti on both sides of the walls: *The Dragon is always watching.* I really fucking hope not. Finally, I emerge, grateful for the sight of Vera's smile that somehow brightens the darkness. "Come on, get inside, will you," she whispers, eyes darting everywhere.

"Alright. Alright." I only manage three small steps before she drags me over the threshold and pulls down the metal shutter behind me. "Who said romance is dead?"

She leads the way up the block of stairs, a strong smell of detergent filling my nostrils. "I haven't got long."

Chapter Eight: The Return of Leotard Man

"How long will you be gone?"

"After this client, I'll need to report back. To him."

"You might as well tell me who he is. I'm already up to my neck in it."

She runs a key card over an electronic scanner, prompting a click. "Remember your promise," she says, coiling her fingers around the door handle.

"Of course."

"His street name is Ass-man."

"And again, of course."

"But his real name is Trevor, Trevor Hartley."

"Trevor Trevor Hartley?"

"God, you're impossible." She swings the door open. "Not many people know his real name."

"I'm honoured."

"Oh, and he's got halitosis, too. Killed a man for mentioning it once. He's always chewing gum and sucking on breath mints, but it doesn't help."

"I don't want to know what he chews and sucks on."

"Now, now, don't be feisty. You did ask." Filtered moonlight sneaks through the blinds, revealing a surprisingly tidy and chic apartment. "I'm a bit of a clean freak. Even when the cleaners have been through, I give it a good going over myself."

"Why does that arouse me so much?"

She laughs. "Because you're a sicko pervert. Coffee or tea?"

I watch her make her way to the kitchen, imagining her offering a drink to her clients. "Coffee, please." Still, the place is unlike the brothels I've seen in the movies, and the bedside table supports only a large vase full of flowers with no sign of an old cookie jar filled with prophylactics. Through the window, though, the street below offers a dirty, grungy feel. "I guess turning on a light isn't an option?"

"If you pull the curtain across, that lamp in the corner should be fine."

Red velvet is the first sign this place is anything other than a flashy stayover. Still, I grab hold of the thick fabric and slide it across, the pay-off being to shut out suburbia's sliminess. *She's a whore, Simon. Can't you see what this is doing to me?* And once again, this place begins working at what little reserve I have, words battering at the door, my filter giving way.

"I want to take you away from all this."

Her laughter is explosive, doubling her over until her cheeks turn red. "Take me away from all this," she mocks. "Fucking priceless." Eventually, she straightens, tears running down her cheeks and hands planted on her thighs. "And you had the nerve to call me corny."

"Fuck you, then."

She turns. "Maybe one day."

Taking my chance, I march across with my chest puffed out. As the rhythmical tune of spoon-against-cup begins, I slide in behind her and kiss her neck. She turns, looking as though she's ready to scold, but her face softens. "Corny, but it worked a treat, eh?" I mutter.

And with that, we kiss for the perfect amount of time. It's everything I imagined it to be and more, silent fireworks exploding around our heads. The life of a failed superhero has its perks, after all.

She offers a smile as we both come up for air. "Drink your coffee, Simon."

"Cheers."

I've only ever kissed three women, one of them being my mother—*Not like that.* And one of the others, I later found out to be a "kiss the weirdo" challenge. The point is, I can still feel her lips on mine, taste her scent at the back of my throat, and even sense her essence coursing through my body. Corny, doesn't even cut it.

All I know is I'm smitten, and if I can't leap from tall buildings, I, at the very least, want to jump into her arms. We can run away and start a life together somewhere. I'd fry chicken from dawn 'til dusk. She could become a florist...or...or even start one of those webcam things. I could cope with that. Maybe. Everyone is doing it now anyway. You can't switch on these days without the risk of coming across your Aunty doing something with a piece of out-of-date fruit. No pun intended.

"I know what you're thinking, Simon."

"Huh?"

"Your eyes are glazing over. You're thinking we could run away together."

Perhaps she could become a psychic. "Maybe."

Her face hardens, dissuading me from going in for round two. "You have two unconscious goons at your place, both unlikely to forget your face in a hurry. Faster than a rat up a drainpipe, word will get around that Bum Fluff is missing in action, and when his bloated body finally comes to the surface, there will be questions. And people talk around here, Simon. They're made to. And for the love of God, when The Dragon finds out some nutter in a leotard is prancing around his streets preaching to bring back hope, he will put this chain of events down to more than just a coincidence. You will become a target, Simon. There'll be a bounty on your head."

"In that case, I better get on my horse and ride out of town, good lady. But I ain't—I say I ain't—leaving without yer!"

"Fucking idiot." She buries her head into her hands.

"That fucker at my place... He saw your face, too, Vera."

"I'll give him credit." She shrugs. "Get him to keep me out of it in return for—"

"Right. Yes, good idea." *Shitty idea. Another spit roast on the cards. Fuck this shit!*

"But I doubt he'll keep your little encounter to himself, not with most of his teeth missing." Vera starts shaking, looks unsteady on her feet, watery eyes full of panic. She turns, grasping the countertop. "I can't think straight. Too much—"

"Chaos. Would another kiss help?"

She shakes her head. "I have to get ready, I'm going to be late."

"I'm sorry for all of this, Vera."

With that, she rushes into the adjoining bedroom, frantic, and wiping at her eyes through heavy sniffles.

What a fucking mess! Reformo—he'll come into your life and fuck it over even more. With thoughts rushing by of the countless men that have been here before me, I slump onto the bed and let my eyes close for a while. If only the voices would stop. Still, I take what respite I can, holding onto thoughts of clean streets and smiles full of hope.

"I'll come back when I can," she says. "We'll fix a plan."

I lift my head to see *Crystal* in the doorway. "Wow. You look—"

"Don't." She brushes herself down and opens the iron door. "Your money is in on the kitchen counter, and more Fentanyl if needed. The bread might be out of date, but there's egg and ham in the small refrigerator if you get hungry. I'll lock up downstairs. No one should bother you. Hopefully."

"I love you."

The door closes behind her, and even though I've spent most of my adult life in my own company, I suddenly feel lonelier than ever.

A plan? What kind of plan? Either way, I doubt our ideas will align.

As her heels clip-clop down the stairs, a million thoughts rush through my head, none of them rational. Everything I've tried to change, all the good I've been attempting to bring, has only led me further down the rabbit hole of chaos. Exhausted, I close my eyes, again offering myself to the dark.

The familiar four walls of my old bedroom surround me, poster-less and unmarked. At the sound of Mama's voice, I nudge the small box under the bed and pinch at the skin under my thigh. "Shh, now." A warm breeze blows through my window, bringing the sound of children's laughter.

She's coming!

It's as though the walls are closing in with each of Mama's footsteps. I hold my breath, eyes on the handle, praying for it not to move. Heart in my mouth, I will for her to keep going, to pass my door, but the footsteps stop, and I hear her manic breathing. As the door swings open, Mama gives me that stare, the one she gave me when she found the dirty plate in my cupboard and the bramble stain on my best shirt. "It might seem like a little thing to you, Simon," she'd said, "but that's how it starts. It's a slippery slope. A slippery slope, and one that GETS MY FUCKING GOAT!"

I shuffle forward on the bed. "Mama?"

"Can you smell something funny, Simon?"

Crinkling my forehead, I sniff at the air, knowing in my heart of hearts this is just part of the charade. "Coming from outside, I think, Mama."

"Hmm. That's what I thought at first. Only when I stepped outside, I could only smell cut grass and cooking meat. But inside"—she mimics my loud, dramatic inhales—"there's an overwhelming smell of piss."

I pinch down harder on my skin, trying to maintain eye contact.

"Can you smell it, Simon?"

Sniff. Sniff. "A little. Still think it might be the drains, Mama."

"It's extra strong in here, though, don't you think?" She takes a stride towards the bed, eyes burning into me. "Either you have pissed yourself again, Simon, or there's another explanation. Which is it?"

Turning my stare to the ground, I swallow hard. As if to solidify my gesture of defeat, the kitten offers a high-pitched meow. I cower, my mother's heavy breathing intensifying.

"Stand up, Simon."

"No."

"STAND UP, SIMON!"

Bolting upright, it takes a few seconds for me to realise where I am, the heavy-set velvet curtains setting my mind straight. Bittersweet relief washes over me as I kick off the damp sheets. Nearly two in the morning, according to the clock on the far wall.

Quitter. Quitter. Quitter.

"Why won't you ever leave me be, Mama?"

I knew you'd turn out like him. No backbone. Happy to sit on your arse while the world turns to shit.

"But I did try, Mama." I throw my legs from the bed and make my way towards the kitchenette. "And look where it got me."

I only tried to do right by you, Simon. Show right and wrong and give you a code to live by.

"It was too much, Mama. I was so lonely."

People only let you down anyway. And as for that two-bit whore you're shacking up with now, I can't even—

"Don't call her that, Mama. I love her."

She's probably taking one up the arse right now.

"Mama!"

Can't believe you love a whore more than your own mother.

"It's different, Mama."

The world is going to the dogs, Simon. It breaks my goddamn heart at how little you care. This is not how I raised you.

"But I tried, Mama. And I made a promise to Vera." I stick my head under the tap and swallow some water. "Can't break a promise."

But you can break one to me? A promise to a hooker is worth more than a pledge to your mother? You have to pick up the reins, Simon. You must restore order.

"I can't, Mama."

Quitter.

"Mama."

Weak as piss.

My fingers clamp around the bench, but I can't stem the flow of tears. "You were so hard on me, Mama."

All for love, Simon. All for love.

"What about Vera?"

You're a pity project, Simon—a kitten in a box.

"I don't know anymore."

Quitter.

"Fuuuuuuuuck!"

Quitter. Quitter. Quitter. Weak as piss. Weak as piss. Quitter. Quitter. Scared little boy who pisses himself. Weak as—

"STOP!" The entire countertop vibrates as I bring my fist down. SMACK!

Several mouthfuls of water later, I stash half the notes into my pocket, drive another dose of Fentanyl into my side for good measure, and head towards the velvet curtain. Pulling it back reveals not a soul below, but I know as well as anyone that means nothing. Inhale. I lift the window and stick my head out, gauging the distance to the puddled streets below. Exhale. Feeling powerless without my cape, I lower myself down until my legs are dangling several feet from the pavement.

Three.

Two.

One.

The landing is solid but sends a fresh surge of pain up my left-hand side. Before long, though, I'm back in the shadows, albeit as a civilian, en route to Hope Street, staying low along walls, the familiar soundtrack of this shitty town on full volume. My last encounter with Janice and Alf plays out in my head as I arrive at the red door. This will be interesting.

KNOCK, KNOCK.

Who's there?

Dog Shit Man. Surprise!

I knock a little louder, ear to the door.

KNOCK, KNOCK, KNOCK.

Finally, a light turns on upstairs. I hear muffled voices and a window sliding up.

"Morning, Alf."

"What the fuck? Do you know what effin' time it is?" He screws his face up even tighter, eyes bulging from their sockets. "It's you. It's you, you fucker."

"Who the hell is it?" I hear Janice grumble.

"It's the fucking Leotard Man."

"Dog Shit Man?" she asks. "The fucking cheek of it!"

With that, the window slams shut, and I hear feet pounding against the stairs.

Dog Shit Man in a Leotard—another hit coming to a cinema near you.

After another series of thundering footsteps, the door swings open. Alf offers a snarl, his fingers tightening around the black handle of a knife.

"That's a bread knife, Alf."

"What?"

"The knife you've got there. It's a bread knife."

He lifts it for inspection. "Janice, get me a steak knife."

"That won't be necessary, Alf," I say, holding my palms out in a gesture of peace. "Listen, I need a favour."

"You what?"

"I know, I know, the audacity, especially after the little stunt I pulled. But listen, I have an exciting proposition for you."

"It took Janice ages to get rid of the smell from the shag. I should rip you a new one."

"What does he want, Alf?" Janice yells from over his shoulder.

"The fucker says he's got a proposition for us."

"If it's anything to do with that gimp suit, I'm out." She arrives at the doorway, wearing a hairnet and a scowl, the requested steak knife slotted in her tiny left hand. "You've got a real cheek, you know. I've still got the smell in my nostrils. Any faith in the pigs in blue and we'd have called them on you."

I hold my hands up higher. "Part of the reason I'm here, Janice.

If you want a job done properly and all that." I begin counting the cash, making a meal of it, observing as the couple gradually wilt. "How about a thousand?"

Alf's eyes sparkle. "What for?"

"Just for a new suit, but one with a few more modifications."

"Get inside, love," Janice says, almost giving me whiplash as she drags me across the threshold. "You can't be seen around here carrying that sort of cash."

My eyes water as staleness hits me for six. "Only, I need it soon."

"How soon?" she replies, eyes fixed on the notes.

"A thousand notes soon."

"Well, I've plenty of material." She makes a clearing for me on the couch. "Might be able to put something together. Have you got a specific design in mind?"

"It just needs to be better than the last one and, you know, with a mouth hole to breathe."

"For a grand, love, you can have as many holes as you like." She claps her hands together. "Tea?"

"No thanks."

"Alf, make some tea."

"Not likely," he says, slumping into an armchair lined with head grease.

"It's fine, Janice, thank you. I just need that suit."

"Alf, you will make that bloody tea."

"I fucking won't." Defiant, he switches on the TV and crosses his arms.

"Funny thing," Janice says, dragging Alf from the couch by his left ear. "My friend Doris from bingo said she recently ran into some 'tosser in a leotard'. She said he made her crouch down in the cold to pick up all of her Polly's 'little pebbles'. I could hardly keep a straight face when she was telling me."

"It's just a matter of self-respect," I say in defence.

"Little runt on a rope she drags around. Can't stand the little fucker."

"I really need that suit, Janice."

"Of course."

Avoiding the mug of swill that Alf plops down next to me, I give Janice a quick run-down of requirements. She nods and reassures me throughout, but as I try to explain I'd like a cup sewn into the suit, she stares at me, blank. "Wouldn't a flask be easier to conceal?" she asks.

Over that minor hump, she lights a cigarette and heads upstairs, leaving Alf and me to sit in silence, the television saying enough for both of us. An overweight and shiny game show host runs up and down a glittery staircase, breathing hard down the microphone and making the most of every double entendre and cheap pun. *Hands firmly on your buzzers, gents. Oo-er missus. Are those real, love, or is that where you carry your shopping?*

A little after five-thirty, close to clawing my eyes out, the grating sound of the sewing machine finally cuts out, and upon hearing the first creak of the stairs, I all but jump from the couch.

"You're wasting your time around here," Alf says.

But he will not dampen my excitement. "A blind eye here, a blind eye there, and before you know it, we're hiding in the broom closet eating tinned peaches."

"It's an extra twenty for the tea," he says.

"I've finished." Janice announces.

I turn to see my new cape draped across her arms. It's everything I imagined—a glossy and functional second skin, no longer looking like a cheap fancy dress throwaway but a proper hero's costume. The large 'R' sewn into the centre, surrounded by a ring of flames, is an off-list addition but one that makes my heart sing.

"I hope you don't mind. Think it adds a certain something."

"I love it, Janice."

"And I've added a couple of extras, figuring you might need them, you being a superhero and all."

Alf chokes on the stale air.

"It's fantastic. Absolutely top notch. Can I try it on?"

She mirrors my excitement with a vigorous nod. "Upstairs,

first on the left, there's a large dressing mirror in the corner."

Falling up the first few stairs in haste, I offer my thanks, renewed visions of saving the world flittering through my head. It's just about bringing order, reminding people about dignity and self-respect, I tell the crowd. The room hosts a single bed packed rows high with toilet rolls and cigarette cartons. In the corner stands the mirror, blocked by a mannequin with one arm. Adrenaline flooding through me, I give it a right hook to the jaw—THWACK—and proceed with stripping off as fast as possible.

Here we go. Reformo is reborn.

An arm through. *Come on, come on.* Two arms. A leg—*Oh, it's a thing of beauty.* And...another. It's tight, but a much better fit than before, allowing me to crouch and stretch without feeling like my balls are in my throat. The cape is the perfect length, too. Everything about it screams superhero. "Reformo, bringing hope back to town."

"Is it okay?" Janice shouts from the bottom of the stairs.

"Sensational, Janice." Reformo is back, back to save the day. "Absolutely sensational."

"I am quite pleased with myself."

Giddy, I skip down the stairs, launching from the fourth, cape swishing behind. On landing, I plant a kiss on Janice's cheek and coil my fingers around the door handle. "I pledge to bring order back into town."

"Can you start by not slinging dog shit through our letterbox?" Alf yells from the living room.

"Ignore the old bastard," Janice whispers. "He's riddled with gout."

"I am sorry about the poo, though," I say. "Anyhow, what are you going to do with the money, Janice?"

"Well, we are running a bit low on cigarettes and toilet rolls."

The cold breeze stings my face as I open the door, but my body remains warm. I feel like a million pounds, perhaps that second dose of Fentanyl kicking in. "Thank you again."

"Just be careful out there, son. It's getting worse. And if you do get into trouble, there's a little something sewn into the padding down your right arm." I can't feel a thing as she taps against it. "Don't worry," she says. "There's about ten layers of linen between you and the blade."

I run my fingers over the slight bulge on the outside of my suit. "Steak knife, perchance?"

She winks. "Something with a little more bite. I used to keep it under the bed, but it's too tempting, what with Alf lying next to me." She winks again. "I think it's better off in your hands. Velcro pocket near the wrist for quick release. Good luck, Reformo."

And with that, I disappear into the very early morning, avoiding the streetlamps, senses activated to "Fully Heightened Mode" as I try to establish my bearings. Across the road, a young couple is going at it hammer and tong in a shop doorway.

"Don't put it up there, you dirty bastard," I hear the woman cry. "And the name's Jenny, not Jacky." A bit further along, someone's taking a piss against Miley Cyrus's face on a bus shelter.

Sorry, Miley, but priorities and all that. I continue on my way. *What's my plan here anyway? A civilised chat with Butter Balls, a plea to her human side?* That guy had said, *"Bad to the bone she is, not an ounce of compassion."* And look how things turned out with Bum Fluff. My head spins with chaos as I approach the unlit launderette, searching for a good spot to hide, a solid vantage point.

"Want a blowjob?" a voice says from the darkness.

I spin around, unable to find the source for this indecent proposal. "No, but if you let me know where you're hiding, I'll see you right."

"Up here, mate."

The voice leads me to a dilapidated building a few yards to my left. "Where?" I ask. A series of shuffles and cusses fill the night, followed by the clatter of bottles, until a head pops out over the edge of the flat roof—one that looks like it's been on max setting in a microwave.

"Hey!" he says.

The hair on his head and chin is long and dry. It points in all directions, defying established laws of gravity, as though frenzied in its attempts to escape the undeniable smell this creature kicks off. His skin looks like puckered leather, and a single brown tooth stands defiant in the gummiest grin. "I'm *really* good at blowjobs," he says, bouncing his eyebrows up and down.

"I'm sure you are, but I just need a hiding place."

He sighs. "There's a wooden crate down the side. Hoist yourself up."

Following the advice of my new friend, I move the crate in place and scramble up the side of the building to find a makeshift bed; nothing more than a bunch of dirty rags, his pillow, much the same.

"Now knock it over."

I do as he says and turn to face him again. As if holding the rest of his tattered clothes in place, a stereotypical and oversized dirty overcoat hangs from his shoulders, finishing way past his knees. He offers me an opened tin of beans, a rusty spoon poking from the lid.

"No, thank you," I say, a shudder running down my spine upon spying a milk bottle half-full of yellow liquid towards the far corner of the roof.

"It's piss." My new friend offers a gummy smile. "Toilet's out."

Before you know it, you're living in a shit heap—a fucking hippy, collecting your piss in empty milk bottles.

I nod with a polite smile. "How long have you been sleeping here?"

"A few weeks. Pigs moved me on from my last spot but did me a favour really. Nobody bothers me up here. I see everything, but it's as though I'm invisible to others." He taps me on the shoulder with one of his grubby fingers. "Look, you can see all the way from the bridge to the old industrial estate. Not much to look at, but it's better than staring at misspelled graffiti down some piss-stinking alley."

"Indeed." I'm running out of things to say already. *What are your plans for tomorrow? Bit of a chilly snap we're having, isn't it? Did you watch the game?* "It's freezing up here."

"Heating's out, too," he says. "Who are you supposed to be?"

"The name's Reformo. I'm bringing hope back to town."

"Are you on crack?"

"No."

"LSD?"

"Certainly not."

"Mushrooms? Ritalin?"

"No."

"Then you must be straight-up out of your goddamn mother-fucking mind. Ain't no chance of hope rearing its head in this shit hole of a town."

Eyes sweeping across the launderette, I crouch down low. "Here's a fifty, I'm sure you'll spend it wisely."

He looks at me all wide-eyed and grateful. "Not likely. What are you looking for, anyway?"

"Trouble," I reply. The wind fires up, sending my cape flapping around my shoulders. *Look at that timing. Perfect.*

"Well, you're in the right place." The vagrant taps me on the shoulder again and holds his hand out, probably enough bacteria under his fingernails to wipe out an entire alien species. "I'm Reggie. A pleasure to meet you."

"Likewise, Reggie," I say, nodding and leaving it at that. "You heard of Butter Balls?"

"Uh huh. Made the mistake of asking her for a twenty once, and she gave me four bunches of five, if you know what I mean. Couldn't see out of my right eye for a week."

"She has a certain reputation, for sure." It suddenly occurs to me that my source, Tom, could have said anything to prevent a beating. Perhaps he's even setting me up. An ambush. "She owns the launderette, right?"

"Yup. And I'm guessing you being here now is no coincidence."

"Looks and brains, Reggie."

"It's a curse, I tell you. She done you wrong?"

"She ever alone?"

He shakes his head. "There are usually at least two others and more popping in and out all day. Never seen a soul carrying any washing in or out, mind."

"Why are people so afraid of her?"

"Some people are afraid of spiders. Some people are scared of things that go bump in the night. But every fucker and their dog fears a visit from Butter Balls." Reggie shoves some beans into his mouth, more of the sauce collecting in his beard. "Can't imagine the kind of life that could turn someone so sour, and that's coming from me. But I figure that woman was born bad. You can see it in her eyes. Word on the street is she once killed someone for not giving her a wide enough berth on the pavement."

"Sometimes word on the street is exaggerated."

"You'll know it's true when you lay eyes on her. Carries meanness around her like a black cloak." He wipes at his beard and sits next to me, feet dangling off the edge. Nothing to see here, just your local tramp and everyday superhero sitting on a shed roof, shooting the shit. "Always thought she'd make a good right-hand woman for the devil," he says, following with a muted snicker. "But she'd likely stab him in the back the first chance she got."

We sit in silence like old friends, time seeming to stand still. Stars above offer indifference and bring thoughts of irrelevance to my efforts, this place being nothing but a speck on the ever-spinning rings of chaos. *Small steps make climbable ladders, Simon.* And just as I'm about to tell Mother we'll need a bigger ladder, a star zips by, cutting the night in two.

Reggie clears his throat. "You see that?"

"Uh huh. I still don't want a blowjob, Reggie."

"Eh?"

"Nothing."

"Second one I've seen tonight," he says, his glistening gums on full display. "Now, don't get me wrong, I'm not one of those hippie types with a hard-on for star signs or tea leaves, but I've not seen one around here for years. And then two in one night."

"Maybe you just haven't been looking."

He shakes his head and scrunches his face up. "What else you think I got to do all night but stare at the fucking sky? Ain't like I'm fighting the ladies off with a shitty stick or walking the red carpet for my latest premiere. No, I'm telling you, something good is coming. A shooting star is a sign of hope. And by Christ, it's long overdue."

"I hope so, Reggie. I hope so."

He nods. "Good things, I tell you. And you're a good person, I've got intuition for these things."

"Trying." No longer feeling insignificant, instead encouraged by the heavens, I pick the suit from my arse and settle in for the long haul. Hours spent in front of the television as a nervous kid, wishing I could escape through the glass screen, I've seen my fair share of stakeouts. But nothing could have prepared me for this, the electricity in the air and palpable tension.

My name is Reformo, and I'm bringing hope back to town.

There's every possibility I won't see the day through, and even though I know the stars will continue shining, I can't help but feel a deep connection to them. I feel lightheaded, a mixture of excitement and dread at what will most likely be my most explosive confrontation yet. It's an important moment, and—

"What the fuck, Reggie?"

"Sorry, that's the beans."

And just like that, all the build-up is lost behind an invisible wall of death. My eyes begin to water, and my stomach churns. "That isn't normal." I gag. "Isn't human."

Reggie shrugs, pinkness showcasing his solitary tooth once again. "That's my superpower, I guess. What's yours?"

I can't help but laugh out loud. "My sense of smell," I reply, holding my nose and gagging once more. Childish, vulgar, and unbefitting of a superhero, yet it feels utterly essential. Such a strange set of circumstances to bring us together; this time in the morning, on a small roof opposite a twenty-four-hour, non-operational launderette, but it's safe to say that I love this guy.

We're just kids who have lost their way, adulthood a far cry from the symphony of arm farts and snail races in the school playground. The bouts of laughter that brought tears to our eyes, making it almost impossible to speak, nothing but a distant memory. People get older and meaner with it. The bullying begins—*The weirdo with the mental case of a mother*—and then you're on your own, not invited to places, eating lunch at the school canteen surrounded by empty chairs, fantastical images playing in your mind of parades down the streets, and chants of your name.

"Where are you, kid?"

I turn towards Reggie and smile. "What's your favourite memory? As a kid, I mean."

He shrugs and looks to the stars again. "Ain't too many. Mother died before I knew her, and my old man used to beat me pretty hard. Slapped a lot of the good stuff out, I guess."

Trauma, coming-of-age, bad choices, good choices, and the relentless rollercoaster of adulthood—all part of the baggage trying to drag us down. *Chaos, Simon. Chaos.* We fight and do our best, but we're only fucking human. "Just one memory," I say, offering Reggie an encouraging nod. "Go on."

Running a hand through his beard again, as if in deep thought, he offers a deep sigh before turning and revealing the child in his eyes. "There was this one time," he says. "Me and Jason...Maher. Yeah, that was it, Jason Maher." A smile breaks across his face, lines of stories with faded ink drawn across his forehead and under his now glistening eyes. "We decided to cut school one day. No plans or wild exploits in our heads. Just for fun, you know. But Christ, it got dull quickly. Walked the streets for hours, as bored as fat kids with a bowl of veggies." The smile deepens, a tear escaping from his right eye. "Not sure how we ended up near Sadie Harper's house, but we put it down to fate at the time. Prettiest girl in town by some goddamn margin, let me tell you. But her mother, well, she was in another goddamn world. Supermodel territory, if you know what I mean. An arse to die for and breasts that could suffocate a man. Anyhow, don't judge me, but we had this idea of stealing some of her panties off the washing line."

I shake my head, offering a disapproving sigh. "Consider yourself judged, Reggie."

"Hey, we were kids. Dumbasses. Even a wink from the TV weather girl caused a hard-on in those days. So, we snuck down the side of the house and heard running water coming from inside. 'The shower,' Jase said. The house being on a slope, the steamed-up window above was just out of reach, so he offered to lift me on his shoulders on the condition I return the favour. Of course, we spat on our palms, shook hands, and I climbed aboard. And as though fate struck again, there was a magical patch of glass completely free of condensation."

"So you got an eyeful?"

"Goddamned frosted shower screen, would you believe?" He laughs and shakes his head again. "Refusing Jason's plea for a go, I pressed my nose against the glass and waited, filled with excitement and as horny as a three-balled tomcat. Finally, the water flow began to slow, until it... Until it..."

"Go on!"

But his shoulders are already going, rhythmic jostles—up and down, up and down. A half-wheeze, half-laugh explodes from his dry and cracked lips as he wipes more tears from his eyes with a dirty wrist. A far cry from the weathered old man that first greeted me with the offer of fellatio, I see the child, folded over and guffawing, already disillusioned by the lottery of life but holding onto a glimmer of hope. Finally, he composes himself and looks back towards the stars. "Jeez, I can't remember the last time I laughed like that."

"For Christ's sake, will you finish the story, Reggie?"

"Everything happened so fast. I heard Jase offer a high-pitched cry of 'Fuuuuuuuck.' And not before copping an eyeful, I crashed to the ground in a heap, only to look up and see Sadie Harper's mother staring at me with her hands on her very shapely hips. She didn't say a word, just raised an eyebrow."

"Hang on a minute then. Who was in the shower? Mister Harper?"

"Nope. That might have given me a couple of nightmares, but the sight I saw kept me awake for weeks. It was all around school the next day, Sadie telling everyone I'd been perving on her Great Grandma."

"No way!"

"Uh huh. She'd been staying there while the family found her a home to move into."

"Holy shit. And you saw—"

"The works. Every wrinkle, every age spot, the swinging titties, and the hairless wonder."

"Jesus Christ."

"It was weeks before I could tickle my pickle again."

He turns to look at me, and I'm the one to go this time, laughter taking me back to another time. He follows suit, his face creasing more than ever, gums on full display as tears leak down the caverns in his cheeks. We laugh like children, without bounds, consumed by the moment, our past and future on ice, if only for a moment. Only the sound of an engine snaps us back into reality.

"That her?"

"Car looks familiar," Reggie replies. "You got that look back in your eye, Mister. I mean—what was it again?"

"Reformo."

"What did she do to you, anyway?"

I watch the car pull up, taking note of the registration: BB4LLS. My skin prickles, and the knot churns in my stomach. *I need you to say it, Simon. I need you to say I promise.* After what feels like an eternity, a man exits the driver's side and walks around the vehicle, snapping his head left and right before opening the rear passenger door.

There she is. Butter Balls.

Five foot two at most, but built like a panzer, shoulders like boulders, hands like melons, and fire hydrants for legs. She clicks her fingers in the air, and the two lunkheads congregate by her side, all but bowing at her feet. Her voice is loud and brash, but even with the help of the breeze, her words don't quite carry.

"Does the shop door lock from the inside?"

"Think so. Most of them do, don't they?"

"Fancy earning yourself a fifty, Reggie?"

I hear the spoon clatter against the tin. "Whoa, wait a minute, pardner. These days, I could just about work my way into a paper bag if whisky was involved, but I doubt I could fight my way back out."

"No fighting, I promise. Just need a little distraction."

"So, I don't need to bring this?" he says, holding up the tyre iron.

"On the contrary, Reggie."

Chapter Nine: Butter Balls

Tucked in behind a garbage can, I study the three of them through the window, the two lunkheads sitting wide-eyed on the centre bench, Butter Balls spreading something out before them. Their voices are muffled, but it doesn't take a genius to work out they're not discussing which laundry powder is best for whites. From behind the car, Reggie gives me a sign that he's ready to rumble. Time for action, and with a hobo as my sidekick, what could go wrong?

Inhale. Exhale.

I'm so sorry, Vera, my love, but Mama's right: Can't sit back and watch, or you're only as good as them.

You're just part of the chaos now, a quitter like the rest.

I hope you'll find it in your heart to forgive me.

Three.

Two. *Wait, wait, wait. What if it's a trap? Others hiding in the shadows, ready to rush me? Did Tom and Bernie blab, I wonder? Nah, they'd be too shit scared, surely.* I glance over my shoulder and offer a final nod to Reggie. *Okay. Okay.* Heart in my mouth, I raise my hand, count to three one last time, and bring it back down.

SMASH!

The relative silence of early morning crashes around us, an explosion of shattering glass bringing a sense of urgency and panic to the air. The alarm on the car sounds, offering a high-pitched wail as if the vehicle protests at being woken from a slumber. Lunkheads one and two are on their feet, making a rush towards Reggie, who flicks the bird as he heads for the shadows. "Suck my dick," he yells, without earnestness on this occasion.

"Bring that fucking turd before me, so help me God," I hear Butter Balls scream through the glass, eyes bulging from her massive head.

Run, Reggie, run!

Dirty coattails flap around Reggie's worn-out shoes as he continues running in anything but a straight line, dark water splashing on either side of him. The lunkheads are closing in, but I've no doubt my new friend knows this shitty little town and all its seedy hiding spots like the back of a bottle of cheap whisky. I wait until all three disappear into the shadows before turning my attention back to the launderette, hoping Reggie will keep them occupied for some time. Returning early and empty-handed would certainly not be in their best interests.

BOSS FIGHT.

My body offers a violent shudder as I study the powerhouse still sitting on the bench, shaking her head as she returns to her business. It has to be now. No time for hesitation. But Jesus Christ, look at the arms on the fucker. And the tattoo-covered, tree-trunk legs have me wondering whether anyone has ever been brave enough to venture between them.

Focus, Simon, I mean Reformo, for fuck's sake.

Inching closer, tucking in behind the signage, I feel inferior, no match for the tank inside. My heart thunders, blood whooshes in my ears, and my limbs feel as leaden as in the black water. *Come on. Come on!*

Weak as piss, just like your father.

Shut up, Mama!

The position gives me a clear view, allowing me to see the four piles of notes spread across the bench. She starts on a fifth, occasionally licking her stubby thumb to ensure traction.

You have to promise me that's the end of it. Promise me you'll stop.

It's for the greater good, Vera. One day, we WILL sit on that bench and hold hands, you'll see. I'll make this town great again or die trying.

Tensing my muscles, I unfold, preparing for battle. She doesn't see me yet. As I grab the door handle and pull, I consider the possibility of trying to reason with her, perhaps offering a shoulder to cry on, an outlet for whatever traumas brought her to such a dark path. We probably have a lot in common, able to form a union of—

"Where shall I send your remains, fuckhead?"

"Beg your pardon?" I say, giving her the benefit of the doubt as I close the door behind me.

"Only one person ever came into my office without knocking or giving the sign, and they left in a bin bag." She continues counting cash without looking up. "Was it you who busted up my car?"

Quite a ridiculous size for a launderette, if truth be told, especially considering no clothes get washed here. "Not exactly, but I did have a hand in it, so to speak."

"Then you're as good as dead, *so to speak.*"

"I thought we could talk." Inching towards her, I raise my arms and uncurl my palms. "Let me introduce myself formally."

"What is this—fucking prom night?" She slams a knife down on the table. "There, that's my introduction. Now what the fuck—" She stands, looking me up and down, and I swear I see a morsel of trepidation behind the one eye that works. But the line of scar tissue extending across her left cheek and running down to her neck grounds me very quickly. "It's you," she continues. "You're the fuckwit in the leotard."

"Reformo, actually, but my PR campaign is still picking up steam."

"Sticking your nose where it don't belong."

"Doesn't."

A snarl from Butter Balls commences a pre-battle stand-off, the air around us electric. FZZZZ. Yet amid such tension and impending chaos, one question won't let me be: Why Butter Balls? The woman has a glass-fucking-eye, for Christ's sake. What about Popeye? That one works. She looks like a hardened sailor, and right now, she seems angry enough that her eye might pop out and roll across the floor between my legs. Words rattle around my head, ticking time bombs of information that must be released. "Tell me, have you ever thought about—"

"ROOOOOOOOAR!" She's on her way, red-faced, knife in hand, ready to slice and dice. For a split second, I wonder where she keeps the bin bags, but it soon dawns on me that I've neglected the golden rule of striking first.

Oh shit.

"I'll fucking kill you," she cries.

For carrying bulk, I'm impressed with her agility, everything working in harmony like a well-oiled machine. *Wait for it. Waaaaaaait for it.* As she draws within three feet, I sidestep, narrowly missing the knife as she takes a swipe and bounces off the machines. THUD!

Now's my chance. POW! Direct hit on the jaw. "Eat that, motherfucker." But other than her widening eyes, there's no reaction.

Oh shit.

Loading the punch with everything I have, I swipe again. KERPOW! Bang on the magic spot. This time, her atlas of a face creases into what looks like a smile.

BIFF. BAM. KAZAM.

Fuck! Fuck! Fuck!

Before I can react, sausage fingers latch around my throat, her grip only getting stronger as I try and wrestle her arm away. "Metal plate for a jaw," she whispers into my ear, bringing her knife-wielding arm towards me. "I've already returned from the dead twice; what made you think you were worthy?"

My head—it feels like it might explode. Continuing to lash out and fend off the knife, I hear and feel things popping along my neck. Darkness begins closing in, and it feels like I'm in the water again. I coil my fingers around her thick wrist, but my arm is growing weak, the blade drawing ever-closer towards me.

Weak as piss.

Offering a grunt, Butter Balls rams me hard into one of the machines, causing it to wobble. "I asked you a fucking question!" Hot coffee breath rushes over my skin. "You think you're suddenly a tough guy because you put on a stupid costume and give yourself a silly name?"

Yeah, that was the idea, lady. "I am Reformo." I swallow hard.

"And you think you're the first to try it on? I've seen off far bigger and stronger than you, you lanky fuck!"

"Is it too late to talk?" I utter, my words inaudible.

She snarls again, and I feel the blade puncture my skin. Warmth runs down my cheek, accentuated by her quickening breath as she senses a kill. This is it, this is how I'm going to go. A much more dignified ending than dying with a tea towel around my knackers, but still, I thought this fantasy would play out a little longer.

Quitter. Quitter. Quitter. You have to stand up and make a change. Only the loudest voices get heard, Simon, and if everyone kept their mouth shut—

I tried, Mama.

If everyone gave up.

It goes against everything I believe in, but the thought won't leave me be, and I know if I don't act fast I'll die with it in my head. Gritting my teeth, I pray to whoever is watching for forgiveness as I bring my knee into her nether regions.

THWACK!

Her eyes widen, and her grip around my throat relaxes. "You fucker," she says. Still, she yanks her other arm back and brings the knife towards me. SWISH—and a miss.

My move, bitch.

And once again, swallowing my pride, I get the knee off— THWACK. Direct hit, but this time, an even more desperate look behind her eye. *Hit and fucking sunk, baby.*

Breath rushing from her, she crumples, knife bouncing to her side. "How could you?" she groans.

"I am Reformo." Hands to my throat, sucking in the stale air, I rest against one of the giant washing machines, watching her writhe on the floor. Painting my blood across the tiles, she kicks out, reaching desperately for the knife. I'm not proud, far from it. Never hit a lady; that goes without saying. But I guess even if one has a knife to your throat, there's an unwritten rule you should still not kick her in her lady bits. "You left me no choice," I say.

"As soon as I get up, I'm going to skin yer," she cries. But her voice sounds hollow.

"You're not going to stop, are you?" No sign of the lunkheads as I turn towards the window, but I know I'm running out of time. "No hope of trying to talk you around, I mean?"

"Gonna cut your dick off and feed it to my Bobby."

As I weigh up my next move, I can't help but hope Bobby is a dog, not a child or an unfortunate husband. Either way, neither option sits well.

Christ, first a man-child and now a lady.

With fingers coiled around the back of the washing machine, I grit my teeth and pull. Some give allows me to bring it to a quarter tilt. "You wouldn't fucking dare," Butter Balls cries, attempting to push up to her elbows.

Wanna fucking bet, lady? Come on. Come ooooooon! A series of crackles and pops run through my arms as I heave with all my might. Blood drips into my mouth, offering a salty and metallic warmth. *Come on. Come on. Come—*

"EEYAAAAAAAAGH," Butter Balls cries, her face contorted in agony. And as she begins pushing at heavy steel—her efforts futile—there's a realisation in her eye that she's well and truly fucked. "This can't be. This isn't right." She looks up at me, probably wondering how she was toppled by a *fuckwit in a leotard*. "You can have the money on the bench." Gritting her teeth, she lets out another eerie wail. "I could take you on... You could be my right-hand man. More money than you've known."

"No."

"Then what do you want?"

"I am Reformo, and I want to restore order."

"Order? What does that even mean?"

"I want people to pick up their dog shit. I want people to park in front of their own houses. I want people to keep their music down. I want—"

Butter Ball gives a pained laugh, still trying to squirm free. "You're not right, are you, kid? Dropped on the head at the hospital, were you? Shaken like a bag of popcorn? Some kind of childhood trauma?"

"No. I just want respect. I want consideration. I want—"

"Christ, what did your parents do to you?"

"What?"

"For you to become so fucked up," she says. "What did Mummy and Daddy Reformo do to you?"

"Just shut up, will you!"

"Come on, spill." Her smile returns. "Let's shoot the shit, chew the fat. We can swap stories, plot our revenge on the only fuckers supposed to care."

"Leave them out of this." Somehow, I feel the advantage slipping away. She's pinned under a washing machine, yet still, she has the upper hand.

"Did you not get enough of Mama's titty? Or too much titty, perhaps?" She stretches again for the knife, but it's just inches out of reach. "Or was it all about Daddy?"

"Shut up! Shut up! Shut up!"

"Hitting a nerve, am I?"

A thousand thoughts rush through my head, all the moral baggage accompanying being a superhero. But if I let her go, I know she'll only return to her old ways. Call the cops? *Had an incident last month, and it took two hours for a pig to show up.* Even if they did eventually make it, Butter Balls more than likely has them in her pockets. Can't think straight. Can't—

"Just let me go," she says, still trying to free herself. "It's what Mama would want."

"Stop talking." *What did I think would happen, that she would come quietly?* "Just stop fucking talking, will you?"

"You'll have a chance if you leave now. Not much of one, granted, but at least you can get out of town, perhaps have one last suck on Mama's titty before you're brought to your knees."

"Stop talking!"

"You're a fucking joke, kid." She lunges for the knife again, her fingers less than an inch away now. "A Mama's boy with a hard-on for Superman."

"STOOOOOOOOOOOOP!"

"Mama's boy. Mama's boy. Mama's boy."

Her words play on repeat in my head, even after she gets back to her struggles. I feel my teeth grinding, my jaw beginning to ache. As I draw close, my nails dig into my palms, and I'm suddenly sweltering in the suit.

"I could be your Mama. You can even have a go on my titty if you let me go."

Her fingertips touch the knife's handle, but only briefly, my kick sending it sliding across the floor into one of the machines. CLANK! Like a game of spin the bottle, we watch as it performs one final stubborn spin, coming to rest with the blade pointing centre stage towards the final act.

Butter Balls snaps her head towards me, face twisted in anger. "Nothing but a fucking Mama's boy." I expect she knows the game is up, her street cred now worth less than a Blockbuster membership card. "Fucking fucker. Screw you and your Mama. Pervert in a suit. Weak as piss!"

"What did you say?"

"I said you're as weak as piss!"

My boot catches her square on the nose, prompting an audible crack. For a moment, she stops writhing, and her eyes widen as if, once again, I've stepped over the line and broken the rules. "Just you fucking—"

There's no crack this time, more of a dampened squeak as my heel connects with her misshapen nose. Emitting a garbled cry, she tries to grab my leg, but I whip it away and bring it down even harder. SMASH!

"Weak as piss," she rasps. "Weak as fucking piss."

With all my might, I stomp on her bloodied face again, her flailing arms unable to slow the impact. And again. And again. And again. "I'm not like him! I'm not like him! I'm not like him!" With a deflating whoosh, her arms fall to her side. The face is a mess, almost unrecognisable.

Yet still, she manages to raise a defiant middle finger on her left hand and continue her chanting, albeit in the form of incomprehensible and bloody gargles. *Weak as piss. Weak as piss. Weak as piss.*

I'm past the point of no return, almost an out-of-body experience as my heel repeatedly crashes into her face. The whimpers dampen further, but it makes no difference as the words are in my head now, bouncing around with ever-increasing intensity. *Weak as piss.* All thoughts of Vera and the superhero code of conduct disappearing behind a veil of red mist, I scramble on all fours towards the knife. *You have to set an example, Simon.* Only a laboured wheezing comes from behind as I wrap my gloved fingers around the handle.

Knife in hand, I make my way across the blood-smeared floor, glancing towards the streets in case her "security" has given up on their search. I'll never forget the reflection that confronts me in the window, just another traumatic memory forever burned into my psyche. "For the greater good." And as I crouch down, beginning to carve the knife through my fallen villain's neck, that's how I'm able to justify my actions. I'm intoxicated with hate and high on trauma, the lines between reality and fantasy a blur. I'm no longer lurking in no man's land, a moral high ground of uncertainty, but charging towards the enemy, screaming, "I'll do whatever the fuck it takes!"

Sweat drips from my chin onto the bloodied floor, and my muscles sing as I work the knife through gristle and bone. The blade gets stuck halfway, so I withdraw and start from the other side. As I saw further, I'm taken back to Mother's house, tasked with cutting down some of the branches of next door's tree that had started to hang over into our garden.

Parking in front of our house, and now this. They're laughing at us, Simon! If your father had done something earlier, set an example, this sort of thing wouldn't happen.

They're only branches, Mama.

Only branches? What next? Let their dog shit in our yard? Invite them around so they can piss all over our shagpile?

Can't do it, Mama.

Put your back into it, Simon.

I am, Mama. The branches are too thick, though.

Too thick? Too thick? What are you—a man or a mouse?

I'm trying, Mama.

Try harder, Simon. Try harder. Nothing in life for being a trier, only a doer!

My arm aches.

Weak as piss. Just like your—

Finally, the head separates, and I lift it in the air, the dirty ceiling light offering a glint of animation to the left eye. "I did it, Mama, see." My breathing is heavy and erratic, but the euphoria fades as the red mist dissipates, and I'm left studying the bloodied lump in front of me, listening to the soft splash of blood into the pink puddles beneath. "For the greater good. For the greater good." I repeat the words again as I let the knife clatter to the floor. Falling back against one of the machines, my stomach offers the promise of a gag.

A noise from outside prompts me to snap my head towards the window, reality keeping me pinned to the spot. Studying the darkness, I wonder where I go from here. I can tell myself my actions were for the greater good, but I was on autopilot back there, lost in a haze of trauma and bottled rage. None of this was part of the plan.

You have to fight, grow some balls. You have to set an example!

I raise the severed head in a toast. *Is this not good enough for you, Mama?*

Beginning to wipe the blood from my eyes, I turn towards the voices that aren't in my head. Morning light is still far from its daily struggle, but I can just make out two silhouettes through the lettering on the window. No third one appears in tow, and that offers immense relief. *Good on you, Reggie.*

Side by side, the goons march towards the launderette, their shoulder span casting a formidable sight. With every yard they draw closer, I will for my adrenaline to return, but I'm still half-floating, trying to come to terms with the carnage surrounding me. *Sometimes, things will get worse before they get better, Simon.* Understatement of the fucking year.

The first lunkhead begins a jog, realising something isn't right. Perhaps he sees the body sprawled across the floor or the "'twat in a leotard". He shouts something to lunkhead number two, prompting him to launch into a sprint. They appear to be racing now, their apparent pursuit of machismo never far away, especially in this seedy little world.

You forgot to lock the door, Simon.

Don't think it would have made much difference, Mama.

Suddenly, I want nothing more than to be by Vera's side, wrapped in that cotton-wool feeling again. I want to shoot the shit, chew the fat, with someone who cares. *I think I love you.* It's fantasy land, I know, but it doesn't stop me from wanting to give it one last visit before what inevitably comes my way.

Christ, why does it hurt so much?

Even as the door slams open and the fools almost fall over themselves, I offer no reaction. They, too, freeze, their attention shifting from the bloodied body on the floor to the head I hold in my hands.

"What have you done?" the one on the left asks.

"He's cut her fucking head off," the one on the right says.

"I can fucking see that," the one on the left replies.

Another stand-off ensues, the three of us exchanging glances. They've likely seen worse, even carried out more inhumane and grisly deeds at the command of Butter Balls, but she's unable to speak or offer a click of her fingers. The one who gives orders is incapacitated. *Decapitated.*

"Now what?" I say, pushing off the washing machine, grateful that my legs support my weight.

Lunkhead number one looks towards lunkhead number two.

Lunkhead number two shrugs and offers the severed head another glance before mumbling, "Maybe we should get help."

"We are the help, you muppet. Fuck! We are deader than country music."

Having no fight left in me, I can only think of tossing the head towards them and making a run for it. "Catch," I yell. It's a clean throw, but an even cleaner take, lunkhead one using cat-like reflexes to grasp the head and bring it towards his chest. He panics, tossing the bloodied mess to lunkhead two, who reaches for it, but his not-so-shit-hot reflexes fumble the catch. The head lands in a puddle of goo with an undramatic thud and begins to roll. "D for donkey," I scream, grabbing one of the stacks of cash and throwing the door open.

Glancing over my shoulder as I run, cape flapping behind, I expect to see them giving chase, but the streets remain empty. Perhaps they're still too overwhelmed with shock or thoughts of what will happen to them for such a balls-up. *We are deader than country music.*

"I'm Reformo. Hope will live here again."

But is that really the best I can do? D is for donkey? It's okay, but hardly worthy of a superhero or the occasion. Something about their boss losing their head or how to get ahead in the launderette business. A missed opportunity, for sure, but such sharpness will become second—*What the fuck am I talking about? I've just cut off a drug lord's head, and I'm worrying about my level of wittiness.*

Inhale. Exhale.

Approaching the winding path, I slow to a walk, offering one last look over my shoulder, feeling a morsel of relief as darkness wraps its blanket around me. Yet upon seeing the freshly scattered needles further down the track, Mother's voice adds the usual cacophonous percussion to an otherwise rare quiet moment.

A blind eye here, a blind eye there—If everyone did that—Chaos everywhere—It starts with you—As weak as piss like your—Rinse, rinse—Nothing in life for being a trier, only a doer.

"I cut a fucking head off for you, Mama. What more do you want?"

My outburst silences her, further calm washing over me as I spy Vera standing at the water's edge, holding her hand out towards me.

"You came back for me, Vera."

Promise me you'll stop all this silliness. For Christ's sake, Simon, you're not a superhero.

I wonder if I've gone too far. Is this no longer the realms of superhero territory, just the clumsy attempts of a desperate vigilante taking on almost an entire town? Self-doubt and paranoia consume me, thoughts that I might be doing more harm than good, that this place might be truly unfixable. But just as I feel myself sinking into an unclimbable hole, Jayden steps out of the darkness and takes Vera's hand. "Wee-formo save day," he says, eyes full of hope and wearing what looks to be a clean diaper.

"That's right, little man. I am Reformo, and I'm bringing hope—"

My stomach churns as their silhouettes fade, and aside from Bum Fluff's dead and bloated body somewhere in the depths, it's just me again. *You're better off alone.* I know there's no backing out now. I'll see this through or die trying. After all, a broken promise to my love has to be worth that.

After hiding Butter Balls' cash behind a loose brick in the wall, I perch on the edge where Bum Fluff once did, doing my best to ignore the fresh pile of dog shit near the concrete holes and focussing instead on the gentle ripples forming across the blackness. The calming effect brings a heaviness to my eyelids until it becomes a struggle to keep them open. Thinking I'll steal just a few minutes of rest, I lower myself to the ground, the breeze rushing over my exposed skin, but the suit ensuring the worst of the iciness doesn't make it through. Images of the night begin running through my head—the blood, the bone, the fluids on the floor—but exhaustion has been coming for me for hours, and red gives way to black. I'm floating. Aimless. Directionless—

Sirens wake me.

At first, I put it down to just another "for show" performance, but consciousness lends to the wails of an ambulance. Cussing myself for sleeping on the job, I scramble towards the path, feeling unprepared and dangerously exposed. Word must be getting around town that I'm no longer just a "'twat in a leotard" but a bona fide villain slayer. Paranoia overwhelms giving me the feeling I'm not alone.

Eyes in a thousand places, ears all around.

Nevertheless, something bad has happened under my watch, and that can't be allowed to happen. Reignited adrenaline courses through every part of me, and by the time I emerge from the path, sucking in air and ears ringing with urgency, I feel like I'm floating. Streets look empty, too late for the night creatures and too early for the day walkers, but the raucous wail is beginning to draw people from their beds, dirty yellow light falling across the glistening concrete.

The flicker of red in the distance stops me in my tracks. I can't move, can't breathe. Intuition? My superhero senses raising the stakes? Heart pounding, the vein in my head drumming a ferocious beat, I finally set my legs into action again, swinging myself around the wall into MacArthur Street. Still trying to convince myself it's just paranoia, I pump my arms and legs as fast as I can, the morning nothing but a blur as I race towards the warm red light.

That can't be. No, this just can't be.

But as the first few people come into sight, my heart sinks.

"Excuse me. Excuse me!" Ignoring the looks and murmurs, I hustle to the front of the small queue until I'm standing outside my old place, watching two men carrying a stretcher from the house next door. It's Violet, only just recognisable. It's all I can do not to throw up as I lunge towards her, but just as soon as I find my feet, I'm yanked to the side by a burly officer with the thickest eyebrows

I've ever seen. "Wait!" I scream at him. "I just need to talk to her."

Before he can tell me to shut the fuck up and start his questions about my curious get-up, I hear a series of garbled moans coming from the stretcher. It's the same chant over and over, almost incomprehensible, but not. "He came back. He came back. He came back."

"And the boy?" Heart in my mouth, I look to the house, waiting for another stretcher to appear. "What about the boy?"

"Excuse me sir, but—"

"What about Jayden?" I scream.

The cop swings me around to face him. "Sir, I'm going to have to ask you to—"

"What?" Teeth gritted, ready to knock someone into next week, I front up to him. "What are you going to have to ask me to do?"

Heads begin turning towards the latest show, a series of elbows and murmurs ushering on the rest of the crowd. "That's him," someone says.

The twat in the leotard.

But I feel the shift, some eyes no longer mocking, some lips not twisting into abhorrence. The cop feels it, too. I see it in his eyes as he runs them over the crowd. Tittle-tattle travelling fast, rumours working their way through the drug-filled veins of town. He turns his eyes on me again, looking me up and down like the penny is finally dropping. Perhaps the butchery at the launderette is already topic number one at the station, closely followed by the disappearance of Bum Fluff. "Leotard," he mutters.

Some brave soul at the back of the crowd even begins to clap, but stops after three, slinking back into the shadows, likely en route back home to triple-bolt his front door. Patience running dry, I grab the cop by the throat and bring him close until our noses touch. "WHERE'S THE FUCKING BOY!?"

"Gone." The cop swallows hard, his Adam's apple a shard of regret in his neck.

The ground rips away, and I'm back in the void.

Gone. Gone. Gone?

I can't breathe, that same unbearable pressure on my chest, but with no Vera to help me to safety. I'm on my own, sinking in the chaos. Mother stands above, hands on her hips, shaking her head. *Quitter. Quitter. Quitter.*

"He went in the first ambulance," the cop says. "About five minutes ago."

Jesus fucking Christ. "Is he okay?"

"Some broken bones, and his face is all bloodied and swollen, but I think he'll be alright."

I'm so sorry, Jayden. I'm so goddamn sorry. "What happened?"

As the cop eyes my grip, I release him. He snaps his head left and right and back again. "More than my job's worth this."

"Your job ain't worth shit. Not around here anyway."

He wilts in apparent agreement before taking one last look around. "It was the partner, Terry. Nasty piece of work. All boozed up by the smell of him, violence on his mind. Tried to get to the kid, but Violet said she got in front of him. Looks like she paid the price for it." He looks left and right again, his shoulders dropping. "Punctured lung, by my guess, and two broken eye sockets. Her head is pretty banged up. While she was on the floor, Terry started on the kid, screaming he was going to kill him. A kid, for Christ's sake." The cop looks down to the ground as if all the blind eyes are beginning to catch up with him. "Don't know how the poor lass did it, but she said she squirmed across to the other side of the house to get the gun. Not exaggerating one bit when I say the entry wound was square in the middle of the fucker's forehead. Like she was a sharpshooter or something."

"Good egg, Violet. Good egg." Perhaps she always meant to miss. Maybe she could sense the hope I was exuding. Just part of the show to make sure Terry didn't give her another beating. And the cop in front of me, too, his demeanour beginning to change. Behind the fear, bravado, and layers of guilt, there's a twinkle in his eyes, like the one I imagine he used to get when sitting in front of the TV watching superhero shows, nursing a mug of cocoa. Likely been on the wrong side for so long, but there's still time for him. *Small steps make climbable ladders.* He swallows hard. "Did you do it? I mean... all that business in the launderette?"

The crowd's murmurs build as I begin slinking back into the shadows. "I don't know what you're talking about."

A thousand eyes. A thousand eyes.

"Reformo," the cop whispers.

And with that, I turn to run, cape flapping around my shoulders. Everyone will be talking about events, the public, the police, the lunkheads, even The Dragon himself. But my thoughts return to Jayden, all beaten up, his tiny little arms trying to fend off Terry's attacks.

Where was Reformo when all this was happening? What happened to my fucking super senses?

Pressure builds behind my eyes as I picture the boy looking over the brute's shoulder, waiting for his new hero to smash open the door in the nick of time and save the day.

Things will get worse before they get better.

"But he's just a kid, Mama. Just a little boy that should be playing with toys, not eating his food through a straw. It's all my fault. If it weren't for me—"

What are you going to do about it? Get even or piss yourself?

"Mama!"

Don't you dare quit on me, boy!

But none of this was supposed to happen. Violet and Jayden wouldn't be in the hospital if it weren't for me. Anger swells, overwhelming me, stopping me in my tracks a few feet short of the path to the water. Fuuuuuuuuuck! The graffiti-covered wall to my right is asking to be punched, and the spray-painted half-assed attempt at a dragon steals the last of my reserve.

"Not fair."

THUMP!

"Not the way it was meant to play out."

WHACK!

"Two fucking shooting stars!"

WHALLOP!

They've parked there again, Jeff. Can you hear that music? Mowing their lawns at this time of day, Jeff. SMASH! *Their leaves are dropping in our yard, Jeff. Jeff! Jeff!* Simon, get your elbows off the table. Simon, you can't eat ice cream in here. Simon, look what you've done now. BAM! *No, I don't want other people trudging through my house. I don't care if other people have their friends around.* POW! *Bloody bastard dogs barking all day, Jeff. Can't you do anything, Jeff? Jeff? Can't you be a man for once, Jeff? Jeff! Jeff! Jeff!* WHAM. *Jesus-motherfucking-Christ! You and him—just the same—weak as piss.* WHOMP!

"GETS MY FUCKING GOAT!"

"Shut up, dickhead," someone yells back through a second-floor window. "Trying to get some fucking sleep around here. Goddamn fucking sirens blasting all night."

Tears fill my mask as I let the wall take my weight. I miss Vera. I want to find her, run back into her arms, and search for shooting stars before morning light steals them. But I broke a promise. One made to a woman who looks like she's had far too many broken already.

Are you crying over a whore, Simon?

"I feel so alone, Mama."

Better off that way. No distractions.

"But Mama, I—"

Stop crapping and get cracking. Otherwise, the chaos will swallow you.

"I don't want to do this anymore."

You carved some fucker's head off. You can't quit now.

"I didn't mean to."

You didn't mean to? Parking in a disabled spot, elbowing someone in the street, even drinking from the wrong glass—all things you can apply that sentence to, but not decapitation, Simon. You cut her fucking head off!

"I can't do it, Mama."

You fucking can, and you fucking goddamn will. God help me,

Simon, I won't be responsible for my actions if you quit on me. If you turn out like your father—

"I'M NOT MY FATHER!"

Then man up and finish what you started. You made your mother a promise, and you will—

As footsteps emerge from my left, Mother's voice fades out. I snap my head around to see a giant of a man approaching. *Jesus Christ, doesn't this town ever fucking sleep?* Whistling to my right gives way to a shorter man, a human pit bull of a creature with shoulders almost big enough to lie across, a baseball bat grasped tight in his right fist. Making a slapping sound with his lips, brute number three approaches from straight ahead; chiselled jawline, ice-blue eyes, his skin covered in more scars than a blind welder. He holds a gun in his right hand and a look in his eye suggesting this is as far as my little fantasy goes. "Mamaaaaaaaaaaa," he sings. "Oh-oh-oh-oh." Sinking to his knees, he offers jazz hands. Thinks he's bloody Nicolas Cage, giving it all the camp. "Just killed a wo-maaaaaaaaan. Put a knife against her neck, ripped her head off, now she's dead. Mamaaaaaaa."

"Don't give up the day job. Just fucking shoot me and put me out of this misery, will you?"

He stands, transitioning to a dance that I wholeheartedly believe he considers majestic. Finishing with a spin, he offers a well-manicured hand. "They call me Dreamboat," he says. "And you, I believe, are Reformo."

I'm going to be ended by someone called Dreamboat. Fuck my life. "Just do it."

"Too easy," he says. "It would take all the fun out of things, and Butter Balls was all about the fun, wasn't she, guys?"

"Uh huh," they say in unison, playing their parts well: Lunkhead three and four.

"How rude of me, so sorry." Dreamboat takes his hand away and slicks back his hair. "Allow me to introduce Shortass and Cinnabon."

I offer the lunkheads a glance, earning a snarl from both.

"Cinnabon. Get it? On account of the size of his fists." Dreamboat performs another spin, following up with a sorry attempt at a moonwalk. "Except those will break your teeth, not just make them sing." He runs a hand through his shiny hair again and offers a few more aggressive chews on his gum. This kid would clean up if there were an award ceremony for overacting. "You know, I was never a fan of Butter Balls myself. I always found her a little uncouth. But orders are orders, you understand."

"Heads must roll," I say.

"Quite." He looks me up, down, and back again. "Love the suit. Who's the tailor?"

"No more small talk. Let's just get this over with."

He nods, but instead of leading the charge, he raises both arms, palms facing his goons to hold them at bay. One of them groans, likely knowing what's in store. "I used to get bullied at school," Dreamboat says, turning his stare to the wet pavement. "Can you believe that? Me." CHEW. CHOMP. CHEW. "I mean, look at me, for Christ's sake. But, it might surprise you to learn I wasn't always this smooth and as devilishly—"

Kick his arse, Simon! I can't take much more of this. Johnny Depp, he ain't.

There are three of them, though, Mama.

Ain't a brain cell between them. Nothing behind their eyes but a dial tone.

The size of them, though. Even in prison, I never fought—

Knew you'd turn out like him. No backbone. Happy to sit on your arse while the world turns to shit. Just like your weak as piss father!

I'm not him. I'm not him. I'm not him.

Prove it. It's do or die, Simon. Do or die.

I'm so tired, Mama. I just ripped someone's head off.

And these guys will rip yours off if you don't kick their arse. DO OR DIE!

It's as though time is slowing, Dreamboat's words continuing to spill out, but only as a drawl. As though my superhero senses are in tune like never before, I feel the breeze with such intensity and each tiny raindrop through my mask. I turn to the goons to see their stares still on me, veins standing out in their necks and arms as they prepare for battle. I can hear them breathing and even see their nose hairs tickled by the breeze. Their faces are stoic, yet I swear I smell some fear in the air. The shorter one stands with his right leg forward, contrastingly skinny to the rest of his bulk. Material on the trailing left leg seems more strained—padding, perhaps? As for Cinnabon, he looks about as reactive as a snail cooking in the sun.

Turning back to Dreamboat, I ready myself for war, no longer as fearful. Do or die. For Jayden, Violet, Vera, and all the people too afraid to venture outdoors. It's time to end the chaos and honour my pledge to Mother.

"... nothing growing up, bar an abusive father and a mother with a penchant for—"

"A shooting star," I scream, a finger raised towards the sky.

And even before I see the scars running down Dreamboat's chin, I throw my best punch—KERPOW—snapping his chiselled jaw to the left and sending him crumpling to the ground. The gun slides from his grasp, and he lets out a moan. But before I can follow through, Cinnabon is on me with surprising speed, a giant arm locking around my neck, chin digging into my skull. Dragging his left leg behind, Shortass begins a belated approach.

It's on.

I can't breathe. My neck crackles as Cinnabon increases the pressure, his tobacco breath lingering in my nostrils. Shortass smiles, the perfect villainous grin, his eyes carrying promises of all sorts of violence.

Mete la barbilla. Mete la barbilla.

It's the voice of my Spanish friend this time. *Tuck your chin. Tuck your chin.* And just as Shortass readies the bat, Luca's demonstrations are crystal clear in my mind. Three options, but as Luca so eloquently put it, "If in doubt, agarrar las malditas nueces." *Grab the fucking nuts.*

Grasping the arm around my neck, I tuck in my chin and, with my spare hand, squeeze my fingers around his ball sack, yanking with as much force as I can muster. He caves almost immediately, and I take my chance, twisting his arm behind his back and spinning him into Shortass's swing. There's an almost comical hollowness to the sound of the end of the bat connecting with Cinnabon's skull. THWUMP. And just like that, his eyes roll back in his head, and he collapses to the floor in a gangly heap.

HOME-FUCKING-RUN, BABY!

Shortass's face twists in disbelief as he looks at his boss still on the ground and back at me again. The gun is in no man's land, a few inches from Dreamboat's splayed fingers, and almost dead centre between us.

FIGHT.

And I'm charging, cape snapping in the wind, adrenaline back in full flow. Shortass makes the mistake of stepping back, his left leg buckling as he readies his swing. *Three. Two.* And just as the bat starts slicing through the air, I drop and sweep. THOK! A perfect hit on the back of the leg brings him down, the bat smashing against the tarmac. He squeals and scrambles, desperately thrusting the end of the bat into my chest as I attempt to mount him. THWACK! Pain rips through me, my left side igniting, a scream trapped in my throat. Sensing my weakness, Shortass tries the same move again, but I snatch at the wood and force the other end towards his throat. Using all my weight to keep him pinned down, I push the bat towards his neck, but he's stronger, and he knows it, that same abhorrent smile creeping across his lips. *Luca, help!*

Codo. Codo. Codo.

And to my friend's chants, I slip an *elbow* through, catching Shortass on the outside of his eye socket. THWUMP! He lets out another cry as magnificent red spills from the cut. Our struggles continue, the bat nowhere near his neck, but the distraction enough for me to get another elbow through, catching him in the same spot. THWACK! And again. POW! And again. SMACK! Blood paints his face and wells in his eyes, his frustration evident as he growls and crashes hard against the ground. It's like trying to ride a bull on heat. I'm losing balance, slipping, and if he gets on top of me, I'm fucked.

Our eyes meet, electricity fizzing in the air between us.

FZZZZ. He smiles, sensing the shift. Could I? Not again, surely. But it's *do or die*. Swearing that after this point, I will abide by the superhero code, I bring my knee into his nuts, his mouth dropping open, his eyes all but spinning in his head. "You cheap arse, motherfucker," he squeaks, turning to his side.

I think he's crying.

"Sorry," is all I can say, "but, but... Ah, to hell with yer." And with that, I pick up the bat and swing it at his head. A cross between an intake of breath and a choke—PHWAR—emerges from his lips as the wood finds his nose. For just a second, I think he's out, but then he turns his bloodied face towards me, a pleading in his eyes, small rivers of red between his teeth. "Please don't. I have a dog."

Ain't a brain cell between them.

I'm inclined to agree with Mother at this point. First, he would have been wiser to play dead, hoping I don't take another swing. Second, using his dog as his mercy reason for letting him live, when he could have said kids or something other than a four-legged shitting machine, gives dumb a whole new meaning.

He offers another groan, reaching his arms out. Bat in hand, I study the lump before me, imagining his own mother wouldn't recognise him now. His face is already beginning to swell, and there are large gaps where his teeth should be. As for his nose, it's nothing but a bit of gristle. "Please. Her name is Christie. She's only got three legs."

Man up, Simon. Man up. Finish what you started.

But he's not fighting, Mama. He's down. And he's got a three-legged dog.

And what do you think he will do when he gets up? Offer to buy you a drink? Let you pat his dog? FINISH HIM!

His eyes grow wide as I step towards him. "Please." Squirming on the ground, he begins shaking his head like a dog with a newspaper. "No. No." He raises his big arms in defence again. "The Dragon will have you for this. He'll dance under the moonlight wearing your skin. Make you wish you were never born."

I offer a snicker and bring the bat over my shoulders, pieces of my life flashing before me. One particular image stands out from the montage of disappointment: Mother in my bedroom raising her foot over that tiny cardboard box. *No, Mama! No!* I remember snapping my head away, blocking my ears with my hands, but I still heard that box crumple. *Mamaaaaaaaaaaaaaaaaaaaa!*

Anger courses through my veins quicker than any street drug could. My fingers tingle, my muscles ripple. Shortass opens his mouth to offer one last plea, but it never escapes his bloated lips.

SMASH! SMASH! SMASH!

Breathing heavy and erratic, the taste of blood at the back of my throat, I take a step back to study the lifeless body. So much violence, so much blood. *Things will get worse before they get better, Simon.*

How bad do they have to get, though, Mama? How many people have to get hurt or die? All I want is for this to be over, for the chaos to end. But this town is unrelenting, layer after never-ending layer of nastiness. And I feel he is toying with me, like a kitten with a mouse. "Dragon, where are you? Show yourself!"

The only answer I get is the sound of a hammer cocking. "Never turn your back on your enemy. Golden rule number one," Dreamboat says.

"Look, a shooting star."

He smiles. "Point taken, but I'm back in the director's chair now." Pacing, gun pointed in my direction, eyes not leaving mine, he's also back in actor mode, milking the scene for all he can get. Still, I sense nervousness in his performance, the knuckles of the hand holding the shaking gun already turning white. And on closer inspection, the weapon looks old, not an antique by any means, but not the type of thing you'd find in the latest Nicholas Cage movie. Perhaps acquired from a robbery or through a dodgy deal in a darkened alley with a geezer with an eye patch—*a Captain Jack Sparrow of sorts,* Mother would say. But *nobody comes close to Johnny Depp.*

"Are you sure that thing shoots?" Anything to buy time.

"Oh, yes. Notched a few up with this one," he says, proud. "I call her Marisa, after Marisa Tomei, on account of how many hearts she's stopped."

"Marisa Tomei? Of all the women in the world, you chose someone who took a role in *Wild Hogs*?"

Narrowing his eyes, he rests his finger on the trigger. "Apologise!" He looks possessed, as though I've just told him his mother sucks cocks for cans of spam.

Entrar en sus cabezas. Get in their heads. "No."

His hand begins to shake harder—uncontrollable—and once again, I find myself wondering if my enemy has ever really used a weapon for anything other than a threat. "Apologise," he says again. "Apologise to Marisa, and I'll make it quick."

He could have shot me twenty times by now, but I'm guessing he wants the scene to go as planned: Me on all fours, begging for my life.

"Apologise," he cries again, lowering the gun barrel towards my lower half.

"Fuck you, and fuck Marisa Tomei!" I make my charge, holding my arms out defensively.

Dreamboat steps back, his face twisting as the ear-splitting explosion fills the night. BANG! I grimace, prepared to go down and die like a hero, but I'm still running, still charging towards a terrified-looking Dreamboat, his hair out of place, his blue eyes projecting anything but coolness. He lifts the gun, managing to get off another shot. BANG! Heat surges up my right arm, the force twisting me around. I'm still here, though. Still—

"Fucking die, for Christ's sake," Dreamboat sings. He swings the gun at me, but I'm too quick, ducking down and launching an elbow into his midriff. WHAM! He crumples fast, a rush of air expelling from his cheese factory of a mouth. PFFFT. And in a move Cinnabon would be proud of, I take Dreamboat's back, wrap an arm around his neck, and bring my lips close to his ear.

"Marisa Tomei, for the love of God."

He tries to whip the gun around, but I grab his other arm, locking my fingers around his wrist. And while a stray dog takes a shit near the entrance to the water, I take a romantic ride on the "Dreamboat," up and down the street.

YEEHAH!

He squeals and flails, but I'm tighter than a cobra. "Now, if you'd said someone like Sophia Loren or even Ingrid Bergman, I might have had more respect for your weapon." He offers an incoherent rasp, dropping to his knees. "Grace Kelly? Marilyn Monroe?" Relentless, he continues his efforts, but I think he knows, in his heart of hearts, he overacted the part and missed his cue. "Even Kate Winslet at a push." Finally, he begins to tire, and just as Luca taught me, I wrap my legs around his midriff, and we fall back against the ground.

THWUMP! It takes less than five seconds before the gun falls from his grip.

"A shooting star," I say, watching the end of the trail carry across the sky as I squeeze.

Not wanting to repeat a mistake, I push the limp body away and stagger across to the gun. *You must set an example, Simon.* "My name is Reformo." BANG! A river of delayed red begins leaking from the centre of Cinnabon's head. Shortass is next, taking one in the neck—BOOM—the gun offering a dodgy recoil. I send another one his way just in case, this time taking an eye. BANG! "And I'm bringing hope back to town."

Awakening from his little nap, Dreamboat groans and opens his eyes. He attempts to scramble to his feet, combing a nervous hand through his hair.

BANG!

A high-pitched and delayed cry echoes down the street as he thumps back against the ground, studying the fresh hole in his pants. "These are Armaaaaaaaaaaani." After another series of whimpers, he looks up at me, eyes wide and full of knowing. "But I shot you. You should be dead."

"Man of steel," I reply, noting the sharpness working through the material along my right arm. The dent near the top of the blade where the bullet hit is hardly visible, but this would have ended on a very different note without the knife. *I love you, Janice.* "The scars on your neck and chest," I say, raising the gun. "How did you get them?"

"The arcade," he replies. "Please, I'm just a fake, just a player. I'm not the one you want. Did I tell you I have a dog?"

"And I suppose it has three legs?"

"No, four. But it has a food allergy and—"

BANG!

And just like that, Dreamboat is no more. The ringing in my ear gives way to silence, nobody sticking their head out of the window complaining about the noise, no lights flickering on, no footsteps rushing to investigate. "I'm getting rid of the rot. Do you catch my drift?" *Now, THAT's a worthy catchphrase.*

I consider hiding the bodies, dragging them into the long grasses near the start of the walkway, but it was only a short time ago that I cut off a head in the middle of a launderette, so I figure the time for discretion is out the window.

"Simon?"

"Vera?" Half-expecting it to be my mind playing tricks again, I turn. "Vera, it's really you." Drained of any remaining adrenaline, I only want to collapse into her arms. She looks like an angel.

"I was at the water, hoping you'd return." She breaks down. "I heard gunshots...I thought—"

"It's okay, Vera. It's all okay." I rush towards her, arms out, desperate to feel her against me. She came back for me. Once again, she came back.

"Oh, Simon." She all but folds, mascara running down her pale cheeks but failing to disguise the—

"Your face. What happened to your face?"

She buries into me, shoulders rising up and down. It takes a while before she finds composure, her swollen lips still quivering. "Lost his temper. Said I was late for the last client and started asking questions. He didn't believe a word I was telling him. Oh, Simon, I've never seen him so angry." Threatening to go again, she takes a few short, sharp breaths and squeezes at my arm. "I think he means to kill me, Simon, I really do. Said he would hurt my family, too."

"I promise I won't let anything else happen to you, Vera." Considering the last one I made, I hope the gesture comes across as sincere. "I'm sorry I wasn't there to protect you."

"If one of his heavies hadn't arrived to take him to a meeting, I'm sure I'd be dead already. I snuck out through the window as soon as he left."

"I'm sorry. I'm so sorry." My words sound pathetic, but they're all I have. "You're safe now. Reformo will protect you."

"You broke your promise."

"For the greater good. I'm sorry." I reach for her cheek, but she pushes my hand away, the same look of self-preservation drawn across her face as when she first turned to face me in the darkened alley.

She wipes a tear away. "You shot Dreamboat."

"Didn't like his singing."

"You're not going to stop, are you?"

"No."

"And it would do no good me telling you to leave? Even if I begged?"

"No, Vera. I'm going to fix this town, bring order—"

She begins to sob again, only more violently than before, flailing her arms against my suit. I try and comfort her, but she yanks her wrists back and begins pounding my chest even harder, her bloated face glistening under the last of the moonlight. After what seems like an eternity, her little balled-up fists starting to sting a little, she relents and pushes me away. "We can't stay here," she says, heading towards Finnegan Street. "It'll be light soon, and we're sitting ducks."

"Where are we going?"

"I have a client who owns a factory. It's up for let. He said we could use the basement to lie low for a while."

"In return for what?"

"In return for my stamp collection, what do you think?" She walks fast, her head snapping towards the slightest of sounds.

"Wait." Chasing after her, running my fingers along my right arm, I begin stuffing the knife's point back into the fabric, managing to slice through my glove several times. It takes a bit of fumbling, but finally, all that's left of Dreamboat's efforts are a few exposed black and white threads. "Can we trust them?"

"Who?"

"Your client."

"If he ever wants his dick in my mouth again."

"You could have just said yes."

We don't speak another word as we approach the industrial part of town, trying to beat the sunrise. All the way, I feel the urge to declare my love for her. Still, I manage to keep the words in my head until we reach our destination: a depressing and crooked-looking building with holes the size of barrels in the windows and a surrounding stench that would make even the rats think twice about setting up shop.

"I love you, Vera."

Ignoring me, she begins working at the wooden door, huffing and puffing, ramming her tiny shoulders at its thickness. "Open, you fuck. Why won't you fucking open?" She throws her fists against the heavy wood and begins crying again, offering a howl to the last of the moon.

"Here, let me," I say, easing her away. Tensing my muscles, I step back and rush the door, sending it screaming on its hinges. It offers a satisfying WHAM as it slams against the internal bricks, prompting a sprinkling of dust from the ceiling.

Reformo to the rescue!

"Simon."

"Yeah?"

Her mouth opens, but no words emerge. Instead, she walks past me, heading towards a mechanical elevator resembling something from an Eli Roth movie. I make to follow her, my superhero senses beginning to tingle.

"Vera, I'm not so sure about this. Could be a trap."

"What choice do we have?"

It gets difficult to breathe, a heaviness to the air, as if—as if it carries the burden of wrongdoing. "Vera." The noxious odour of detergent is strong, but I swear I taste blood at the back of my throat. "Vera, I—"

"Simon, I meant what I said. I think I love you."

There she is, her toughened exterior giving way to a vulnerability only I am privy to. She wraps her fingers around the rusty handle of the makeshift elevator and lifts her head towards me, all glassy-eyed, her shoulders dropping. I nod and join her, grateful she doesn't try and resist a kiss on her forehead. L-o-v-e. And although hairs prickle on the back of my neck, and everything about what we're doing screams danger, her scent still brings a wave of calm that I imagine would transform even a really pissed Hulk back to mild-mannered Doctor Bruce Banner. Together, we slide the iron door across and, side by side, step into the mechanical jaw en route to our temporary hideaway.

You can't trust a whore, Simon.

Can't trust anyone according to you, Mama.

A small circle glows a dirty orange as Vera presses the adjacent button, clanking the elevator into action. After a short delay, the air tasting nastier by the second, our descent to the basement begins.

You're a fool, Simon. Have I not taught you anything? Have you given up? Weak as piss.

About halfway down, Vera opens her mouth to say something, a solitary tear rolling down her cheek. "It's okay," I say, putting a finger to her lips. But as soon as the cage descended, I figured something wasn't right, even without Mother's narration. If truth be told, and if I'd have paid attention to my superhero instincts, it's been written across Vera's face since turning up out of the blue at the water's entrance. But love is blind, they say, and I've been unable to let myself believe she might deceive me in such a way.

No distractions, Simon. No distractions. Rinse! Rinse! Rinse!

As we sink into the guts of this decrepit building, I consider myself alone again, and most likely out of lives. I hold no malice towards my love, only a feeling of grief. *A case of self-preservation in a town where the last of the dogs are fighting for supremacy.* Perhaps she does even love me. Maybe this will leave a wound from which she'll never recover.

Feeling as far from a superhero as possible, it's as though realisation is finally dawning that all my romanticist ideas of saving the world are crumbling around me. Hopelessness fills the cage, and like Kryptonite to Superman, the exposure to such despair leaves me feeling weak—*as piss*—and vulnerable.

"I fucking hate this place," Vera says as the elevator clanks to a standstill.

Adjusting to the even dimmer light, I can just make out the silhouette of a man holding a gun. "Step out of the elevator," he says gruffly.

I turn to Vera, but her stare finds the floor. "Is that him, is that Ass-man?" He looks like his body has been chiselled from stone, such effort causing said sculptor to offer a half-assed effort when they got to the face. Unless they were going for something abstract, a Picasso-esque version of Quasimodo.

As Vera rattles the iron door into submission, a high-pitched cry from somewhere beyond confirms the previous tingling of my senses. And another. And another.

"I would have protected you," I say to Vera as she enters the darkness.

"I'm not worth it," she replies, brushing past the heavy with haste.

I'm scared, Mama.

Knew you'd turn out just like him.

But I killed people for you.

Back to being a quitter now, though, eh? I should have known. All those crumbs on the countertop, dishes on the sink. Once a quitter, always a—

I tried, Mama!

Got distracted, though, didn't you? The smell of a cunt making you forget about your pledge.

It was more than that.

A whore's a whore, Simon. She could change her hair, put on a dress, even try and walk like a lady, but it'll never change the number of dicks she's had inside her.

I loved her.

And look where it got you.

It's all over, anyway. They mean to kill me, Mama.

Don't you dare quit on me.

But, Mama, what can I do?

Quitter. Quitter. Q-u-i-t-t-e-r. Quitter.

I'M NOT LIKE HIM! I'M NOT LIKE HIM!

From the bowels of the darkness, I hear a drilling sound and another elongated cry, throaty and desperate, filling the air with further hopelessness.

"I won't ask again. Step out of the elevator," Quasi says.

On their turf and likely severely outnumbered, I step from the cage, another wave of weakness washing over me as I stare into the abyss. I'm unprepared, as good as blind, my powers drained.

"Move," the burly man says, raising the gun towards my head. Unlike Dreamboat's relic, it looks like it's just been stolen from a Nicholas Cage set.

He may have my soul, but he doesn't have my spirit.

Only a sliver of silver makes it through the tiny basement windows into a room that, in contrast to the crumbling brickwork outside, is a network of wooden beams. A guy in a sharp suit and shiny black gloves takes centre stage. Six heavies beyond him, and some poor guy tied to a bolted-down chair—clothes all torn, face all bloodied up, a puddle of lumpy darkness at his feet. *Beefcake? The one in the alley, the one who tried to mug Vera. Yeah, it's him!* The large ruby ring and gold buckle on his sneakers help seal the deal, but it's the partially visible tattoo around his neck—H-U-G—that could never be mistaken.

You're a dead man walking, a fucking ghost.

"Please bear with me a second," the one in the sharp suit says, lifting a finger of the hand not gripping a drill—Ass-man, I assume, AKA Trevor. A walking stereotype, just like in the movies, the pimp always being the best dressed. But I guess you wouldn't buy a Ferrari from a Skoda dealer. I find myself wondering, in all the chaos, why go to the trouble of having an expensive-looking tailored suit only to get so lazy with the name? I mean, for the love of Christ, Ass-man is only one up from the likes of Flesh Peddler and Pussy Monger.

The sound of the drill—BZZZZ—brings me back. Likely knowing it's the end of the road, Beefcake offers a series of moans and begins thrusting his back into the chair. "I'm sorry," he says. "It was a mistake. A mistake." He coils his remaining fingers around the arms of the chair, wide eyes darting around the room as if looking for a miracle to present itself. Advertising anything but, a small table to the right supports an assortment of blood-soaked implements.

"I fucking hate you," Vera says.

"Love it when you talk dirty," Ass-man replies.

She bites at her lip again and marches towards a small room in the corner. Full of defeat, I track her path, noting the trail of darkness running parallel and leading to an iron door in the far wall, knowing no good could ever occur behind such an ominous-looking portal. A bit further along, an unlit box declares a less sinister-looking doorway as the emergency exit.

"Everything I do is for you, baby," Ass-man shouts after her.

On her way past, Vera offers me a look but can't hold it for long, and I'm sure I hear the beginnings of a sob as she speeds to a trot.

I still love her. Still would give my life for hers.

As the noise of the drill fills my head, blocking out Mama's response, I turn my attention back to Beefcake in time to see a string of pink saliva leaking from the corner of his mouth. "Please," the big man cries. "It was just a mistake."

Ass-man sighs, dropping his shoulders. "You're really beginning to bore me now. Where's your fight gone? Where's the guy that came in offering to fuck my mother?"

One of the heavies offers a snicker, quickly extinguished by a stern look from the boss.

BZZZZ

"Don't do this," Beefcake cries. "I have kids."

"Liar."

"I might."

"And I might have been the Duke of Cornwall's fluffer in a previous life. Might don't mean shit. And kids or not, you fuck with me, you're as good as dead."

The big man's pants grow a shade darker. "I can get you five grand by sundown."

"I can make twenty by then. And what kind of gangster talk is sundown anyway? Are we back in the Wild fucking West? Yeehah, motherfucker!?" Ass-man looks to his cronies in expectation, a subsequent titter breaking out for his joke, mirrored guffaw from behind reminding me I still have a gun pointed to my head.

"I told you, it was a mistake. I didn't know who she was. It was dark and—"

"Booooooooooooring."

Ass-man tilts the torture device until the drill bit sits on the underside of Beefcake's swollen right eye. He leans towards his victim, simultaneously running his eyes across his crew, perhaps to make sure they're watching for a demonstration of how he rewards betrayal.

"I'll leave town," Beefcake cries. "You'll never see me again."

Squeezing the big man's eye open with the fingers of his left hand, Ass-man offers a smile. "Nobody will ever see you again, punk."

A high-pitched scream fills the area as shoes scuff against the wooden floor. Some heavies smile, and some look away. A few seconds in, Ass-man offers a cuss as the drill bit slips, whipping to the left and sending a spray of Beefcake's blended eye across the room.

"Keeping fucking still," Ass-man cries.

Focussing on the globule of glistening pink mucus on the ground, I try and clear my mind, rationalise some form of plan. Down by the water, I managed three of them, but there are seven of the fuckers in here, not including the boss himself. And Dreamboat was nothing but a pretender, an actor playing the part, whereas Ass-man seems the real deal, his heavies being "prime" beef.

Mama?

Doing his best to dampen Beefcake's instinctual fight for survival, Ass-man mounts the big fella and clamps his head still. "This is a new fucking shirt," the boss screams, forcing the drill bit back into the leaking socket. As Beefcake offers another desolate wail, my mind again runs off on a strange tangent, perhaps to lighten the load. Torture, blood, and death—all par for the course for the hardened pimp-cum-gangster, so why wear a clean shirt? An apron over his clothing would surely be a bare minimum. Even a sheet of plastic. All good points, but why the fuck am I so concerned with Ass-man's laundry bill when I'm up to my neck in shit here and sinking fast?

"AAAAAAAAAAAAARGH"

To the sound of Beefcake's innards processing like a smoothie and the grinding of his socket bone, I close my eyes, searching for a happy memory. But all that comes is another outburst from Mother, her face all twisted, full of rage and disappointment. *You're fucking useless, Jeff! You're not a man, what even the fuck are you? As useless as your pissant of a brother. And what kind of example are you setting your son? Letting people walk all over you your entire life, how do you even fucking live with yourself? How do you breathe? You're a maggot! Dead inside. IT GETS MY FUCKING GOAT!*

Bonded by fear and habit, they endured, whatever initial alignment of planets that brought them together, nothing but a speck in time. As Father absorbed such relentless abuse, I could never quite gauge what he was thinking or even if he thought at all. His eyes never gave anything away.

Another muted cry drags me back just in time to see more splatter raining onto the floor. "Jesus fucking Christ, will you just die!" His face glowing beetroot red, Ass-man brings the drill back down again, putting all his weight behind it. BZZZZ. SKKKRT. Finally, Beefcake's legs cease their movement, and his pleading ends. And just like that, Beefcake has left the building, his probably fictitious kids now fatherless, and his hopes of leaving town before *sundown* at a bloody end.

Ass-man removes his knee from the dead man's crotch and takes a step back to admire his efforts. "Get him out of my sight," he finally says. As the heavies get to work, the boss turns to me, giving me his best tough guy look, one he's been likely practicing in the mirror since being able to wipe his own arse. "What do you think?"

"I think you're going to need to boil wash that shirt," I reply, responding with my "seen it all before" superhero smirk. "You're in luck, though. I know the owner of a launderette, but she might lose her head over the state of it."

Ass-man smiles, showing off a gold tooth I missed the first time. "So you're the guy? The super-pooper-scooper cum litter-picker-upper cum twat in a leotard?"

"Easy for you to say. And although the others have a certain ring to them, particularly super-pooper-scooper, I think I prefer Reformo."

"Reformo it is. Sounds a little like a child's playdough."

More forced titters emerge from the heavies as they carry Beefcake away to an unceremonious funeral. There may be black plastic bags and a barrel of acid involved, but little chance of tears or cucumber sandwiches.

Mama? What now?

A glance behind shows Quasi with his gun still pointed at my head, a look on his face suggesting he wants me to try something.

"I wouldn't," Ass-man says. He's in my face as I turn, all up close and personal, wiping a smear of blood from his cheek with a shiny pocket handkerchief. "Shot his father last week just for swiping a bag of coke."

"Been looking for a reason for a while," Quasi says, pressing the muzzle against my head. "Shot him in both hands and legs and then in the head. And that was my dad."

Ass-man smiles. "You're causing quite a stir in this town, Reformo."

"I've only just started."

The smile widens as he moves in even closer. "Once The Dragon hears of this, he'll likely make me his right-hand man. This town will be mine, and all will fear me."

"Jesus Christ, your breath, perhaps." I recoil and screw my face up. "Now I know why they really call you Ass-man."

The smile wavers. "You might think you're tough, all dressed up in your little Halloween costume, but a few minutes in that chair, and you'll be begging for mercy."

"Why? Are you going to breathe on me?"

"Tiresome," he says, searching the room to see if anyone shows signs of a smirk. "One question, though. Why? What's in it for you? Are you working for someone? A competitor wanting in?"

"I just want order, an end to the chaos." *So scared, Mama.*

"Crystal said something about that kind of crazy talk."

"Her name's Vera." *L-o-v-e.*

He nods. "You're not the first client to fall for her, you know. That's what she does, that's why she's the best."

"I'm not a client."

"That's what they all say. Although, admittedly, she did get quite defensive when you cropped up in conversation. Closed up quite a bit"—he drives a fist into his palm— "until she burst like a dam."

"Hit a lot of women, do you?"

"What would you consider a lot?"

"Just get on with it; put a bullet in my head."

"We don't need to be so hasty." He looks over my shoulder and offers a nod to Quasi. "My morning has just opened up."

Mama, I don't—

Ice-cold water in my face has me squinting.

Christ, my fucking head!

Along with the restraints fixing me to this chair of death, the table of bloodied tools is the first thing I see.

Don't want to die, Mama!

Told you not to get mixed up with that woman. Nothing but a whore.

Thought she loved me.

You know what thought did. And yes, it's the end of the fucking line, Simon. I'll be seeing you soon.

More icy water fills my mouth and works its way down the back of my suit. *Fuuuuuuck!* I tense my muscles, but my futile struggle against the restraints only serves as a cruel reminder I have no real powers, that earlier taunts of me being just a "twat in a leotard" are well grounded.

"Wakey, wakey, rise and shine, Reformo."

No severed fingers at my feet, just a ring of darkness and a strong smell of detergent, its pungency failing to displace the taste of death at the back of my throat.

Show no fear. Show no fear. "Kiss my arse...man."

"He's back and still with the dad jokes." Ass-man hovers his hand over the table, a look on his face like a kid in a candy shop. "This might hurt a little." The audience of heavies close in, as though the first show was just a prelude, and this is the main event. Between hulking shoulders, I see Vera, her face pressed up against a dirty pane of glass.

I think I love you, Simon.

I guess I'll never know the truth. Perhaps it was all Ass-man's idea, just part of a ploy to keep tabs on me, see if there was something to the rumours around town, Vera nothing but a pawn in his game.

I'm used to looking after myself around these parts. Dog eat dog and all that.

Ass-man lifts the pliers from the table and turns his stare towards me, the same excitable look dancing in his eyes. "I was going to remove the mask, but I think it maintains an air of mystery. And I'd rather take down the superhero than the spotty comic-reading freak who no doubt hides behind such a costume. Any last words before we dance, Reformo?"

"Do you get behind the teeth when you brush? And have you ever considered flossing?"

"Dogged with the comedy, aren't you?"

"I do my best...Trevor."

Ass-man swallows hard, his right eye developing a sudden twitch. Over his shoulder, I see one of the heavies biting his lip, trying hard not to laugh.

"What did you just call me?"

"Sorry, do you prefer Trev?"

He wraps a hand around my throat, veins popping in his neck. "Who fucking told you my name was—" He cuts off, turning his attention to the grimy office window in the distance. "Someone bring that whore out. Now!"

Oh, well fucking done, Reformo. Like always, the words just couldn't stay in your head, could they? It would be funny if it weren't so tragic.

"I had a suspicion there was more to it," Ass-man says, releasing his grip and pacing the floor. "She plays the game well, but I saw something different in her eyes when I asked her to bring you here. What? You two getting all cosy playing house? Sharing gossip over dinner? Kissing her goodnight and sending her on her way to give some fat cunt a handjob?"

"Don't you dare talk about her like that!"

"And what are you going to do about it, Reformo?"

"I'm going to fuck you up."

"She's mine, not yours."

"She's not a fucking puppy."

He sneers and shakes his head, his fingers white around the pliers. "This is real life, kid, not a fucking comic or a Hollywood movie. You're about to find that out." At the approaching clip-clop of heels, Ass-man snaps his head towards Vera, that same vile smile creeping across his face. "Bring the whore here. Let's give her the best seat in the house."

Although she can't bring herself to look at me as the heavies drag her towards the stage, I can see Vera's eyes are red-raw. She's shaking, unsteady on her legs. I want to tell her everything will be okay, but that would likely be another broken vow. *Promise me, Simon. Promise me you'll stop all this silliness.* Even in the alley with the more animated version of Beefcake looming over her, she never showed fear like this. It's a whole new level of vulnerability that makes me incredibly uncomfortable.

"Hurry," Ass-man yells.

Offering a grunt, the heavy thrusts Vera forward, and as though she was nothing more than a baton passed in a race, Ass-man grips her arm and yanks her towards him until they're almost nose to nose. "What else have you been saying, huh? What other bile has been leaking from those cum-soaked lips."

Keeping her stare on the ground, she shakes her head. "Nothing."

"You told him my name was Trevor. What else have you been saying?"

She shrugs and mumbles.

"LOOK AT ME WHEN I'M TALKING TO YOU!"

Vera's head whips to the left, saliva spraying from her lips. Our eyes draw level for the smallest of moments, but there's no comfort, only a crushing realisation that she was right about any prospects of a happy ending.

"Leave her alone, you shiny fuck!"

Attention back on me, Ass-man comes in fast, driving the pliers towards my mouth. I feel nothing at first, only numbness. *Show no pain. Show no pain.* But suddenly, it hurts like hell, the sting spreading across my face, the taste of metal at the back of my throat. And I know there's so much worse to come.

"Make sure she watches," the sharp-suited fucker tells his audience of heavies, encouraging the nearest bong-eyed lunkhead to step forward and clamp a massive hand around Vera's tiny jaw. With sleeves up to his elbows almost, the red-faced thug squeezes, encouraging a garbled cry.

"Get off her. Leave her be!"

The guy looks at me and smiles, revealing metal filings where teeth should be. What next? A little man arriving on scene, steel-rimmed top hat in hand? The floor to open up, dropping me into the jaws of a shark? *Fuck me.*

"Don't you see, my dear?" Ass-man says to Vera. "Love of my

life. My treasure. My whore. Nobody can protect you as I can." As if about to ask for her hand in marriage, he bends down on one knee before her. Instead, he turns to me, pliers at the ready, nodding to the heavy at my shoulder. Before I know what's happening, tobacco-flavoured fingers are in my mouth, prising my jaw wide open. Once again, that god-awful smile breaks across Ass-man's face, his hair now as frantic as the look behind his eyes. "And this is all the thanks I get."

The heavy behind forces my head into the back of the chair, his hands stretching my jaw further. It feels like my fucking head is going to rip in two. "Sit still," Ass-man yells, trying to work the pliers into my mouth, metal gliding across gums and grinding against teeth. Behind him, I hear Vera's muffled whimpers, but they only fuel Ass-man's rage. "Sit fucking still!"

Gripping my jaw tight, he pinches the pliers down on one of my bottom teeth and pulls. "Music," he says, prompting Karen Carpenter's voice to fill the room with moans about *Rainy Days and Mondays*. As pain explodes across my gums, I find myself wanting to bring her back just so I can scream in her face to shut the fuck up and tell her to find something worth grumbling over.

"Simon!" Vera screams.

Ass-man's eyes light up. "Simon?" Raw pain rips through me, nerve endings on fire. My head lolls back and forth at the mercy of the metal instrument.

Mama! Mama!

Sweat rolls from Ass-man's brows as he yanks this way and that. "It looks a damn sight easier in the movies," he says. "Should have gone for the old-fashioned kneecapping. If it's not broken, pardon the pun, don't—"

CRACK.

He recoils, inspecting the fractured tooth in the grip. "Fuck it. Pass me the bat."

Vera lets out another series of muffled protests, her heels scratching against the wood. "He threatened my family, Simon!" Over Ass-man's shoulder, I see her dancing with two of the heavies, throwing her little balled-up fists every which way. "Said he'd kill them all. Get the fuck off me!"

See, Mama. She does love me.

"Keep her fucking quiet, will you," Ass-man says, snatching the metal bat from one of his thugs. He wipes his hair back from his eyes and takes position on his knees, readying his swing. If it weren't for the blood on his shirt, he'd look like a father home from work, lining up to play a little softball with his son. "Which leg first, Simey?" he asks. "I guess it makes no odds." That fucking smile, like the cat that got the cream, but oh, what a story he will have to tell. And word will travel fast to The Dragon that the "twat in a leotard" is no more, and Ass-man will become a goddamn supervillain.

One of the heavies behind lets out a high-pitched cry, and as his head disappears behind Ass-man's, I know there's only one thing that elicits such a response—he's taken one in the knackers.

"Will you keep the bitch quiet," Ass-man yells.

"Trying, boss," the heavy croaks.

Like a mosquito, Vera's relentless. She kicks, bites, and scratches, but her blows have little effect against the swarming giants. "I love you, Simon," she cries from the pack. It's all futile, of course, but it only makes me love her more, her betrayal just part of the spiralling chaos consuming everything in its path. "I love you!" she cries again.

"Never seen her like this before," Ass-man says. "Almost brings a tear to the eye."

I feel so fucking helpless. This was supposed to be my show, not some low-budget James Bond rip-off. *Luca? Luca!* But my little Spanish friend has nothing for me, no words of advice to break free from my constraints and single-handedly take down eight villains. Ahead, early morning light spills through the tiny windows but offers no reprieve from this nightmare. Even Mother's voice is staying quiet, realisation this seedy little building will be the end of the road for Reformo.

"You have to choose," Ass-man says through gritted teeth.

"Fuck you."

"Fine. Left it is."

The taste of death is strong as I swallow, but there's a look in Ass-man's eyes that he intends to draw this out for as long as possible. Ready to swing, he eyes me again, but as though Vera's cries are like fingers down a chalkboard, he rakes a gloved hand through his hair and snaps his head towards the crowd of lunkheads. "FOR THE LOVE OF CHRIST, KEEP THAT BITCH QUIET!"

Offering a series of cries, she spits and lashes out, but as a giant fist—THWACK—finds her face, she crumples to the ground, her cheek smashing against the wood. Our eyes meet, and I mouth for her to stay down. Instead, she screams and drives her heel into Ass-man's side.

"I just want to enjoy the moment," Ass-man says, swatting her kicks away. "Is that too much to ask?"

He jumps to his feet, draws a gun from the back of his pants, and points it towards me. Tensing my muscles for impact, I screw my eyes shut so tight, they ache. *Be seeing you soon, Mama. I did my best.* As my pitiful life flashes before me, Vera fills the room with another high-pitched scream.

This is it. This is the—

BANG!

Mama? Mama, are you there? Mama?

If it weren't for the throbbing in my gums and the ringing in my ears, I would assume I was dead. And that same tormenting morsel of light beyond my eyelids. Slowly, I unscrew my eyes, only to see Ass-man kneeling before Vera, his head resting on her side. "Look what you made me do."

No! No, no, no, no.

"Vera!" *This can't be real. Can't be happening. Just part of the game.* "Get up. Vera!"

You're thinking we could run away together, aren't you?

"Vera, please." Muscles crackle as I writhe in the chair. "Vera, don't you dare be gone!" My stomach swells at what feels like a thousand simultaneous kicks in the nuts. I snap my head to the right, offering a dry gag. "Veraaaaaaaa!"

"This is all on you," I hear Ass-man say, his voice distant and empty. "All on you."

"Get up. Get up. Get up. Please, Vera. Please!"

Promise me, Simon.

"Fuuuuuuuuuuuuuuuuuuck!"

Her eyes are still on me but as dead as a doll's. Unplugged. Disconnected. Yet, I can't believe she's gone. From the small hole in the side of her head, a trickle of blood traces a path across her nose and cheek, pooling on the dirty wooden floor next to her open lips.

"Noooooooooo!"

Grief and anger overwhelm. *CHAOS. CHAOS. CHAOS.* I can't breathe. I'm back in oblivion. "I'll kill you! I'll fucking kill you!" Teeth gritted, veins popping in my neck, I struggle against the ropes, visions of tearing off Ass-man's head filling my mind. "You're fucking dead!" At Ass-man's request, one of the lunkheads steps forward and strikes me hard across the temple, but it does nothing to dampen my fury. "I'LL TEAR YOUR FUCKING EYES OUT!"

Ass-man stands and turns towards me, wiping a tear away with his blood-smeared handkerchief. "And she was such a good little earner."

Blood whooshes in my ears, encouraging an accompanying throbbing in my gums. As my muscles ripple and Lycra stretches, I picture the suit tearing and the restraints giving. "Fuck you! Fuck you! Fuck yooooooooooou!" I half-expect a laser to shoot from my eyes, burning a hole through Ass-man's chest. "You fuck! You fuck! You fuuuuuuuuuuck!" A scream builds inside me, big enough, I imagine, to make the whole fucking building shake.

"Whores like that are hard to come by, let me tell you." Ass-man places the handkerchief back in his pocket and finds his smile again as if he has grieved for long enough. "But once The Dragon hears of this, I imagine I'll be swimming in them."

I roar until my voice fades, but there's not even a sprinkle of dust from the ceiling. I struggle against my restraints, but my suit remains intact. And only burning tears emerge from my eyes. "Jesus fucking Christ!" Spider-Man can swing across buildings, Superman can laser through metal, but I can't even work my way out of a crude knot.

"Get her out of here," Ass-man says, giving his deceased beloved a tap with his shiny shoe. "Make sure you take the jewellery off first, it cost me a goddamn fortune."

"Fucking animal!" Thrashing my head against the back of the chair, I let out another wail. "Why did you have to fucking kill her?"

Ass-man lifts the gun towards me. "I had no intention of doing so, but her little performance grew too much to bear." He steps forward, driving the gun's muzzle into my forehead. "You must have made quite an impression."

"I was supposed to protect her."

He pushes the gun into my skull. "No, that was my job."

"Call that protection!?"

"That's on you, my friend. She was fine before you turned up."

Quasi begins dragging Vera away, a shoe working loose, her body carving a path through dust and grime. "Just do it. Do it," I cry. Ass-man's right. All this time without me, she'd survived just fine. *What's the alternative?* "Kill me. Pull the fucking trigger. Do me a fucking favour and end this chaos once and for all."

Ass-man removes the gun from my skull and coils his finger around the trigger. "At least your grief will be short."

"No cheesy parting words, no fucking 'we're not so different after all' speeches. Just do it!"

His smile stretches. "Oh, don't worry. I'm ready to collect my—" To the sound of *The Godfather* theme tune, Ass-man begins patting at his jacket. He brings a cell phone from the right-hand pocket, his forehead creasing as he studies the display. Keeping the gun pointed at my head, he lifts the phone to his ear. "Yeah?"

On the other side of the room, Quasi releases Vera and reaches for the iron door. Darkness awaits within, a single ray of light stretching far enough to allow the briefest glimpse of a plastic rim. Jayden in hospital, and Vera in a barrel. So much for bringing order back to town. *What the fuck, Mama?* But she remains quiet.

Ass-man nods, eyes not leaving mine. "Yes," he says. "I understand." Blood drains from his face. His forehead crumples. "Yeah, he's not going anywhere. Do you need an—" His arm falls to his side, but he continues studying the clutched phone. "Address."

One of the heavies taps him on the shoulder. "Boss?"

"The Dragon," Ass-man says. "He's coming."

The heavy swallows hard, his eyes growing wide. "Was that... him?"

Ass-man offers an imperceptible shake of his head. "One of his grunts."

It's as if the entire entourage is in dire need of a blood transfusion, all bravado taking off on early retirement, a newly-found cowardice working through the ranks.

"He's actually coming here? The Dragon?" Quasi says, his voice breaking mid-sentence. "When?"

"Tell him we can handle it, boss," another of the lunkheads suggests. "Ring them back now and tell them."

"It's not a fucking quote for car insurance, you stupid prick, it's the fucking mob. King of the fucking Underworld. You don't ring the fuckers back. Besides, the number will already be void."

"Why? When?"

Staring at the ground, Ass-man appears a million miles away, his dark eyes emphasised further by his now pallid complexion. All suaveness has gone, and even his suit appears duller as if draining of colour. And I swear I see a little trickle of darkness running from his hair.

"Boss. When?"

Like a lousy actor unable to break a habit, Ass-man shakes his head and lifts his stare. "This evening. He wants to take care of Reformo, AKA *Simon*, himself." Offering a sigh, he lets his shoulders and the gun drop. "I need a fucking drink. If anyone needs me, I'll be at the club."

"What about him?"

"Lock him in with the dead—two on him outside the door at all times in two-hour shifts. Pitbull, Baby Face, you've got the first watch. The rest of you...get some sleep. We'll need to be on our toes."

"Fuck's sake, I'm knackered," one of them whispers. Baby Face, I assume, not a hair on his head and cheeks like a chipmunk playing the trumpet. From behind him, a growl emerges, one I trace to the thug wearing a scowl and a massive leather jacket that still looks two sizes too small. Pitbull, I'd bet my right nut on it.

Leaving the disgruntled pair behind and confirming my guess, the other heavies begin heading towards the lift in a huddle of shoulders and murmurs. Pitbull offers another snarl and Baby Face more hushed cussing.

Vera's dead. Vera's dead. Vera's—

"The Dragon. Coming here," Baby Face says. "He's real then. Not a myth."

Pitbull spits out a ball of phlegm that explodes next to my right foot. "Believe it when I see it."

"You heard the boss. See his face when he took that call?"

"Doubt he'll come himself. Probably just send some of his goons."

Baby Face nods. "I liked Vera, she was a good egg. A shame really."

"Nah," Pitbull says. "A whore can never be trusted. Good riddance, I say."

"Fuck you," I yell.

"No, fuck you," Pitbull replies. "And your mother."

"My mother's dead, you prick."

"Well, I'll fuck her 'til she isn't then."

"Fuck you!"

"No, fuck—"

Wake up, Simon.

But it hurts, Mama.

Are you a man or a mouse, like your weak as piss father?

I'm so tired.

Tell them that. They might let you go.

They killed her, Mama. My only love.

No substitute for a mother's love, Simon, especially not from some two-bit whore. Do you forget what she did?

She had no choice.

There's always a choice, Simon. She sat back and watched, just another casualty of the chaos. NOW GET OFF YOUR SORRY LIT-TLE ARSE AND BRING AN END TO IT!

I can't see a goddamned thing except for the image of Vera's head resting on the darkened patch of wood. Gone. My Vera. Just like that. All those fucking shooting stars for nothing.

I love you, Simon.

Fuck this. Fuck it all! And with every breath in my body, I make one last promise to ensure she didn't die in vain: The Dragon will fall.

Taking a deep breath, I try and compose myself, but the smell that fills my nostrils induces hysterical panic. Blood begins pumping impossibly fast around my body, and a small grenade explodes in my head, sending ripples of pain behind my eyes and across my temple.

Lock him in with the dead.

It's as if my senses are picking up the slow disintegration of the bodies in the barrels—FZZZZ. There's a scream in my throat, but I take my frustration out on the rope, continuing to get nowhere fast. This fucking place. This goddamn fucking town!

I am Reformo. I am Reformo. Wee-formo save day.

The chant helps, but I know I must leave here fast. A clash with the archvillain is inevitable, but I'll stand no chance if it's in his arena, heavies on tap. Holding my breath allows my superhero senses to pick up a trickle of tinny music and the unmistakable gentle rumble of someone snoring.

Come on!

The rope is tight, cutting off the circulation to my hands. They're numb, like useless fucking balloons tied to the end of my arms. Still, I grit my teeth, muscles tearing and popping as I try to make something happen. *Come on. Come on.* There's some give, but not enough.

Something with a little more bite.

Janice, I fucking love you! Is it possible the chain-smoking and puckered-faced old dearie could save my life twice within twenty-four hours? My muscles burn, and my fingers ache as I continue fighting against the ropes. I grimace, driving my teeth into my lip, wanting to scream again but not needing the attention. *Come on. Come the fuck on!* Pain surges across my wrists and arms, but I persist, finally grabbing the cuff area with my fingers.

Focus your mind.

And as my fingertips brush across Velcro, I'm filled with an urge to cry. *Reformo! Reformo! Reformo!* Bending my right wrist until it feels close to the point of dislocation, I bite down harder on my lip, forcing my index finger through the gap. Never has anything sounded so sweet as the tiny hooks separating—TSSSSSCHHH-HHHRT—allowing the handle of the knife to slide into my hand.

See, Mama! I'm not a quitter.

Don't just sit there then.

It's far from over, but as I begin working the rest of the knife out, being careful of the sharp serrated blade, things look a hell of a lot better than they did a few minutes ago. Vera. My Vera. A dent in the steel lets me know I'm nearly there. One final pull, and—it's out.

Got it, Mama. Got it! Now what?

My superhero senses have the answer, and I begin sawing at the rope, gyrating my left hand up and down. *Fuck, yeah!* I can hear the blade working its way through, envisaging the tiny splaying fibres.

Reformo! Reformo! Reformo!

Ignoring my burning muscles, I find my rhythm and up my tempo. Noxiousness continues filling my nostrils and will likely stay with me forever, but I have no intention of it being the last thing I smell. Beyond the door, over the tinny music, I can still hear at least one of the heavies snoring. Both may be asleep if I'm lucky enough, but I already know how dangerous hope is.

Come on. Come— Holy shit, I've done it. I'm out. That was too easy. More bite than fucking Jaws.

The frayed rope around my chest provides no contest for the

blade and my renewed enthusiasm, and in only a matter of seconds, it falls to my side. But just as my luck seems to be turning, the snoring stops. I pause, breath held, expecting footsteps and the door to be flung open, gun pointed at my head.

Silence.

A change of guard? I've no idea how long I've been out. What if they check in on me? What if they—

The snoring starts again, and I return to work on the rope around my feet. Within seconds, I'm free, albeit in a dark room surrounded by dissolving bodies, guarded by two men with arms like legs. And a thought flashes across my mind: *What if the door is locked?*

Lock him in with the dead.

Of course it's going to be locked, you silly fucker. There's no way Ass-man would take any risks, not with The Dragon visiting town. All of that for nothing. What now? What now, you stupid fucking idiot? What are you—

The door quietly clicks as I turn the handle. Shit on a stick. I've heard of brawn over brain, but that's really taking the piss.

Ain't a brain cell between them.

Holding my breath, I move the door slightly ajar, expecting it to be slammed back in my face. But no cries from Baby Face, and no barks from Pitbull. Two pairs of shiny shoes just a couple of feet away, and as still as death. *There's no way. There's just no way.* I can hardly believe my luck as I open the door wider, exposing wide-open mouths and vulnerable slouches.

Don't just stand there gawping as if nothing is happening, Simon. That's what your father used to do.

I'm not, Mama, I'm thinking.

Stop crapping and get cracking.

I am, Mama. I am.

Knowing the clunky lift could wake the dead, my eyes settle on the "Emergency Exit" sign across the room. *What would Batman do? Leave in peace, or take the fuckers down while he had the chance? If nobody was watching, that is, if he had free rein. Both will have guns, no doubt, but if I can get hold of one—*

Pitbull's eyes snap open, and he jolts forward, removing the trouble of a decision. He looks confused and childlike, but a knife through the throat—SCHLUK—provides a gritty reminder of his lost innocence. Blood spills over his sausage fingers and the stretched fabric of his shirt as he clutches at his neck, eyes wide and desperate.

I offer him a gentle nod. "You can't swim against the tide. Catch my drift?"

He tries to speak as he slides to the floor, perhaps something about a goldfish with digestion problems or a blind cat. His horizontal dance begins, feet slipping and sliding against the bloody floor, allowing me to reach for the exposed gun in the rear pocket of his pants.

BANG!

"Oi!" Just as wide-eyed, Baby Face emerges from his slumber. He reaches behind his back, but such reflexes count for nothing if one's actions are broadcast by the word "Oi."

BOOM!

And just like that, his feet are once again still.

In desperate need of fresh air to wash the smell of death from my nostrils, I wrestle the knife from Pitbull's throat and make haste towards the emergency exit. Not going to lie, it did cross my mind to take a gun, but it just isn't the superhero way to carry one. And addressing the massive fucking elephant in the room, I've already stretched the limits of superhero conduct by sawing someone's head off with a knife, something I imagine would be a nightmare for superhero HR.

Brightness forces a painful squint as I push the doors open. Still, the cold air feels cleansing as it rushes over my limited, exposed skin. Grateful to be above ground again and keen to stay that way, I ascend the stairs to the street. It's still quiet, but soon people will feel brave enough to leave their houses, albeit with eyes in the back of their heads. *What's the plan, Reformo? Soon every bad motherfucker in town will be after your blood, including The Dragon himself.*

Chapter Ten: The Dragon

I feel vulnerable and exposed. Unsure how long I was out in that horrible little room, I have to hope I have an hour at least before any changeover. But what if they heard the gunshots? A desperate thought crosses my mind to knock at Janice's door, but with eyes in a thousand places, I consider it too much of a risk to them.

So damned tired. I just need to close my eyes. The Dragon will no doubt be well rested, well fed, supercharged, and ready to kick my arse. I have nowhere to run, nowhere to—

I see everything, but it's as though I'm invisible.

Of course! Reggie, King of the blowjobs.

As I emerge from the tired, old industrial estate, a beautiful sight almost brings me to my knees: Someone picking up their dog's shit. A strange thing for most to get so emotional about, but to me, it's everything, especially after all that's happened. *And wait...isn't that—it is, it's Poppy!*

Mama, do you see?

Small steps make climbable ladders, Simon.

I can't take my eyes away. Even as the old lady leads Poppy across the street, a bag of shit—*Just pebbles*—dangling from her wrist, my legs feel weak.

Hope. Worth sticking your neck out for.

If I make it out of this alive, there's no doubt what happened to Vera will haunt my waking hours and dreams—such a brief snap-shot of time to share, but one that will carry years of grief. We were just two lost souls who found each within the chaos, a dramatic encounter that even the heavens noticed.

But now is not the time to grieve.

All I have is now and tomorrow, and my mission still stands. "I'll avenge you, Vera. I promise we will sit on that seat together, holding hands and searching the sky for shooting stars. We will."

The sight of the swinging dog shit has lightened my mood, and as I head off towards Reggie's place, there's almost a spring in my step at the thought of him offering me a blowjob. I up my pace, dogs beginning a chorus of barks as if picking up on my renewed optimism. The public may be undecided, but the dogs seem right behind me.

"I am Reformo. I'm bringing hope back to town."

Rowdier still, the dogs respond by increasing the frequency and volume of their barks. Maybe even they've had enough of the restricted once-a-day walks and looking at each other's shit mounds.

There it is!

Even from two streets away, I recognise the flat roof of the building. The elevation helps, the occupying street on a slight hill, accounting for the panoramic view of the town. "I'm coming, Reggie, my friend." *My* friend. *I have a* friend.

The bottle shop on the corner stops me in my tracks. Again, in any other circumstances in any ordinary town, it wouldn't be much to write home about, but the fact someone has tried scrubbing the graffiti from the shop window makes me as teary as a beauty queen winner. Cuntfac. Why they decided to work on the last letter first is beyond me, but beggars can't be choosers, and I take it as a win.

"Yo, Reformo!"

Just a kid, perhaps twelve, thirteen at the most. So much for staying under the bloody radar. He throws a newspaper onto a lawn and raises his fist in the air, bringing another tear to my eye. *For fuck's sake, get a grip, Reformo.* But part of me knows there's every possibility I might have just helped keep that kid's life on track, that given the inevitable choice between drugs and living clean, he too may strive to end the chaos. I raise my hand in return, keeping it in the air long after he's pedalled off.

Hope.

Doing my best to keep tears at bay, knowing exhaustion and grief are trying to set up home, I set off again. I'm struggling to keep my eyes open as I turn into *Reggie's street*. Still, I feel the slightest spark of adrenaline as I approach the familiar roof, preparing for his proposal.

"Reggie."

Only the wind replies.

"Reggie, how much for a blowjob?"

Silence.

Perhaps he's not at home. Maybe the pigs moved him on. What if the lunkheads got him—beat him to a pulp and left him for dead?

"Reggie." My senses tingle; something isn't right. Urgent and shaky, I move the crate in place and hoist myself onto the roof. "Reggie!"

I try to convince myself he's asleep, nothing but a drunken slumber. But as I draw closer, studying the vomit that speckles his erratic beard, there's no doubt in my mind. He's gone. In his grasp, an empty bottle of premium vodka—the sort that would set you back fifty notes.

I'm sure you'll spend it wisely.

Not likely.

Pain cripples me, the knot twisting in my stomach, rubbing and scratching against my rawness. I can't breathe, suffocating with darkness. It's too much, this is too much. My body trembles as I lift my stare towards the skies and let out a silent scream that echoes inside my head long after I've crumpled to the floor next to my friend.

This isn't fucking fair! I killed them. I killed them both. Fuck! Fuck! Fuuuuuuuuuuuck! Every bit of good I try to do invites more chaos—Jayden, Vera, and now Reggie.

Things will get worse before they—

Mama! Vera and Reggie are dead! How much worse can it get?

No war was ever won without casualties.

But they were special to me, Mama. Reggie was my friend, and Vera was—

A whore! Now stop being as weak as piss and end this chaos. People want order, Simon, they're desperate for it. You saw the lady carrying her poo and the scrubbed-off graffiti.

Two lives gone, and one more in hospital must be worth more than a bag of shit and the letter "e", Mama.

Stop crapping and get cracking. It gets my fucking goat!

Sidling up to my friend and lying beside him, I pretend we're both watching the clouds rolling by. One of the few memories I have of my father was of doing just that, most likely at a stage where the lights behind his eyes were nothing but a flicker. I must have been eight, maybe nine at a push. It was in a field somewhere, possibly on one of the infrequent trips away we used to take before the chaos consumed Mother whole. The rickety blades of a windmill made a not-unpleasant sound against the breeze, but aside from that, I remember it being impossibly quiet. Even Mother seemed content, leaning against a fence in the distance, away from the hustle and bustle of everyday life in a rare moment of peace. And when Father suggested looking for shapes in the clouds, I recall it was all I could do not to cry.

I can't remember what shapes I might have seen that day, but I still recall Father's answer when I asked what he saw: "I see dead people." As we got up to leave, there were also some vague ramblings about this not being the person he was supposed to be. The rest of the day is nothing but a haze, aside from the final words he uttered that day, delivered with a smile and a twinkle in his eye. "In my next life, I'll be someone special. Like a superhero or something."

Since that day, I've been obsessed. Superman to begin with, but there was no stopping me after that—my drawers became stuffed full of comics and paraphernalia. Even my dreams were taken over with thoughts of saving the world. Silly really, bearing in mind I still struggled to tie my own shoelaces and was known to piss the bed every now and again.

Mother got worse quickly, further losing herself in her own world of chaos. Becoming more and more oppressive, she alienated us from all—family, friends, neighbours—until it was always just the three of us living under her dark cloud. Father was no comfort, his flicker all but gone. Before long, it got so their marriage was like a one-sided war of sorts—*No war was ever won without casualties*—uncomfortable, extended periods of silently building tension, followed by explosive bouts of linguistic violence spewing from Mother's mouth. Instead of leaving—*Weak as piss*—Father just took it, absorbing her dark spores until they finally extinguished the flickering light. PSSST.

I hated him for it, maybe more than I hated her.

Something had to give. I couldn't take anymore.

"I'm sorry, Reggie." Tears make their presence known on the icy breeze. "I will be a better man."

Trying. Trying. Trying.

Not long after the kitten episode, I waited at their bedroom door one night, ensuring they were asleep. It could have even been morning, I can't recall, but that's not important. Mother's snoring was as loud as ever. Father's was quieter but audible. He could fall asleep on a washing machine, likely running free in his own little fantasy land. I recall being terrified, feeling sure I wouldn't be able to go through with it. *Weak as piss, just like your father.* And that was the thought that spurred me into action.

I intended to make it look like an accident, not that I had much of a plan. After all, I was nothing but a kid pushed to the limits, a head full of Mother and not much else. Candles. Oh, how she loved them, so many scattered all over the house. Usually white to "cleanse and purify," as Mother used to sing. At least one tiny part of the world could be free from chaos. I used the ladder from the storage cupboard to remove the fire alarm batteries, and then one by one, I lit the candles. Even then, I wasn't sure I'd go through with it, but the sound of that box being crushed kept playing in my mind. Taking a match to anything I thought would burn along the way, I began toppling them all.

SNAP. CRACKLE.

Arms wrapped tight around my knees, I watched the fire take hold from behind some bushes. At one point, I even considered running in and dragging them out. I'd be a superhero, and they'd be so proud. Perhaps we'd even be a normal family again, a rare second chance to get things right. Instead, I ran, all the way to the old railway station and then some, not out of fear of the dark or even getting caught but trying to escape a voice that would never let me be. It wasn't long before I heard the distant sirens filling the night air.

"Please, forgive me. Jayden, Vera, Reggie, Mama, Papa. Forgive me."

The breeze blows across, bringing a concoction of freshly baked bread and the faintest whiff of vomit. A dog barks, a car backfires. Life in this shitty old town continues, oblivious to my sins and losses.

"I will honour my pledge, Mama. But I'm doing it for Vera, Jayden, and Reggie just as much as I am for you." I take Reggie's cold hand in mine, heavy eyes on the clouds again. "That one looks like a rabbit. And that one...a three-legged dog. What do you reckon?" Another tear spills down my cheek as loneliness overwhelms me. "You were my friend, Reggie." Eyelids getting heavier still, I afford myself a moment of respite, shutting out the morning light. "You helped me, and I'll never forget it." Still picturing the clouds rolling by, I'm transported back to that field again, the slow churn of the windmill helping to sedate. I'm sinking. Sinking fast. I do my best to fight, but even superheroes get tired. "I will bring hope—"

Jolting up, I wipe the rain from my eyes.

Fuck.

I hear a voice.

Fuck-ety fuck.

I feel vulnerable and ill-prepared. Footsteps from the right—close—have me drawing my knees to my chest. *Oh shit! He's under me, on the street below. The crate!*

"Yeah, I've checked there... Yeah, and by the water. Wait, hang on a second." As the man ducks into the alley, I hold a hand to my mouth, stemming the wisps of air. But there's no way he'll not climb the crate, just no way, and if he only slightly resembles the gruffness of his voice, I've got my hands full. "I'll call you back," he says.

Sure enough, it isn't long before I hear the first groan. *Wait for it. Waaaaaait for it.* Only as his fingers grab the roof's edge do I drop to the street and sidestep to the corner, preparing to sidle back into the alley. Eyes on the guy as he pulls his massive bulk up the crate, I'm already starting to second guess myself, thinking I should have attacked from above. Even lying down, I could have planted a hefty kick in his face. With a bit of luck, he would have fallen back, striking his head on—

"There's someone up here... I don't know yet, do I? Give me a chance."

That's my cue. Breath held, I climb the crate and hoist myself up.

So far, so good.

"Jesus, the guy stinks... Nah, just a hobo with expensive taste... Look, it's definitely not our guy... Because he's a fucking hobo, that's why... A disguise?... Not unless he's best friends with Tom fucking Savini... Never mind, it's niche... Niche... N-i-c-h-e... Look, I'll call you if I find anything." He thumbs his phone hard and slides it back into his pocket, still kneeling over the body. "Fucking ingrates, the lot of them."

Over his shoulder, I spy the launderette. It's empty. Stranger still, only a couple of heavies walk the streets. My guy stands, offering a simultaneous yawn and fart. "It should be me in charge," he mumbles to himself. "I should be King of this fucking town. The men would kiss my feet, and the women my dick. All hail, King Jeremy." He shoves a hand down the back of his creased pants and commences what I can only describe as an intensive rummage, before bringing it back out and sniffing one of his fingers as though it was a fine cigar.

Hollywood, this ain't. Isn't.

Luca always insisted there was no room for emotion in fights, only strategy and technique. But as my friend Reggie is sent to the ground, courtesy of the fucker's right foot, I only see red.

CHARGE!

It's all so rushed, yet my sweep is perfection. "He." My choke-hold is flawless and deep. "Was." My wraparound is seamless. "My friend."

I squeeze tighter, his face turning red, things crackling and popping in his neck, veins coming to the surface. In desperation, he lashes out, catching me a good one on the chin. SMACK! He throws another, but it glances off my left arm, a futile attempt. DINK. A choky rasp emerges. I think he's trying to tell me something.

"What is it, champ?" Part of me wants to know, but the other part doesn't give a fuck. "The King's speech again?" He continues to writhe, but he's weakening, his face beetroot red and on the way to being a shade darker. Frantic, he taps his hand against my right arm, perhaps an instinctive move picked up from the gym. "Sorry, King Jeremy," I whisper into his ear. "No tap-outs. This is a one-way ticket." And as if on cue, his body goes limp. "This is a one-way ticket," I repeat. "My name is Reformo, and this is a one-way ticket."

Allowing him to slide from my grasp reveals the night sky and the constellation near where Vera and I spotted *our* first and last shooting star. Perhaps she is up there watching me. Maybe she even sent the rain to wake me. Actually, if Vera were up there, she'd be more likely to be involved in a slanging match with Mother, two strong women fighting for supremacy. *Nothing but a whore.* What a battle that would be. *Christ, I'd strip your mother down if she was here now.* Yes, the heavens would soon regret allowing both through its doors.

"This is a one-way ticket." *At last, a line to be proud of!*

I slide the phone from the big fella's pocket. Commando style, I drag myself to the roof's edge and continue surveillance, resisting the urge to look down at my fallen friend. The launderette remains empty, as are the streets now, but the sight of a Hummer parked in the industrial estate turns any thoughts of a rain check with The Dragon into ashes.

It's time to end the chaos, Simon, once and for all.

Mama, is Vera up there with you?

They wouldn't let a dirty whore up here, Simon. Now focus on the job at hand and bring hope back to town.

I'll do my best, Mama.

A woman wearing a high-vis vest emerges from an alley across the street, scooping what looks to be the last of a diabetes-inducing breakfast into her mouth. She fingers whatever juices remain from the carton and slides the shiny digit into the gap above her even glossier chin. The sight of food makes my stomach grumble, and I realise I'm famished, unable to recall the last thing that passed through my lips besides a pair of pliers. *Could eat the scabs of a tramp's head.* "Don't worry, Reggie; I ain't that—"

My heart sinks as the woman throws the carton over her shoulder, all thoughts of hunger fading. Words bounce around my head, beginning their violent assault on my silence, but just as I'm about to burst, unable to hold my tongue, the woman turns, offering a shake of her head.

Do it. Do it!

After looking up and down the street several times, she drops her shoulders, walks over to the carton, and bends to retrieve it. I promised myself no more tears, but I'm unable to prevent a couple from escaping. *Small steps.* Flattening myself against the roof, I follow her across the road, a lump in my throat forming as the litter finds its rightful place.

Order. Order. Order.

It's a beautiful distraction that helps replenish my dwindling reserves of hope. But it is a distraction, and now it's time to *focus on the job at hand.* The Dragon, my biggest challenge yet. I know I can handle myself, but I've been dealing with wannabes, all one step behind the beat, even the dancer. These will be The Dragon's best men. And how many will there be? Armed with a dented knife and a handful of dog shit bags, I'd have to be an idiot to believe my luck won't run out.

Mama?

Stop feeling sorry for yourself and kick some arse, Simon. Rinse! Rinse! Rinse! Crumbs on the countertop. Dishes in the sink. It's just laziness. Get's my fucking goat!

But I just took down that big fella, Mama.

You got lucky, Simon. He got distracted by his shitty finger and the filthy hobo.

Hey, Reggie was my friend!

And now he's dead, just like that whore. No more distractions.

Mama!

You made a pledge, Simon. Remember? YOU FUCKING OWE ME!

Her words ring in my head louder than ever. *Rinse! Rinse! Rinse! Crumbs on the countertop. Dishes in the sink.* Like an overly domesticated version of Mister Miyagi, her chant has been with me for as long as I can remember. It's the first thing I hear when I wake, and the last before restless sleep comes for me. And as much as Mother wants—wanted—the chaos to an end, I want her voice to end too. Safe to say, I hope to find some semblance of peace when all this is over, whatever that may entail.

"My name is Reformo, and I'm bringing hope back to town."

I don't know much about guns, but the one I slide from big fella's jacket pocket looks pretty slick, putting Marisa Tomei to shame. "You compensating for something, King Jeremy?" Levity is short-lived as the big fella's phone begins to vibrate.

Just a number, no name. Car insurance, solar power, or one of the fucking kingpins. What a choice. If I don't answer, they'll get suspicious. If I do answer, they might know it's not the big fella. Either way, I could get rushed.

Fuck it!

I take a couple of deep breaths, working my suit away from my crotch. "Yeah?" I say in my deepest voice possible. "Uh huh...I'll be there."

It looks like the guy was just a dispensable. Nothing more than bait.

He knows everywhere I go and how long I spend there.

A thousand eyes.

I've been summoned for a one-on-one with The Dragon himself. A trap? Ambush? Probably. Call it instinct or super intelligence, but part of me feels there's no way someone as important as The Dragon—his fingers in the orifices of so many dirty little towns—would come all the way down without taking the kill himself. I'm the buzz in his ear and the stone in his shoe. He'll want to look me in the eye as I take my last breath because that's how arch-villains roll.

I lift the gun in the air.

BANG! BANG! BANG!

Vera. Reggie. Jayden.

Long after I release the trigger, the shots echo across town. Curtains twitch, and I imagine arses doing the same, but beyond that, there's no movement. Minutes pass, yet the streets remain clear.

I'm coming for you, Dragon. I'm coming for you.

Do or die. Do. Or. Die.

I toss the weapon aside and lower myself from the roof. There's an eerie feeling about town as I approach the industrial estate. At this time of day, the non-workers—most of the town—usually feel brave enough to venture outdoors, leaving their homes-cum-prison cells behind for a few hours. But this reminds me of an apocalypse, or at least that moment in the movies before the horde picks up the scent, spilling from all directions like pensioners with news of a sale on garden trowels.

A tapping from my left sets my heart racing. It's just a kid. Looks to be about the same age as—*Fuck's sake*—why do I keep getting so emotional? I won't let you down again, Jayden, I promise. The kid mouths something and holds a piece of paper against the glass. As far as I can make out, it's just a shit drawing. Really shit. Nevertheless, I give the kid a thumbs up and return to my mission. The tapping starts again, only louder. Intending to give the kid another polite thumbs up and be on my way, I turn.

Squinting into the morning sun, I step from the pavement, examining the still awful but at least now correctly rotated picture. "Holy crap." If it weren't for the lettering scratched underneath the unidentifiable mutant, I'd still be clueless.

R-e-f-o-r-m-o.

He offers the gummiest smile and begins jumping up and down, his breath continuing to mist the window. Three syllables. Wee-for-mo. I mean, Re-for-mo. In return, I grace the kid with a nod and a swish of my cape, causing his smile to turn to laughter. It's a beautiful moment, only cut short as his mum leads him away from the window, but not without the flicker of a smile directed towards me.

Word is spreading. The tide is turning. Reformo is bringing hope back to town.

Guessing his mum or dad would have helped with the spelling, I wonder how many other families may have uttered my name over dinner. Such a thought chokes me with pride, making all my efforts feel worthwhile. Long after the kid's gone, I continue glancing back to the window, letting myself believe that hope will conquer fear.

It's time, Reformo.

Mind buzzing with a thousand thoughts, I set off towards the industrial estate, more determined than ever. A pledge to Mother has carried me this far, but now I have so much more on my shoulders. Vera. Reggie. Jayden. Even the paperboy, and the kid in the window. All my life, I've been the outsider, the weird one with social disorders, unable to pick up on human nuances. Yet, in the last few hours, I've made connections that will stay with me until my dying breath, however soon that may be.

Two more streets to go.

My life flashes before me, an unimpressive world ruled by a volatile dictator. *I'll poison the fucking thing. See if I don't.* It sounds strange now, but I used to think her behaviour was typical. Although TV reflected a different set-up, with mothers all smiles and freshly-baked scones, I knew that wasn't reality. And even when people told me she was odd, or I overheard their mutterings about her, I still refused to believe life could be so cruel. That is until I saw it for myself in those rare times I crossed the threshold into other houses, not the fake mothers from yesteryear but strong women who still loved and cherished their offspring.

But if all you're exposed to is the human equivalent of an angry mosquito, you get used to the buzz.

Rinse! Rinse! Rinse! Buzz! Buzz! Fucking buzz!

My guess is she only married Father to escape a home of seven sisters. Throw in a single mum who probably resented every one of them, and you've got a recipe for chaos. It doesn't explain why she took her anger out on us, but I suppose it goes some way to delineating her need for order and her frustration at her tiny world for failing to yield.

The buildings ahead look so bleak and desolate.

I am Reformo. I am Reformo. I am Reformo.

I am a product of her, I know no other way. Even when dead, her voice has continued its torment, all the way through incarceration to so-called freedom. I'm not angry, but I want it to end, and that can only happen if I fulfil my pledge.

One more street.

I will avenge you, Vera.

Without the usual percussion of noise accompanying the breeze, the town continues to be deathly quiet—the calm before the storm. I've no idea what I'm up against. *They are but a ghost.* Half-expecting to hear a gunshot, I imagine heavies armed to the kilt, peering down from the grimy windows of decrepit buildings. I'd be dead in seconds, the little bit of metal in my arm just that, not a fucking miracle worker. But I suppose even supervillains have codes, some semblance of moral boundaries. At least one would hope.

Here we go. Do or die.

It's as though this tiny part of the world is standing still. Since my Keanu impression on the top of Reggie's roof, the tension has been palpable, as though those bullets signified a final declaration of war, the battle of Good versus Evil.

Armageddon.

People want their town back, Simon. Are you man enough to give it to them, or are you a mouse just like your weak as—"I'M NOTHING LIKE HIM!" Words bounce off the buildings and fade to nothing, but the mantra continues playing in my head. All my life, I've been telling myself that I'm nothing like him, and now, along with the opportunity to quieten Mother's voice, is the perfect opportunity to prove it.

I AM REFORMO!

Eyes on the heavy wooden door that Vera struggled to open, I thrust my chest out, marching into the industrial estate.

Chapter Eleven: Big Boss Fight

I'm twenty yards away, but still no signs of life. Engaging super senses, I weigh up my limited options, assessing the building for my entrance point. Far from calm and collected—as any superhero should be—all rational thoughts dissipate behind a veil of anger, grief, and thirst for revenge.

This place is evil. This place is death.

Visions of Vera's skull connecting against the wooden floor don't help, making me wish I could rip out the part of the brain that stored such memories. The dead eyes, the magnificent bead of crimson across her nose. We never got our walks on the beach or nights spent making love in front of the fire. Romanticist claptrap, I know, but the thought of her in one of those barrels...

FUUUUUUUUUUUUUUCK!

Get a grip, my silly English friend. There's no room for emotion in fights. Strategy. Technique. Estrategia. Técnica. Focus your mind. Become your enemy. Get in their heads.

I'll never be like him, Luca!

Rinse! Rinse! Rinse!

Mama, I'm doing my best.

Leading towards a broken skylight, a rusty and cracked drain-pipe runs up the entire length of the brickwork. *Really, Reformo? A drainpipe? What next? Look for a bloody dog flap?* I'm a goddamn superhero, for Christ's sake. There could be a way in through the back. *Hell, who am I kidding? There's no element of surprise here, he knows I'm coming. I might as well be blowing a trumpet and waving a banner with my name on it.*

My hand becomes forced as the heavy door creaks open, somehow of its own accord, and in total contrast to Vera's efforts. But for sure, I know it was more than the heavy wood she was struggling with at the time.

Focus your mind.

As if even morning light is too afraid to enter the warehouse, darkness awaits within, prompting a shudder to rattle down my spine. I consider running, finding somewhere to lie low until I can devise a better plan. Or at least come up with one. But what if The Dragon never graces this town with his presence again? What if this is his only appearance? No, it must be now. And if I can take The Dragon down and send a big enough message, perhaps his entire shitty little empire will collapse, too.

Hope.

With my chest still puffed out, I march towards the darkness, that same noxious combination of detergent and death filling my nostrils. Only a few feet to go, a grindhouse-esque montage plays in my head, spattered body fluids to the sound of that god-awful drill and bloodcurdling screams. The sun disappears behind a cloud, reminding me of a kid pulling the blankets to their chin while watching a scary movie.

Do or die. I am Reformo. I am Reformo. I am Reformo.

Still unable to rid the sound of metal on bone from my mind, my left leg buckles as I pass through the doorway. No gunfire greets me, though, not even a baseball to the head, only a man the size of a giant, armed with a silver tumbler. "Drink," he says, lifting it towards me.

"Fuck me, have I walked into Wonderland?" This guy is massive, proper circus stuff. My neck's already beginning to ache from looking up. "What if I don't drink it?" My voice sounds like a chipmunk's in comparison.

"Do you really want to find out?"

Squeak. Even I know my limits. I take the tumbler and swirl the yellowish liquid around, bringing my nose close as if trying to catch its bouquet. "On account of it smelling like a tramp's underpants," —*No offence, Reggie*—"I give it one star."

"Funny fucker, aren't you?"

"Comedy is one of my superpowers."

"And I'm guessing your other one is being an annoying little twat."

"Subjective, but I've never made the best first impression. What does that tattoo on your neck say?"

"Anthony."

"Aw, is that your son?"

"Nah, the last man I killed."

"Right."

"I've got over twenty. Room for twenty more. Drink."

"What's your name?"

"Drink."

"Funny name."

He sighs. "Jesus Christ!"

"Come on, I'm on the verge of being hung, drawn and quartered. Just entertain me for a second."

"It's Sean," he says, eyes narrow and hard. "My name is Sean."

"Sean? Hmm."

"What about it?"

I frown and shake my head. "Nothing."

"You were expecting Titan. Or Cyclops?"

"Maximus, perhaps." I even manage a smile. "Anyhow, what do you like to do when you're not torturing and maiming, Sean?"

"Fucking hell, it's like being on *Blind Date*."

"*Blind Date* for the homicidal psychopath. Go on, just tell me, then I'll drink."

He looks over his shoulder. "Painting," he whispers. "I like to paint. You know, scenery, rolling hills, and all that."

"Nice. Why do you do it, Sean?"

"It gives me a peaceful kind of—"

"The torturing and the killing, I mean."

His demeanour stiffens again, deep lines working across his forehead. "Drink."

"Is it trauma? The voices in your head? A need to belong somewhere?"

He reaches inside his jacket pocket. "DRINK!"

"Very well." I can tell by the look in his eyes I've crossed a line. "To rolling hills." I toast, lifting the glass before swilling back its bitter contents. As in the umpteen movies I've watched, my eyes don't roll to the back of my head, nor do my legs collapse beneath me, even as Sean grabs my arm and yanks me towards the mechanical lift.

This is it.

Mama?

Get your elbows off the table.

What?

You can't eat ice cream in here.

What the fuck are you talking about, Mama?

As Sean begins sliding back the iron door with impossible ease, my mind turns to a melting pot of nonsense, voices and thoughts exploding in my head, offering not a morsel of rationality.

People around here know me as Crystal, but my real name is Vera... Focus your mind... You're different, aren't you?... Want a blowjob?... You can trust me... Wee-formo save day... Simon, I love you... And she was such a good little earner.

Sean nods for me to enter, his face softening a little. "You shouldn't have come here," he says. "It doesn't make any sense."

"On the contrary, this is my destiny, Sean. What was in the liquid?"

"Hell of a cocktail that. Won't kill you, but it will take you close." He looks me up and down and back again. "Enough in that tumbler to render a guy twice your size out of action for a few hours."

So much for a moral code. "I'm sorry, Sean. *That last hand nearly killed me.*"

He offers another smile, what I take to be a semblance of respect. "You know mine," he says, following me in and dragging the door back in place. "What's yours? Real one, I mean, and don't you dare say James fucking Bond."

Nothing to do with the drugs, but my legs start to give. "Sorry, Sean, I'm—I'm going to need a—" As my back scrapes against the iron bars, the giant reaches down and plucks me back up as though I am a child having a tantrum. "Simon," I say, trying to recompose. "My name is Simon."

Sean reaches across and presses the button with a gigantic, veiny arm. "And you had the nerve to take the piss out of mine."

"Tell me about The Dragon."

"A bad arse."

"Jeez, I guessed that. I mean, what's his thing? You know... The Joker and his toxic blood, Thanos and his telepathy. Anything I should be wary of? And what does he look like?"

"Were you actually dropped on your head as a kid?"

The lift offers a promising screech but continues its journey down. "Come on, we're friends now," I say. "Rolling hills and all that."

He shakes his head and shrugs. "Fire. Fire is his thing."

Hate fire. Hate it. Hate it. Hate it. But it stands to reason with a name like The Dragon.

"And as far as his looks go," Sean says. "Nobody's ever seen him without his mask."

"Mask?"

"I've said enough."

A proper archvillain with a mask and everything. "My lips are sealed."

"I admire what you're doing," he says, catching me by surprise as the lift begins grinding to a halt. "Takes balls. But it won't make a difference. People around here carry too much fear of The Dragon."

"A blind eye here, a blind eye there, and before you know it, we're hiding in the broom closet eating tinned peaches."

"Bonkers." Sean slides the iron door across and nods for me to get out. "Off the fucking chart."

I step out into the darkness. "I'll be seeing you, Sean."

"No, I don't think you—"

My bloody head. Fist like a sledgehammer, that fucker. It feels like I'm an inch shorter. And if I'm in that cupboard again, I'll—

"Hello?"

Greys and blacks swirl around me, but beyond the ever-changing blanket, I can make out flickers of orange. Blinking doesn't help, only serving to lend the entire situation a strobe effect that makes me even more nauseous.

"What the hell is this?" Same wooden chair, but it's floating three inches from the ground. No restraints, yet I'm unable to move. "Hey. Answer me!"

WHOOSH. WHOOSH.

Now and again, I feel the slightest touch of warmth through my suit. And is that gasoline I smell?

WHOOSH.

Hate fire. Hate it. Hate it. Hate it.

The drink. What was his name again? Sean. Yes, Sean. Fire. *Fire is his thing.*

Fuck.

WHOOSH.

That one was close, the burst of orange combined with the delayed heat bringing moisture to my eyes. Still can't fucking move. *What was in that stuff?* I need to calm down, to focus. Engage superhero senses... *Now!*

I'm in the main warehouse area, I know that much. The patch of darkness beneath my feet is unmistakable, although now morphing from its original sailboat resemblance to a series of faces, each with their mouths contorted into a scream. *I see dead people.* For a moment, I hear the creak of the windmill and catch the final glimmer in Father's eyes before being quashed forever.

WHOOSH. WHOOSH.

I recognise the table, too, loaded with implements that appear to be melting onto the floor. And the snaking trail of darkness leading to the impossibly far away iron door on the other side of the room.

Need to get out. What the fuck was I thinking?

An image of Vera's head on the wood next to the latest agonised face has the ever-present knot in my stomach tightening. Her neck twists until her dead eyes look up at me. The skin begins to fall off, revealing grey bone. Her lips start to move. "You said you'd protect me."

"I'm so sorry, Vera."

"You promised you wouldn't let anything else happen to me."

"But you betrayed me."

What did you expect from a whore, Simon?

Mama, don't speak ill of the dead.

Probably in Hell right now, taking one in every hole.

Come on! Come on!

But my body is unresponsive. Only my blood seems to be doing its job, whooshing in my ears as it continues circulating whatever venom is in my veins. Orange dances in front of my eyes, and a wave of heat falls across the right side of my face. I try to recoil, but nothing.

"Let me out. Make it a fair fight."

My vision is grainy and unreliable, the slightest speck of light emerging from a room I know to be less than a hundred yards away. Squinting, I slowly sweep my surroundings, stopping as my eyes fall across a dancing silhouette, a blur of orange in their wake. My makeshift prison continues its nauseating spin as I will myself to focus, a moment of clarity revealing several aflame wooden torches tossed in the air by a sinister-looking figure dressed in a black, hooded cloak.

"Hey." Another sweep of the room reveals no heavies, just the pirouetting clown, who I assume to be The Dragon. "Answer me!"

As if I'm looking through water, the figure approaches in a distorted haze of black and copper. They move fast, nothing but a trail of flames and a series of whooshes. Intense heat blankets me, coming and going in waves. *I can't see. I can't fucking see!*

Focus your mind, English.

I try to control my breathing. Deep and slow, I draw in gulps of air, trying to filter out the scent of detergent, death, and gasoline. My heart rate settles, as does the bass pounding in my ear. I'm on the ground again, no longer floating. Vision improves, but only as far as the kerosene container just beyond the patch of darkness.

WHOOSH. WHOOSH.

The cloak flaps wildly around me as the figure continues swaying, spinning, and juggling, a face almost coming into view but snapping away before my eyes adjust. He appears to have his back to me now, mumbling something under his breath.

The ripples in my vision cease, allowing me to make out a large dragon lining the back of the material, flames making embroidery shimmer and almost bringing it to life. There's no doubt this is my nemesis, my boss fight. Adrenaline threatens again, but I heed my Spanish friend's words, trying to remain calm. "Did you hear about the clown that ran away with the circus?"

His mumbling continues.

"They made him bring it back. Buh dum schhhhh." *Get in their heads.*

At long last, The Dragon lets some of the torches clatter against the ground. As far as I can tell, only one remains in his grasp, a single flickering flame swishing back and forth in front of his hooded head. His swaying ends.

"I've got more," I say, continuing attempts to instil some semblance of control. "What do you do if you're attacked by a gang of clowns?" Another layer of obscurity peels from my eyes, encouraging me further. His back still to me, The Dragon appears closer and less distorted, and as I try to move my hand, there's an almost imperceptible twitch of my fingers. "Go for the juggler."

My audience turns, lowering the torch to their side. They mutter an inaudible whisper and begin striding their way towards me.

"Any chance we could talk about this?" Fear rides up my spine, but if my time is coming to an end, I intend to go as any superhero would: with pride and a fuck load of sarcasm. "Come on, pull up a chair. Take the weight of those big clown feet of yours."

Unwavering, The Dragon continues his march, cloak a few inches from the ground, face now fully hidden behind the hanging black hood. As my vision settles further still, I swear I catch a glimmer of silver.

"At least give me a look-see. Come on, let me see those peepers."

Creating a puddle of black, he crouches and reaches for the kerosene. The cloak draws up his arm, revealing red, puckered, and scarred skin, his hand resembling an English man's attempts to cook meat on a barbecue. My stomach drops. The room begins to melt. The sight of the twisted and charred flesh has taken things up a notch.

Hate fire. Hate it. Hate it. Hate it.

Unable to take my eyes off the snaking and discoloured skin, I follow it as far as the material will allow. Authentic, bona fide fucking burns, no doubt. Not the kind of thing you get done at the arcade, like all the up-and-coming gangster wannabes, pants around their ankles, throwing gang signs like they're going out of fashion.

It's all I can do not to beg for my life. Inhale. Exhale.

But gasoline fills my nostrils, prompting another wave of panic. As instincts kick in, I see my right foot move, but only as far as the outer patch of darkness.

Focus. Become your enemy.

Inhale. Exhale. "Two cannibals are eating a clown. What does one say to the other?"

The Dragon stands, burning torch in one hand, kerosene in the other. "Does this meat taste funny to you?" he says, his voice emerging as a terrifying guttural growl.

The real deal. I'm face to face with a so-called "ghost," yet all I can do is fucking blink and crack dad jokes.

Don't just sit there then.

But I can't move, Mama.

You're giving up, Simon. I told you, you're just like him, just like your—

With a roar, I thrust myself forward, only managing to lift my back an inch from the chair. Trying to finish the job, I claw at the armrests, but my hands are useless lumps of flesh thrashing against the wood. "You're a coward. Nothing but a fucking coward!"

The Dragon lowers his head, making a grotesque swallowing sound. Burning torches circle him on the floor, lending an even more sinister effect to the show. And as I continue fighting against my body, he begins another series of raspy mumbles that sound more final than his other incoherent utterances. He stops, ripping off what appears to be a silver mask and tossing it to the other side of the room.

Silence.

I imagine cinematic music playing in the theatres, a haunting and saddening end to all hope. Couples clinch, and even the men get teary. Young hoodlums who have talked through the entire film are suddenly silent, giving each other the side eye.

The Dragon flicks his head back, sending the hood to his shoulders and the music up a tempo. "Coward," he says. "You think I'm a coward?"

His face swims in front of me, almost dream-like. Twisted, patchy, and discoloured, the reveal is overwhelming. Unlike those poor burns victims on TV who have been through several reconstructive procedures, The Dragon's face is as raw and grotesque as it gets. One partial eye remains, and the mouth slopes to one side as if someone put him in the fridge shortly after he began melting. There's no hair on the scalp, only more uneven and puckered skin. Looking at him makes my skin crawl, and thoughts of the pain I'm about to endure, make me wish I was already dead.

"Coward," he utters again, following up with another extended half swallow, half choke. "Like the kind of person who sets fire to his parents' house and runs off into the night?"

It's as though the words take time to find their way through, fighting over each other and having to reshuffle themselves back in order. Processing is next, to put meaning to them, to try and make sense of the crispy motherfucker. *How does he know? It's not possible.* I'm jolted back to a different time, knees drawn to my chest, sitting behind the row of bushes, considering my next move.

SNAP. CRACKLE. POP. Run!

You've pissed yourself again, Simon.

Fuck off, Mama!

"I'll give you fucking coward!" He takes a mouthful of kerosene and comes at me with the torch raised, cloak flapping behind.

WHOOSH.

I feel each hair on my face burning, nerve endings beginning to fry. Writhing my body against the chair, I try to turn away from the fire. It's futile, I can't move. A sharp concoction of fuel and burning flesh fills my nostrils and throat. *Make it stop. Make it fucking stop!*

As the heat begins to relent, I prepare for another blast, managing to coil my awakening fingers around each armrest, praying I'll pass out. Swear to God, I can hear my skin continuing to sizzle.

I don't want to die. I don't want to die.

Focus your mind. Enfoca tu mente.

You can get fucked, too, you pot-bellied Spaniard. Nothing but a fucking marshmallow here, and you're asking for composure. Go fuck yourself. Jódete!

As The Dragon offers a series of throaty rasps, I finally feel brave enough to open my eyes, the skin around them screaming its reminder of the fire. But it's as if such intensity is plucking my mind from the murky darkness. The cloudy film is dropping, my vision now clearer, sharper, the letters on the container clutched in The Dragon's left hand now in high definition.

Superhero vision engaged.

This time I manage to move both legs, and the growing sensation of my fingertips digging into the wood offers further hope. My body is awakening.

Come on. Come on!

The Dragon's hacking continues, but it's beginning to wind down, more space between each convulsion. Soon, he'll be spraying me with his dragon breath again.

Like the kind of person who sets fire to his parents' house.

Words that haunt me and prompt a thousand questions, but right now, I need to get out of this goddamned chair. *Small steps make climbable ladders, Simon.*

Come on. Come the fuck on!

I begin raising myself from the wood, right foot outstretched, left ready to take the majority of my weight. My arms shake with effort, but it's working. Ahead, The Dragon begins to unfold, running the back of a crinkled hand across his mouth.

And runs off into the night.

I'd at least have a chance if I could just stand up. A slim one, yes, but sitting here, I'm just a Sunday roast in the making. Almost there. Almost—

"What shape did you see in the flames, Simon?"

I fall against the wood, my strength leaving me.

The Dragon's laugh is gravel. "Taken the wind out of your sails, haven't I? Burst your little fucking superhero bubble."

There's no way. No way. This is not fantasy land. Must be the drugs, the—

"Cat got your tongue?"

No, but it feels like something has, something far more evil than a little kitty-kat. "But—but there is no next life. And there's no coming back."

The Dragon laughs again. "Is that what you think this little scene is? The ghosts of your past coming back to haunt you? One has to be dead to become a ghost, Simon."

"Not possible. Uh-uh. No fucking way." I try to get up again, but my muscles are jelly. "Police said you were dead. Told me they found you and Mama next to the bed, holding hands."

Offering a smile, The Dragon swills the kerosene in the container. "A nice little touch, don't you think, bearing in mind how fond of each other your Mama and Rodney were."

"But—no. That doesn't make sense." *He's my brother, Simon. It's only now and again. Better than him sleeping on the streets, don't you agree?* "The police said—"

"Anything to close the investigation. Two bodies burned beyond recognition, that was enough to warrant a round of coffee and donuts paid for by dirty money."

Questions bounce around my head as The Dragon takes another mouthful of kerosene. *What the fuck? What the fuck? WHAT THE FUUUUUUUUCK?! All this time and*—"But I'm your son," is all I can think to say, thoughts of Reformo on hold.

He studies me as if my words evoke some semblance of humanity, an inkling of doubt. But just as fast, he spits on the torch sending the flames towards me.

WHOOSH.

I scream and squirm, searing pain approaching a never-ending crescendo as my body continues awakening from slumber. *In my next life, I'll be someone special.* I feel my skin beginning to bubble, something leaking down my cheek. The chair screeches along with me, almost toppling back at one point.

Fuuuuuuuuuuuuck!

And finally—mercifully—the blast stops, but my skin continues to smolder.

"My son. Yes." The Dragon places his hands on his knees and releases three more violent hacks. "Are you forgetting you left me for dead, *son?*" He bows further, using a portion of his cloak to stifle his coughs. "Smoke everywhere when I woke. The fire was already busying itself, working into a frenzy. My first thought was to jump out the window, but then I remembered my pitiful excuse of a brother and his pathetic pleas for a bed for the night." HACK. HACK. HACK. "It was fate, Simon, don't you see? I wanted more than to be just the nervous widower of Margaret Dooley, frightened of his own shadow. Oh, so much more. And I fucking deserved it! Christ knows I put in the time. Do you see where this is going, son? Do you catch my drift?"

Catch my drift. Catch my drift.

Peas-in-a-mother-fucking-pod.

With every second, I feel my strength ebbing back. Still, I don't want to risk making a premature play and the chance of crumpling to the floor at his feet. Figuring I need to buy myself a little more time, I nod. Truth is, though, I get it. "What doesn't kill you makes you stronger."

"Exactly. I wanted out. I didn't want to be Jeff-fucking-Dooley anymore—a pathetic little man known for being frightened of his own fucking shadow. And all courtesy of her. No, I wanted to be someone different. A new identity, someone special." HACK. HACK. "Dragged my pissant of a brother from the shed all the way up those fucking stairs, all while those flames whipped around us. He didn't know what was happening, probably chasing unicorns." Another wave of violent coughs creases him in two. "By the time I reached the bedroom, the fire was rampant. I could barely breathe." HACK. HACK. HACK. "It took every ounce of strength and determination to crawl out that back door. But do you know what kept me going?"

Thoughts of the pledge made to Mother helped keep me going, even during my darkest times during incarceration. Made from guilt, not love, though—a way to appease the voice in my head. And I've often considered the development of such a romanticist persona to be part of my own escape plan—about leaving the old Simon Dooley behind. So I get it, more than I care to admit. "Thoughts of being a badass?"

He smiles. "That, and all the bottled rage. Absorbed all of it, Simon, filling my reserves of hate and anger. It was just a matter of time before it bubbled over. And when the opportunity came, I took it. Left us both for dead and crawled away into the darkness. Found my place there, too." HACK. HACK. HACK. "Amazing what difference some crispy skin, a throaty voice, and a brand new persona can make when you turn to the dark side. And I tell you, Simon, it was magnificent. The fear in their eyes as they ran them over my charred neck and arms. Whatever their size, their reputation, they would fall at my feet." SWALLOW. HACK. SWALLOW. "People idolised me, some even trying to duplicate my scarring and voice. So you see, son, I didn't have to wait for the next life to leave

Jeff Dooley behind."

The tiniest part of me wants to reach out to him, but I can see it in his eye, he's too far gone. "You could have just left. Walked out the door anytime."

"Jeff Dooley would always be Jeff Dooley, nothing but a ghost, an ineffectual weakling, institutionalised by a dictator. In a way, you saved my life, gifting me the chance to become who I am today. And how can I hold anger towards the one who set The Dragon free?"

This is all on you. All on you.

I perform another sweep of the room in case I missed anything before.

"Just me and you, son. Family only." He walks away, hand to his scabby chin as if in deep contemplation. "Thought we could talk, shoot the shit, now that your mother isn't breathing down our necks. I wanted to tell you that I forgive you, Simon. I've been waiting for this moment since you got out of prison—and when all this *chaos* started, I knew you had something to do with it. Wanted to give you a chance to join me, to come over to the dark side. Father and son, shoulder to shoulder, imagine it." About forty yards away, The Dragon turns, offering another lopsided smile. "And you'll fit in nicely once those scars heal. Call it your initiation."

"My name is Reformo, and I'm bringing hope back to town."

"But chaos is so much more fun. And after all those years of oppression, don't you feel the need to release? To let all the bile out?"

"I made a pledge to Mother."

"You'll never stop the chaos, Simon. Be part of it, embrace it. The more you try to control things, the more out of control you'll feel, just like *she* was."

"If I say no?"

"Then you'll force my hand."

"Drug me then kill me? Is that the code you live by?"

"I live by the code that keeps air running through my frazzled pipes."

"Weak as piss."

The Dragon's face twists into more grotesqueness. "What did you just say?"

"Mother was right. You're as weak as piss."

"Your mother was a fucking psycho!"

"This from the guy wearing a *Harry Potter* cloak and spitting flames towards his only living kin."

"Don't make me do this, son."

Get in their heads. "A blind eye here, a blind eye there, and before you know it, we're hiding in the broom closet eating tinned peaches. Bastards next door parked in front of our house—"

"Stop it!"

"Someone's cat has taken a shit on our front lawn, Jeff! What are you going to do about it, Jeff? Jeff! Jeff! Get up off your lazy arse and do something, Jeff!"

The kerosene in the container sloshes around as The Dragon's breathing becomes erratic and wheezy. He looks pained as if my words are tiny daggers plunging through scar tissue and opening old wounds. It indicates that our exchange is ending, that the battle to end all battles—good versus evil—will soon begin.

"Idiots down the street playing their music again. Kids playing cricket down the street. It gets my fucking—"

I see it in his eye. What's left of his mind. Snapping. The Dragon takes a swig of kerosene and makes his run. Praying my legs will support me, I grip the armrests, ready to thrust myself up. *Use your opponent's weight and momentum against them, English.* All about the timing, Luca told me. If you get it right, you can take anyone down, regardless of size.

Ready. Wait for it.

As The Dragon inches closer, I make my move, staggering towards him. My father. *My enemy.* It would be perfect if it weren't so tragic. Two people born from the same trauma, one drawn to the light, the other to darkness. He lifts the torch towards me, fried cheeks puffed and ready to blow, no sign of Jeff Dooley behind his one dark eye.

But I am Reformo. I am Reformo.

Enough in that tumbler to render a guy twice your size out of action for a few hours.

Fuck you; I'm bringing hope back to town.

With just ten yards between us, my left leg gives a little, momentum keeping me up. I still feel about two seconds behind the game, so I must time this perfectly.

WHOOSH.

Heat sizzles the hairs on my neck as I duck in, wrapping my arms around his waist and launching from the ground. WHAP! In the movies, you'd expect fireworks, an explosion, a ball of smoke—POOF—one that dissipates to reveal who is coming out on top. But my clash with The Dragon is much less dramatic, silent bar the flapping of black fabric and his grotesque wheeze. In a tangled mess, we crumple to the ground, kerosene splashing as the container flies from the Dragon's grip, flames from the torch licking at my weeping skin.

My reflexes are slow, and he gets the first punch in, snapping my head to the left. He stretches for the kerosene and manages to take in a mouthful, but before he raises the torch, I perform my signature move, catching him on the jaw. POW! His head doesn't move, only a little liquid spilling from his lips. Offering a roar, I lunge, but once again, he's faster and stronger, and in a swish of black fabric, he's on top of me.

"Now who's weak as piss?" he says, spraying my face with kerosene.

As we continue our tussle, more kerosene spills from the can. In his other hand, the torch approaches my face, flames dancing madly above my dampened skin.

Kill him, Simon! Kill him!

I'm trying, Mama. He's stronger than me, though. Those drugs, they—

Stronger? Stronger? That man is as weak as piss, Simon Dooley. Now get off your arse and put an end to this.

"Should have joined me, son."

"Never!"

"Shame. You could have any woman you want. No need for whores."

"Her name was Vera!" Adrenaline surging, I grit my teeth and focus, channelling all the bottled rage and pent-up frustration. Every scolding from Mother, the alienation she created, the loneliness endured. "No more, Mama." The sound of that box crushing underneath her foot, the countless stares of disappointment. "NO MORE!"

It's working! I can feel the heat abating.

Growing as wide as the knotted skin will allow, The Dragon's eye registers the changing tide. I continue pushing his arm back, finally thrusting myself from the floor until, in another swish of black fabric, it's me on top, staring down at the monster my mother created. SLAM! SLAM! SLAM! The fourth smash of his hand against the wood sets the torch free.

WHOOSH!

As the liquid around us ignites, The Dragon offers a throaty laugh. "What shape can you see, Simon?"

"The only thing I see is a frightened little man with a crispy coating." I bring my fist into his jaw, the connection sending his head hard against the wood. SLAM! And another. BAM!

He snaps his head back towards me. "Is that all you've got, son?"

KERPOW! KERPOW!

But The Dragon's smile grows wider, even as orange lights up his eyes. "Come on...you can do better than that." HACK. HACK. "Mama would be disappointed."

"Fuck you!" As I fire more punches, the hungry flames start on my legs, forcing an agonised cry. Filled with rage, I continue my assault, raining down punch after punch after punch. WHAM! BAM! SMASH! "I hate you." BARK. BARK. "Fucking hate you."

Even as the flames engulf us, The Dragon holds that god-awful smile. "Not my first rodeo," he cries. "Not many nerve endings left to—"

CRACK! BANG! WHALLOP!

HACK. "—kill."

The pain is unbearable. I'm at my limit. Offering a deafening scream, I throw myself from the flames, only for more liquid to set alight around me. *Hate fire! Hate it! Hate it!* Guttural laughter fills my ears as I scramble to my feet, the tug on my cape, though, bringing me falling back towards the blaze. "You're not running this time, son."

The first beams catch alight. WHOOSH. CRACKLE.

Filled with only thoughts of escape, I kick out and attempt to crawl, but gristly fingers wrap around my right wrist and pull me inwards. I can't see or breathe, but I hear the kerosene sloshing around and feel it splashing against me. The Dragon's cloak is now alight, as are patches of his skin. I try and snap my hand away, but his grip tightens. Somehow, he finds a smile. "Perhaps it was always meant to be this—"

SMASH!

I swing again with my left. POW! And again. BAM! His grip begins to weaken. WHAM! WHACK! CRACK!

I'm free, on my hands and knees, hoping to find a part of the floor that isn't ablaze. Behind me, Father—The Dragon—launches into a series of bloodcurdling cries, the fire somehow finding new nerve endings to fry. "YOU'LL NEVER BE FREE, SIMON!"

WHOOSH. WHOOSH.

In a father and son duet, we begin singing for our lives, only breaking off to perform the occasional violent hack.

SNAP. CRACKLE. BOOM.

All I can do is half crawl, half drag myself away from the now gurgling cries coming from behind. My pain is beginning to ease, offering little relief. *Not many nerve endings left to...*

WHOOSH. WHOOSH.

Desperate, I lunge forward, managing a couple of weak kicks against the wood before my head drops. "I'm done, Mama. I'm done." And ready to die, I listen to The Dragon's cries grow weaker and the fire taking things up a notch.

WHOOSH. SNAP. CRACKLE. ROAR!

I love you, Simon.

    Vera?

    Get out of there, Simon. Run!

    What? Where am I?

    Run, Simon! Run!

    Stickiness gives to dampness as I open my eyes to the carnage. ROOOOOOOAR!

    It takes a second to get my bearings, but the crackling sound from above and the smell of burning flesh soon has me scrambling to my feet. "Which way, Vera? Which way?"

    Follow my voice.

    I hesitate and spin around, only to find orange everywhere.

    Trust me, Simon. You have to trust me.

    Head down, I stagger back into the flames, following the voice of my love. In seconds, I slam through the metal door and into glorious coolness, heaving in huge gulps of the never-to-be-taken-for-granted-again icy morning air. Tears fill my eyes as exhaustion finally wins its battle, driving me to my knees and the dampness of the road.

    I love you, Simon.

    I'm unsure how long I'm crawling across the tarmac before I feel someone pulling at my shoulders. A tidal wave of black, not orange, comes for me, and I offer no resistance.

EPILOGUE

Vera! Don't go in—

I wake up with a scream in my throat, searing pain across my forehead. One look at my scorched fingers semi-covered in padding brings it all back, a flash-bang of pain and terror that has me tearing the drip from my arm and trying to stand. "What the fuck? What the fuck?" My lips don't feel right at all.

"Alf, he's up. Give me a hand."

"Fuck's sake."

Footsteps pound, a violent rattle drawing my attention to a picture of a wishing well on the wall. Dizziness washes over me, the sea of toilet rolls and cigarette cartons cushioning my fall as my knees give way.

"Get his legs, Alf."

"Give me a minute, Janice, will you?" comes the gruff reply.

As I'm heaved back on the bed, familiar but distant voices continue floating from way above, making me feel like I'm stuck at the bottom of the well in the wall. "The Dragon. The Dragon!"

"Easy, Reformo, easy," Janice says. "You need to rest, love. Alf, put the kettle on, will you? Plenty of milk for the superhero."

"Jesus Christ, it's never-ending."

"Shut up, you big oaf. Here, take a couple of these, love," Janice says, offering me a handful of gigantic tablets and a glass of what I assume is water, a curly straw poking out over the brim. "Now, how does your face feel, petal?"

"Like a very slapped arse," I reply after a generous sip. The fog begins to lift, but the throbbing pain continues. "How long have I been out?"

"A while, love. Thought keeping you here would be safer. The fewer people knowing about your true identity, the better."

"The Dragon?"

"Dead, petal. It was all over the news. Hardly anything left of that building." She offers another of her infamous winks, following up with a smile. "An accident, they reported, but everyone around here knows the truth. And likely much further afield, too. You're a goddamn hero."

My face cracks as I return the smile. "Thought I was a goner, Janice. Toast."

"Your extremities took the worst, and your face is a bit of a mess, but you're alive. That's the important thing."

"How?"

"Well," she says, perching on the end of the bed, "we couldn't send our local superhero out to battle wearing any old suit, could we?"

"Come again?"

She laughs, whipping the duvet with the back of her hand. "Picture this. My Alfie at Christmas, lighting up a Marlboro and putting his feet on the coffee table, ready for the post-roast obligatory movie. I go out to take some mince pies to number seven, but when I come back, the couch cushion is alight. Silly old bastard fell asleep."

"Oi, I heard that!"

"The tea's burning, Alf!" Just as quick as her eyebrows meet, the heavy frown leaves her face again. "Anyhow, I don't know if you noticed, but we like to stock a few things here and there, you know, in case of emergencies."

"I had noticed, yes. Got any tinned peaches by any chance?"

"We have, love. Why do you ask?"

I smile. "No reason."

"Anyhow, they had a deal on this fabric spray, supposed to make your furnishings fire retardant. Coated all the curtains with it, couches, chairs, beds, etcetera. Even thought of giving my Alf a couple of coats." She offers her smile again, tobacco-stained teeth on full display. "Anyhow, he thought me bloody stupid when I started spraying your leo—your *costume* with what was left in a can. Just wish I'd done the gloves, too."

"And the drip? I've not been hobbled, have I?"

"Beg your pardon?"

"Nothing. Just teasing."

"Right.

"Well, anyway, this town is behind you now. People will do what they can to keep it safe, and I'll be able to call in favours here and there."

"I don't know what to say, Janice."

"Say nothing. I hope you like your new suit. It's on me, this one. I've given it the treatment and added a couple of other extras, too. Nothing too flashy, mind, but I'll run through them later. Fit for a hero. A *super*hero."

"It's perfect," I say, studying the glimmer running down both arms. "Janice, I owe you my life. I can't—"

She holds a hand up. "And we owe you ours, pet. Now, I'm just going to the shop to stock up on some food. Anything in particular you like?"

"But it's dark outside."

"Depends on how you look at it." She smiles again. "You don't know what you've done yet, do you? Things feel different out there now. After what happened to The Dragon, and those other creeps, people are afraid to step out of line."

You hear that, Mama? You hear that?

"Janice, can I ask one last favour?"

"Anything, petal."

"I just need to feel the fresh air on my face again."

"Are you sure you're up to it?"

I offer my puppy dog eyes and nod. "Just for a few minutes."

She helps me from the bed, taking the brunt of my weight as I catch sight of my face in the mirror. "There are things they can do," she says. "Facial reconstruction and whatnot. Miracle workers these days, and I'm sure—"

"No, no, it's perfect. As it should be. My mask?"

"Waiting for you downstairs. Mark two, new and improved, just like the suit."

"I bloody love you, Janice."

"Nice to know someone appreciates me," she says, loud enough for Alf to hear.

Aside from an intense prickling up my hands and arms, and a short bout of dizziness halfway, the stairs don't present much of a challenge. Painful and unsightly, my fingers work as they're supposed to. Bar some scarring and throbbing across my skull, I'm in pretty good shape—all thanks to Janice.

"Hold that tea, Alf," she shouts from the bottom.

"Fuck's sake," I hear him mumble.

She turns to me, trying not to move her stare away. "Now, do you want your mask?"

"What are you trying to say, Janice?"

"That you look like that fella from *Nightmare on Elm Street.*"

"Freddy?"

"Nah, it's not Freddy. Now, what's his name. Jason? Oh, it will come to me."

"It's Freddy."

"Nah, definitely not."

"Freddy Krueger."

"Nah."

"I better have that mask anyway."

Returning seconds later with what I can only describe as a piece of art worthy of any superhero, Janice locks her fingers around the door handle and nods. "Ready?"

"Ready, Janice."

As the cool night air rushes over my crinkled face, I can't help but smile. It's never felt so good, never tasted so fine. And there's something different about it, something purer.

You don't know what you've done yet, do you?

"I think I can manage from here, Janice," I say, sliding on the mask.

"You sure?"

"Thanks again. For all that—"

She holds a hand up again, turns, and walks away. "Freddy Krueger," she yells, halfway down the street. "That was it."

"Nice one, Janice."

I plan on seeing Jayden tomorrow—all masked up, of course. And I'll check in on Violet, too, dropping in a bit of cash courtesy of Butter Balls. In fact, I'll likely do the rounds, a bit of PR, if you like. Maybe I'll even talk to the press and get them on side. For now, though, I let my head fall against the back of the bench and study the night sky, hoping for a shooting star. It isn't long before the first one appears. "Love you, too, Vera." And even less for a second to follow almost the same trajectory. "Love you, Reggie. Hope the blowjobs are going well up there."

Tears cloud my vision, but I see no further trails across the heavens. From somewhere close, I hear a bird singing and what sounds like a child's laughter. A little girl rides her trike, legs going like the clappers trying to keep up with her father, who constantly glances over his shoulder and towards the park.

"Look, Daddy. It's him. It's Deformo!"

The excitement that draws across the man's face even over-shadows the girl's look of glee. "Reformo, darling," he says, offering a wave. I watch them down the street and not once does he look over his shoulder again.

Why couldn't you have been normal, Mama?

A new-found peace washes over me, her voice silenced, my pledge upheld. I have a duty now to continue bringing hope to town, ensuring respect and order are maintained.

"I am Reformo."

Such a utopia won't last forever. After all, this is real life, not fantasy land, but at least for now, the chaos is at an end. That said, I know at least one person who should be sleeping with one eye open over the coming days...

AUTHOR NOTE

My debut novel is a tongue-in-cheek story about the long-term effects of trauma and how it never fails to continue shaping us. Life is imperfect, and so are we.

Chasing The Dragon was a thrill to write, a dark concoction of all the genres I've touched on. It is horror, thriller, romance, crime, fantasy, and mystery, with the staple thread of Towsey humour to lighten the load. I hope you fall in love with Reformo as much as I did.

N.B. This is certainly not designed to be a self-help book. Oh, and there are no dragons in it. Or are there?

Mark Towse is an English horror writer living in Australia. He would sell his soul to the devil or anyone buying if it meant he could write full-time. Alas, he left it very late to begin this journey, penning his first story since primary school at the ripe old age of forty-five. Since then, he's been published in over two hundred journals and anthologies, had his work made into full theatrical productions for shows such as The No Sleep Podcast and Tales to Terrify, and has penned fourteen novellas, including Nana, Gone to the Dogs, 3:33, and Crows. Chasing The Dragon is his debut novel.

More from Eerie River

Eerie River Publishing is a leader in independent horror, dark fantasy, and dark speculative fiction.

We are dedicated to publishing anthologies, collections, and novels from some of the best indie authors around the world. Our goal is to become a go-to resource for horror, dark fantasy and dark speculative readers, and to provide a safe space for authors to share their stories.

Interested in becoming a Patreon member?
By joining our patreon, you will be supporting our artists and authors, who work hard to produce high-quality and original content for your enjoyment. You will also get access to exclusive perks, such as early releases, behind-the-scenes updates, bonus material, and more. If you love dark fiction and want to support independent publishing, please consider becoming a patron today. Thank you for your interest and support.

www.patreon.com/EerieRiverPub.

To stay up to date with all our new releases and upcoming giveaways, follow us on Facebook, Twitter, Instagram and YouTube.

linktr.ee/eerieriver

EERIE RIVER PUBLISHING

NOVELS & COLLECTIONS
Chasing The Dragon
The Naughty Corner
Dead Man Walking
Devil Walks in Blood
The Darkness In The Pines
At Eternity's Gate
Beyond Sundered Seas
Path of War
In Solitudes Shadow
The Void
They Are Cursed Like You
SENTINEL
NOTHUS
Miracle Growth
Infested
Helluland
A Sword Named Sorrow
Storming Area 51

ANTHOLOGIES
Year of the Tarot
AFTER: A Post-Apocalyptic Survivor Series
Elemental Cycle: Four Book Series Blood Sins
It Calls From Series
Blood Sins
Last Stop: Whiskey Pete
Elemental Series
Of Fire and Stars
From Beyond the Threshold

DRABBLE COLLECTIONS
Forgotten Ones: Drabbles of Myth and Legend
Dark Magic: Drabbles of Magic and Lore

COMING SOON
Rotten House
The Earth Bleeds at Night

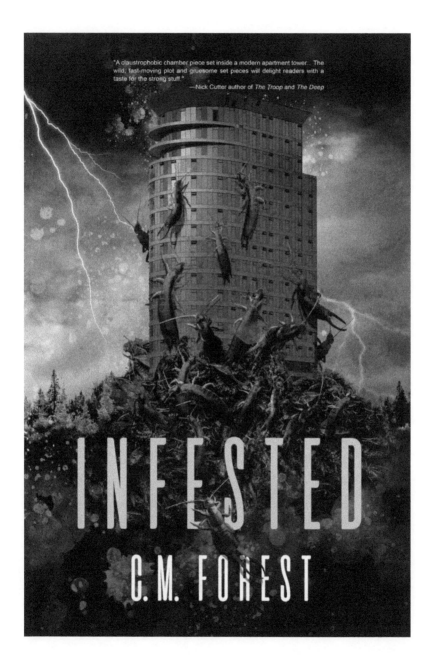

Milton Keynes UK
Ingram Content Group UK Ltd.
UKHW012337010424
440454UK00002B/11

9 781998 112272